Michael Vance's
Weird Horror Tales
Light's End

AIRSHIP 27 PRODUCTIONS

Weird Horror Tales: Light's End
© 2011 Michael Lail

An Airship 27 Production
www.airship27.com
www.airship27hangar.com

Cover illustration © 2011 Keith Birdsong
Interior llustrations © 2011 Eric York

Editor: Ron Fortier
Associate Editor: Ilena George
Production and design: Rob Davis

Second Edition

ISBN-13: 978-0692219119 (Airship 27)
ISBN-10: 0692219110

Printed in the United States of America

10 9 8 7 6 5 4 3 2 1

Contents

CHAPTER ONE

Her left forearm resting on the faux leather armrest of her seat on the bus, itched. Without looking down, she scratched her forearm with the unpainted fingernails of her right hand; something felt wrong. She raised her hand and startled at the white goo on and under her fingernails. Dianne Savage murmured *yuck* and glanced down.

The bloody trench eaten into her forearm was filled with a writhing mass of white maggots flickering in and out like an image jerks when film is misaligned on its sprocket. She screamed and screamed and screamed.

Then she woke up.

Savage sat upright in bands of yellow light thrown from a partially opened Venetian blind on a window of the new WMC twelve-passenger Greyhound bus as it pulled into the Light's End Bus Station. As she did so, a swirl of "dump ducks"—seagulls— startled up from the covered driveway and to the northeast to escape being crushed.

Unshakable discipline, pride, and self-assurance were obvious on her demure, twenty-seven year old, heart-shaped face that was, as always, free of even makeup on the lids of her blue-green eyes except for a light brush of powder. The subtle thin line at the left side of her neck that was the first sign of advancing maturity was barely noticeable.

Savage wore her trademark gray suit with its outrageous, bell-bottomed pants, and her pastel green cloche hat was pulled over her bobbed, red hair, but the suit looked awkward, as if someone who didn't know how to dress a woman had dressed her. Dianne's daily note to herself was pinned to the lapel of her suit.

On her lap lay a copy of the September 1928 issue of *College Humor*, one of the few magazines that had bought several short pieces from her as a "serious" writer. She was fiercely proud to be the only female reporter on the staff of the *Bangor Daily Register*, but her first love was fiction, and she was proud to share space in the magazine with people like the new, rising stars of literature: Robert Benchley, Groucho Marx, and F. Scott Fitzgerald.

1

Between the thumb and forefinger of her right hand, she rolled a tiny piece of paper that was now a tight tube back and forth, back and forth, back and forth, a nervous habit she'd nurtured since her years in an orphanage.

It had been a long, exhausting trip south from Bangor on the relatively new two-lane Highway 1 through quaint New England towns: Wintersport, Stockton Springs, and Ducktrap, with their brick, A-frame filling stations and gravity pumps, curbless streets, clutches of people milling around two or three blocks of cafes, drug and variety stores and, in the larger bergs, a small Vaudeville theater with a new silver screen for silent movies.

The only sounds she'd heard for hours had been the almost hypnotic hurrrrrmmmm of its tires on the road, and the random and occasional coughs, rustling in seats, and snoring from its few passengers, who passed the time looking out of windows, reading, or napping. Dianne had split the tedious hours between reading her magazine and soaking in the beauty of Maine through her window: of the thick forests of red and white spruce, balsam fir, white and red pine, birch, and sugar and red maple that lined both sides of the road, looking like a silent movie travelogue. Most were half naked because they had dropped many of their leaves on the ground in blankets of mottled color. Outside of the towns, the forests were broken only by a random, isolated, and very rustic farm house or rundown barn, or a field of livestock.

Having left half of its passengers behind as it passed from town to town, the WMC bus had rumbled west down Highway 173 through the bleak towns of Hope and South Hope, turning south onto a highway without signage. Then the long stretches of unbroken road were pockmarked with pot holes, and seemed little traveled even for sparsely populated Maine during the final days of Fall.

The reporter had rolled her paper as asphalt was replaced with a hard-packed dirt road, and the bus had traveled east past a street sign that had read "Killingsworth" on the outskirts of her destination. The yellow bands of light thrown between the slats of the Venetian blinds over her window had blinked out as the bus changed positions relative to the sun. Dianne had rolled the blinds up as the Greyhound quickly turned south onto unpaved Neptune Street, and finally east onto bricked August Street in downtown Light's End.

She had stored in her memory the names of the small businesses on both sides of August Street, the main retail business district of the town — most of them bearing the unfamiliar names of "mom-and-pop" stores, not uncommon in Maine — until it crossed Ferry Street. The reporter's photographic memory was a gift from her dead father. The buildings looked clean and well-maintained, with the typical mishmash of architectural styles, and there had seemed an inordinate amount of new construction under way as well, including the bricking of part of the street to the west.

Once past August Street, Ferry split into two roads. In the cup of that "Y" stood her destination: the Light's End Bus Station and Mermaid Cafe, two pentagon-shaped, red brick buildings connected by a covered breezeway where buses unloaded their passengers, luggage, mail, and freight.

The bus pulled with diminishing speed into the breezeway and stopped with a squeal of brakes, and the driver opened the vehicle's doors with the thrust of a handle by his seat.

"Light's End," he announced indifferently without turning his head. Dianne was the only passenger who rose from her seat and walked to the front of the bus.

"Our guys will unload your luggage," continued the driver without looking at the reporter. His stubbled jaw worked on something in his mouth. "Do ya want it carried to the station or the cafe, Miss?"

"I'll wait for it," said Dianne, as she pushed a curl of red hair back into place under her pale green cloche hat. She noticed a slight, unpleasant smell, probably some disgusting kind of chewing tobacco, she thought. "Thank you."

The driver responded with a grunt as Dianne descended the metal stairs and stepped out onto the breezeway. She thought she could feel his eyes following her, but a quick glance over her shoulder proved she was wrong. She waited patiently as two porters, both old men in shabby, gray uniforms, shambled forward to unload the bus.

"That one's mine," she said and pointed when she saw her large suitcase. One of the men lugged it to the reporter with a questioning expression as she reached into the right, front pocket of her pants. She noticed that odd, unpleasant smell again.

"That's all right; don't bother. I can manage," she said, and dropped a substantial tip into his somewhat yellow, upturned palm. "God bless you."

The porter startled at the words as if he'd been stung by a wasp.

Its bell jingled as Savage opened the glass door of the Mermaid Cafe. On either side of the door, very large, plate-glass windows had already revealed the appliances, furnishings, and customers inside.

The reporter was met by the smells of dynamite sandwiches, french fries, onions, meat loaf, hamburgers, and tuna melts. It was October 10th, a mild, pleasant Wednesday afternoon. The Blue Plate Special was meat loaf, and Dianne had arrived after the noon crowd; only a few casual diners were in the cafe. As she moved to the lunch counter, she noticed several heads turned in her direction and conversations ended; she was used to this condescending response to 'pants on a woman.'

The Mermaid Cafe had a ten stool lunch counter ending in six freestanding tables with faux marble tops; several booths were located around the outer walls. Dianne took quick inventory of the customers and staff, and then walked to a red vinyl stool. It was one seat removed from an old man with black- rimmed glasses and close-cropped white hair who, indifferent to the fashion and conventions of 1928, wore an old, off-white dress shirt with blue jeans. His blue Fedora sat neatly by his half-empty plate; and a smoldering Lucky Strike dangled from his left hand. She set her suitcase down on the floor next to a stool and sat down. The old man was chatting with a middle-aged waitress who, dressed in the loose, ankle-length, off-white dress typical of her trade, stood behind the counter, wiping the inside of a just-washed glass with a dish rag.

"Be right back, Chuck," the waitress commented to the senior as she looked at Dianne and then the reporter's dungarees, her jaw gnawing at what Dianne guessed was an unseen piece of gum. She picked up a clean glass from the top of a stacked pyramid of them behind her, filled it with water *fawhhhosh* from a spigot in the counter, and walked over to the reporter.

"Whatcha have?" the waitress asked with a perfunctory smile as she leaned close to Dianne, placed the glass of water on the counter next to her, and removed a ballpoint pen from a pocket in her dress. The reporter wrinkled her nose in recognition of an unpleasant odor as she read the little name plate above the waitress's heart: Mollie.

"What is that you are chewing?" Savage asked with a faint smile as the little unseen bell over the entrance tinkled as someone entered the cafe.

"Gum," said the waitress and nervously looked down as she smoothed a wrinkle out of her dress at her left hip.

"May I ask what kind of gum?"

The waitress looked up at her with a defensive and quizzical expression. "Asafoetida."

"Never heard of it. Well, I don't want *that*. How's the chowder, Mollie?" asked Dianne, and laid her *College Humor* magazine on the counter. "It's a favorite of mine."

"Most people don't notice this," said Mollie with a growing smile, and tapped her name plate with a fingernail painted red. "No better clam chowder, anywhere, Miss," she added, warming just a bit and talking around the tip of the pen and the gum in her mouth. "That, and two sides. It comes with a dinner roll and side salad."

"Okay," said Dianne, taking her hat off and dropping it on top of the suitcase standing vertically on its edge at her feet. "That, and green beans and mashed potatoes with butter, if you've got 'em. And how about a cup of Joe, black?"

"Done and done," the waitress said, and wrote Dianne's order on her pad, tore it off, then impaled it on a vertical nail next to a punch bell in a window cut out of the wall that opened onto the kitchen. The old man to her left leaned sideways with his right elbow on the lunch counter, his stubbled chin cupped with the palm of his hand.

"Excuse me. My name is Charles Walton," he said. The reporter couldn't decide if the four or five day growth of gray beard on his square jaw was intentional, the mark of absentmindedness, or laziness. "I couldn't help but overhear your comment about the chowder. You're from out of town, aren't you?"

"I am," said Dianne with a cautious smile. She noticed his fork, spoon, and serrated knife were carefully stacked on top of his nearly empty plate, the trademark of an organized mind. "How did you know?"

"Besides being the local eccentric, I'm also big on logic — Plato, you know — and sort of an amateur detective; big Sherlock Holmes fan. A retired teacher, so I've got plenty of nothin' to do. Everybody in town knows about the chowder here; ergo, you aren't from Light's End." He unconsciously touched the rim of his glasses with the tip of his right forefinger. "Welcome to our twisted little town, Miss...?"

"Dianne. Dianne Savage," she added as she ran her fingers through her matted red hair to try to add some shape to it. "I'm in from Bangor."

"Are you here visiting relatives, or are you on business? Did I forget to tell you I'm also a lonely old man," he added, pausing to take a drag on his cigarette, "who doesn't get to talk to people much anymore? Nosey but completely harmless."

"I guess you'd call it business," answered Dianne. "I'm a writer, and I'm here doing research for a novel." The punch bell dinged in the window behind Mollie. She turned, picked up a plate of pungent, steaming chowder, and carried it to the reporter.

"Wow, a woman writer!" the waitress said as she sat the plate in front of Dianne with a napkin rolled around a serrated knife, fork, and spoon.

"Whata ya written?" The little unseen bell over the entrance tinkled as someone left the cafe.

"Features for newspapers; mostly interviews," the reporter responded, picked up and unrolled her paper napkin, and chose the tarnished silver-plated spoon. She took a bite of the chowder. "Say, this is good. I've written a few things for some newsstand magazines too, like that one," she added, nodding at her copy of College Humor on the lunch counter. "This will be my first novel, if I can sell it."

"And you're writin' a novel about Light's End?" asked the waitress, rubbing the counter with a towel. "Wait 'til I tell the girls! Hey, can I be in it?!"

"Not about Light's End, exactly," said Dianne and speared some green beans. "I just wanted to use a composite of several small towns on the coast of Maine as my setting, stuck a pin in a map, and here I am. Never heard of your little town before that, Mollie."

"Oh," said the waitress, whose waning smile revealed obvious disappointment. "How long will you be in town, Miss Savage?"

"At least two or three weeks," said the reporter, picking up her cup of coffee and taking a careful, long, exploratory drink. "Maybe more." The little unseen bell over the entrance tinkled as someone entered the cafe.

"Then you'll need a place to stay," said Walton, adjusting his glasses on his Romanesque nose. "Not an easy thing to find right now, considering the big influx of men working on our new storm drain construction project."

"The Van Sanford Apartments over on First Street are really nice and almost finished," interjected Mollie. "She might try there, Chuck. If ya want, Miss Savage, I could call a Dixie cab to take ya there. It's not far."

"That's a very nice offer, Mollie," Dianne said and held up a dollop of mashed potatoes. "Please do. I'll be finished here in a minute or two."

"And while she does that for you," added the old man as he slipped a dime under the lip of his plate, "I'd like to offer my services as well. I'm sort of an unofficial town historian, if you will, and I'd be thrilled to save you some time and effort and share some local color about this aberrant little New England berg."

"Wellll...." began the reporter, her reluctance obvious in her tone, her lowered eyes, and the conscious repression of emotion in her expression. "But I, uh, don't really know you, Mr. Walton."

"Oh, dear me, I completely understand such a response from a young, unescorted lady in a strange town, even one with such piercing, intelligent, green eyes." Walton turned to face the waitress, and winked. "I wasn't thinking... again, eh, Mollie?! I'm so sorry if I offended you in any way, Miss Savage."

"My stars! If I didn't know better, the green eyes comment sounded a little bit like flirting. Thank you for the offer anyway. I think I'll start with the Chamber of Commerce, the local newspaper, and your library."

"He really is a harmless old fossil," the waitress said and handed Dianne a scrap of paper. The reporter looked down at her bill: twenty-five cents. She looked up and smiled at the waitress as she laid two quarters on the counter next to her plate.

"For the best chowder anywhere, and for all of your help, Mollie. Should be enough to encourage you to buy a pair of dungarees just like mine!"

A light breeze carried the ocean's salty tang to Dianne and dispelled the smell of fried hamburgers, boiled hot dogs, and chili as she stood on the a corner of the north side of First Street in the parking lot of Harley's Drive In — a small hamburger stand. Her suitcase and the multicolored, fallen leaves of October lay at her feet as an occasional vehicle traveled east or west on the two-lane, packed-gravel road in front of the stand. Above her, a swirl of seagulls hung just between a scud of clouds as Dianne committed every detail of the Van Sanford Apartments across the street to her memory.

Rectangular, the long, two story, red brick building sat on the opposite corner on a slight uprise of the land that buried its west section half way up its lowest windows. Its slightly recessed middle third was the main entrance to the Van Sanford; in its center was a door set in a ten by ten foot porch topped by a balcony and a red striped metal awning, all supported by two tall, square, brick columns. A smaller version of this porch, balcony, and awning was located on the west and east sides of the apartments, with an odd, aberrant door next to the east entrance. Because of its uneven foundation, the east entrance also required a short rise of stairs to its entrance.

The Van Sanford was thoroughly modern in its architecture, allowing simple, mostly unadorned line to express its beauty. Each of its many single or double windows had its own metal awning, and only the pattern of four white bricks at the corners of an implied square underneath each window on the first floor, and above each window on its second, served as ornamentation. Residential houses sat immediately behind its west side; Quality Motors, a small used car lot, was located on the opposite corner east of the building.

All of this information was critical for a quick and safe exit, if necessary, for an investigative reporter. Satisfied with her survey, Dianne picked up her suitcase and walked across the street to the Van Sanford's east entrance.

As she walked up the short flight of porch stairs, Dianne noticed several large, dirty white trucks parked on the side street next to the apartments; "Ebaugh Construction" and contact information for the company was painted in red letters on the drivers' door. Several men in soiled uniforms were loading tools into the trucks' beds. This was added to her mental file cabinet on everything Light's End as she stepped into the apartment building.

The long white hall stretching before her had a high ceiling with four modern metal light fixtures spaced evenly down its length, and polished oak floors. She thought she could hear the impalpable chittering of electricity in them. Immediately on her left was a door with a louvered, airflow vent above it, and a piece of paper taped beneath a "1A" room number that read: "Office." She sat her suitcase down and knocked. At a muffled "Come in; it's not locked," she opened the door.

"Can I help you, Miss?" said a lanky, sandy-haired man who sat in a wooden swivel chair tilted on its back legs with his feet propped up on a desk in the back third of an otherwise empty apartment. "My name is Gene Sorenson; I'm the manager, if you're looking for a room, and the manager even if you aren't!" He grinned.

"I'm Dianne Savage, in from Bangor, and I am indeed looking for a room," she said, and sat her suitcase down. "Mollie down at the Mermaid Cafe told me you might have some vacancies. Was she right?"

"We won't be officially open until early next year," said Sorenson as he swung his feet off of the desk and stood up. "The second floor and the basement aren't finished. But I do have a few apartments ready if you don't mind some inconveniences, Miss Savage. Will your husband be staying with us as well? Do you have children?"

"No husband or children yet, Mr. Sorenson. I'm here for two weeks or so," responded the reporter as she removed her cloche hat and took inventory of the man. He wore a long-sleeved, blue cotton shirt tucked into the waist of his blue jeans, and a pair of scuffed, black, work boots. Pinned on the left collar of his shirt was an odd, diamond-shaped silver button.

"Oh, dear. We don't usually rent by the week, Miss Savage," he said as he moved to the front of his desk. "But, then again, we aren't really open yet, either, so I don't think Mr. Van Sanford will mind. There are eight apartments on each floor and one in the basement; only the first floor is complete. We'll have seventeen units when we're all done. All of the apartments will be furnished; my wife, Judy, is in charge of that. Would you like a tour?"

"I'd love it. May I leave my suitcase here for the time being?" she said. As he reached and then passed Dianne, she noted he was in his mid-thirties and the odd pin in his shirt collar was a cluster of interconnected crosses forming the overall shape of a diamond. Sorenson stepped around her and was through the door before he turned and said:

"Of course you can; follow me. It isn't far. Walla! We are here!"

He had taken three more steps in the hall, stopped at 3A, the room next to his makeshift office, and had thrown open the door with a theatrical flourish.

"As a woman, you'll appreciate that each apartment has a ten foot ceiling and is a nice 400 to 600 square feet in size. This one is 600. On each floor, there are six, one bedroom apartments like this one, and two smaller efficiency units. All have electrical lighting, some have Murphy pull-down beds; this one does not. Each has its own tiled bathroom with a claw-footed tub, hot and cold running water, and the large ones have a dining room, as does this unit."

"I like the furniture," said Dianne. "Very up-to-date."

"Thank you. I'll let my wife know. All have modern refrigerators and a gas stove in their kitchens," continued Sorenson, "and the Light's End Ice Company just down the street delivers ice for the refrigerator twice a week on Tuesday and Friday. That's included in the rent. All the apartments have doors with louvered airflow vents above them, adjustable from the inside to make our summers a little more pleasant.

"This one," concluded Sorenson, "is the only one I have available now. End of tour."

"Is there a telephone?" Dianne asked, and stepped into the apartment.

"Regrettably, no. Light's End is just a little behind on getting telephone service, although we're working on it. There are only a few scattered around the town. But the telegraph office is close, and our Post Office is one of the most efficient in the county."

"Any chance I can see the rest of the joint?" Dianne asked and smiled, assessing the manager as genuinely pleasant. "If you have the time, of course."

"Well, the floor above is just like this one, and still under construction, and the one basement apartment is occupied. The basement itself is also unfinished."

"I'd still like to look around, if you don't mind."

"Okey dokey," Sorenson said with a frown of inconvenience, "follow me."

As they walked down the hall, Dianne added: "I'm here to research a novel..."

"Really!?"

"Yes, and most writers are generally too curious for their own good. I hope you really don't mind showing me the rest of the place. Who knows, I might use your apartments in my book."

"Well, it won't take long," Sorenson said, and stopped at the intersection of the main entrance with the hall where a flight of steps with oak handrails rose up to the second floor and down to the basement. "The Ebaugh Construction guys who are doing the work upstairs are just now wrapping up for the day," said the apartment manager. "So let's start in the basement." As he began to descend, he said:

"When it's finished, the basement will be our laundry room with the newest ringer washers and two large concrete wash basins with hot and cold water. The ceilings down here are only 6 foot by 6 inches in height, and you'll see the floor joists on the ceiling from the floor above. No washers yet, of course. And since you'll have to take your laundry out while you are here, I'll give you a little discount on your rent. The Seminole Laundry is within walking distance on First Street."

Sorenson and Dianne stood in the doorway to the laundry as he finished his spiel. The reporter noticed a large, oak door with a glass onion doorknob lying on the concrete floor in front of the alabaster wash basins in the otherwise empty, windowless room.

"Your construction guys are a little careless," she said, and walked into the gloomy room. She knelt by the door. "Someone could trip over this. My stars, it's worse than that! Did you know they've bolted the door's hinges to the floor?!?"

"No, that's not possible," Sorenson objected as he knelt by her side. "My gosh, you're right! Now, why would they do that? As a joke? I'm going to have to have a strong word with those boys in the morning." He rose to his feet. "Seen enough, Miss Savage?"

"Was that other door we passed down here to the basement an apartment?"

"Yes. It's entered from outside by the door by the east porch, and is completely furnished, Miss Savage. It has a large living room and kitchen... but why am I giving you my sales pitch since it's rented out already by a widow with a baby? Once a salesman, always a salesman, I guess."

"Do you think we could say hello before we go back upstairs?" asked Dianne.

"Well, I can't see any harm in that since she works at night and is probably getting ready to leave right about now."

Sorenson and Dianne took the few steps to the apartment opposite the laundry room entrance where the manager rapped *nok nok nok* on the door with his knuckles.

"Ms. Willson, it's Gene! Do you have a moment?" A muffled "just a minute" was his answer, followed by a pause, then the door swung inward and open.

A fey young woman in her late twenties stood in the doorway dressed in a light, short-sleeved, powder-blue dress ending just above her knees. She was cradling a baby in the crook of her left arm. Her short, auburn hair was bobbed, and she wore a Grecian headband; her makeup was a little flamboyant for a young mother. The chubby-cheeked baby who held her mother tightly and looked at Dianne with suspicion was also dressed in a lightweight fabric and wore a pink, frilly band around the wisps of her own curly brown hair that positioned a rose in the center of her forehead.

"Margo," said Sorenson, "this young lady may be a new neighbor of yours on the first floor, and she wanted to say hello. Margo Willson, this is Dianne Savage."

"Pleased to meet you, Margo," said Dianne and extended a hand as a greeting.

"Same here," responded Margo, looking at her baby. "And this is Baby Veyda, actin' a little shy this mornin'. So you're movin' in upstairs?"

"Looks like it, if the price is right."

"Oh, oh," said Sorenson with a sheepish grin. "I told you about everything but that, didn't I? Since the laundry room isn't finished yet, let's make it $9 a week."

"Then we're neighbors," grinned Dianne as Margo took her still outstretched hand in her own. "You work at night? Who takes care of Baby Veyda?"

"I do," interjected Sorenson, "or, I guess I should say my wife, Judy, and I baby-sit little Veyda. She's a real doll baby; we love her to pieces."

"Well, I won't keep you any longer today. If you'll excuse me, I think I'll head up to my room and get a little rest. It's been a looong day. Maybe we can get together tomorrow, Margo, for lunch or something?"

"God willing," said Savage as their hands parted, hers dropping to her side.

Her comment was met with a bald-faced but wordless consternation shared between Margo, who glanced at Sorenson with an expression of mild surprise, and Sorenson, who shrugged his shoulders.

Dianne unzipped her suitcase and threw back its panel as it lay on the bed in the quiet of her profoundly beige, new apartment. She looked at its tightly packed contents, but weariness overtook her, and the reporter walked to the one window in the apartment to close its curtains before resting in one of the two chairs in the room. As she did so, Dianne saw a parking lot through the window overlooking the rear of the Van Sanford Apartments to its north. On its far side was an unusually large mound of freshly excavated dirt, possibly ten feet high. Behind that mound and hidden from First Street stood three men; two were beating the living hell out of the third in a silent, horrific dance of violence.

She covered her mouth with her right hand so she wouldn't cry out as one of the men swung his leg back and then kicked his victim *thud* in the stomach with a booted foot. As the assailed doubled over from the impact in anguish, the second of his attackers brought his knee up hard *thuk* into his face, sending him up and then backwards, throwing off a spray of blood as he did so to fall spread-eagled and still on the ground.

Dianne knew she couldn't stop them alone without using the gun in her suitcase and bringing undesired attention to herself, and was uncertain whether the only man she knew in the building, Gene Sorenson, would even try. But she was dead certain of one thing. As both of his assailants moved to their victim's opposite sides and began to ruthlessly and violently kick him *thud thud thud thud* in the stomach and then the ribs, she knew it would do no good to try to contact the police.

It wasn't for lack of courage on her part or of an available telephone.

As the reporter turned to retrieve her gun, her eyes still on the scene below, the two police men stopped their assault and sauntered away.

*..the odd pin in his shirt collar was a cluster of
interconnected crosses...*

Chapter Two

"Will this go out today?" asked Dianne and crinkled her nose at the fecund farm smells of fertilizer, livestock salves and medicines, and of live chicks chirping somewhere from the back of the feed and seed store and telegraph office. She pushed the form she had filled out across the desk to the clerk wearing wire-rimmed glasses that made his blue eyes three times too large for his face.

"Certainly, Miss Savage," he said, as he took a long drag on the cigarette in his left hand, and read the message to himself. "Yes. Yes. That will be fifty-seven cents."

"I would be very grateful if you could read it back to me," she asked, as she adjusted the uncomfortable knapsack she wore on her back. She noticed a stack of copies of *The Citadel*, Light's End daily newspaper, took one from the top and pushed it over to the clerk. "It's very important. And add this to my bill, please."

"'To: Larry Allison,'" he read aloud in a voice that revealed his irritation in having to do so, "'and his address in Bangor, Maine. 'Arrived safely. High hopes of success. DS.'"

"That will be fifty-seven cents, please," he said, staring at the note pinned to her pink, short-sleeved blouse. "I hope you have correct change."

Dianne had gotten out of bed on Thursday, October 11th at the crack of dawn on a brisk but beautiful morning to walk the several blocks east down First Street, then north on Dunlevy Avenue, until she reached Clausing's Feed and Seed next door to the Light's End post office. Sorenson had been right, of course, in his directions; the little, yellowed sign in the display window read: Western Union. Sending her telegram had been painless.

The message in the paper folded and pinned to her blouse that the clerk had stared at read: *Herein is love, not that we loved God, but that He loved us. John 4:19.*

As she left the store to walk back along Dunlevy Avenue, she mulled over the dilemma that always faced her as an investigative reporter and a Christian woman. Although she had not lied about researching Light's End for a novel (she actually was writing a book on small towns in Maine), she had also come to write an expose of its notoriously foul red-light district, Bishop's Alley. There was also no Larry Allison. It was a fictional name for her editor at the *Bangor Daily Register*, Jim Copeland, created to protect her identity when she was working undercover on a dangerous story. The address she had used could not be traced back to the newspaper either.

It was a moral question that would have to wait for resolution on another day. The reporter had reached her second goal of the morning, the red bricked Standard Grocery Store just east of her new apartment. It was the work of only moments for her to choose a dozen brown eggs, a half pound of salted butter, a small loaf of white, sliced bread, and a quart of whole milk, all locally produced, to carry back to the Van Sanford with her in the reporter's formerly empty knapsack.

The fallow young man at the cash register looked at Dianne with the same suspicion and reticence reserved for outlanders that he'd given her the night before when she'd paid him for several packages of bandages, cotton pads, and a small bottle of iodine. When she had said: "Thank you, and God bless," he looked at her as if she were an alien from Mars.

Dianne's walk back to the Van Sanford was uneventful and gave her an opportunity to add to her photographic memory some of the sites and businesses she wished to make pictures of later in the day. She ascended the steps of the east porch whistling the tune "There's a Rainbow Round my Shoulder" that she ended at the yellowish, artificial light in the hallway. She cracked open the door to 3A, and said:

"Vernon? It's Dianne Savage. Are you decent?"

Well-muscled and shirtless, Vernon Thomas sat on her bed, poised to spring up and flee through the door or fight for his life, depending on who stood in the doorway. His left hand lay unconsciously on the wide bandage around his otherwise naked ribs. Another cotton swath was wound in and around the matted black hair on his head, and small cotton pads were taped to the left corner of his mouth, on his right cheek, and over his right ear. They did not cover a number of black and blue bruises on his body.

"You look like you're feeling better," she said as she tossed the rolled up newspaper on the bed next to Vernon where it partially unfolded itself and lay still. "Do you like eggs and toast for breakfast?"

"Sure; yeah; thanks," Thomas answered, his face and body relaxing. "I could eat a little." He got up from the bed, found his shirt draped over a chair' on a bed post, and slowly and painfully put it back on. "It's gotta be better than buffalo fish."

"Do you feel like telling me what happened now?" asked Dianne, as she walked to the kitchenette, removed her knapsack, sat it on the counter next to the apartment's small sink, and began unpacking her groceries. "Do you drink coffee?"

"Don't rightly feel like coffee, ma'am, but thanks for offering. They beat me up because they said I knew too much and talked too much," Vernon answered as he picked up the newspaper. "It's safer for you if you don't know much more, Miss. Myself, I'm on my way to hop the afternoon train out of this stinking little hellhole."

"Well, I forgot to buy coffee, now that I think of it, Mr. Thomas. Are you a working man?" asked the reporter, as she turned on the oven and then pulled a small iron skillet and a spatula from an otherwise empty cabinet above the stove. "Do you have a family?"

"Ebaugh Construction brought me in paying good money to work on a big water and storm drain project for this rottin' little slum," said Vernon with a noticeable sneer as he laid the newspaper back on the bed. "I'm from Ada, Oklahoma, ma'am, and move around from job to job right now. No family to speak of; no wife nor kids."

"Water and storm drain system?" asked the reporter, as she turned on the gas burner to the stove, set the skillet on its little yellow and blue flame, and added a pat of butter and then six eggs, breaking one after another on the edge of the skillet, then throwing the shells in the sink. "Could you set the table, Mr. Thomas? You'll find plates and forks and stuff right over in that drawer. Something screwy going on with the construction?"

Holding his side with his left hand, Thomas rose and moved to the drawer that Dianne had indicated, his eyes never leaving her. He opened the drawer and removed two off-white plates, forks, and knives. Then he said: "You're pretty sneaky, tryin' to get me to say something anyway. Pardon me for askin', considerin' how you half-dragged and half-carried me up here last night and patched me up and all, but why do you even care?"

"Like I told you last night," she said, as the construction worker carried everything to the little metal table with a faux marble top between the kitchenette and the bed. "I'm researching little towns for a book, Mr. Thomas. No one knows you're here, and you won't catch me telling anything you might say to me to anyone else, and I'll be long gone from here before the book is published, and under a penname, at that. So I don't

"Do you drink coffee?"

think I'm at any risk."

"I'm no expert, but I've worked this kind of job before," Thomas said as he sat down at the table. "And I can tell you that the tunnels they're buildin' are way the Hell too big, excuse my language, and there are way too many of 'em for this size town. It don't make any sense. Usually when there's a scam, it's when someone buys cheap materials, or don't even do some of the job they're supposed to, but here they're using the highest quality stuff and doing too much work for a storm drain. It must be costin' a ton of money."

"Too much?" asked Dianne as she ladled eggs on his and then her plate.

"Yeah. Like why are they stringing electric lights in storm drains, and even digging big tunnels under Bishop's Alley; that isn't even in the city limits?" He didn't eat as much as swallow the eggs and toast on his plate.

"Bishop's Alley? What do you know about Bishop's Alley? Have you been down there, Mr. Thomas?" Although he bowed his head, Dianne could still see the construction worker's cheeks blush crimson where there were no stained bandages.

"Well, uh, I..." he tried to begin, then raised but turned his head so he did not look at the reporter. "I mean to say, jest a couple of times for a beer or two and a dance with one of the flappers, jest to let off steam. But that's all I know about the place, except it's no place for a lady like you, Miss Savage.

"I suspect it's time for me to go," he continued and stood up. "I don't have any way to really thank you for what you did for me, and I know I owe you big time for the bandages and breakfast and everything. So I'll tell you I was comin' here to meet one of those Alley gals who lives here when the two thugs caught me and beat the Hell out of me, excuse my language. If you want to know more about that lousy garbage dump, you could ask her."

"Right here at the Van Sanford, Mr. Thomas? What's her name?"

"Whoosh," Vernon blew out between his lips. "Don't rightly know. Calls herself Margo Willson, and lives on the first floor. Please do me a favor and don't mention my name."

According to her wristwatch, it was 10:30 in the morning when Dianne removed the tools of her trade — a small notebook and pencil — from her knapsack, closed her apartment door quietly behind her, walked west down the first floor hall to the stairs, and descended. But her persistent knock on the door of Margo Willson's basement apartment earned her nothing but red, sore knuckles, so she walked to the laundry room; no one was inside. She stood in the laundry, weighing her options. There was too little time for a comprehensive walk around downtown Light's End taking photographs, as she originally planned before the brutal beating the night before had thrown her schedule off kilter. Nor was she in the mood for interviewing the Chamber of Commerce Manager; such past interviews in similar situations had convinced her it was too much work to strip the salesmanship from the man down to the dismal bone of something she could actually print. She anticipated that securing a map of the town would be the best result from the meeting. That left a trip to the town's library for research in its archives on Light's End and Bishop's Alley as a viable option.

Whistling "Mack the Knife" to herself, she left the otherwise silent laundry room and ascended the stairs, then left the Van Sanford through its main entrance onto First Street.

As described by Sorenson, the Annie Gamwell Municipal Building that housed the town's library as well as city offices had been a brisk ten minute walk away to where it stood on the northeast corner of Dunlevy Avenue and August Street. It was a rare chilly day with a sky of scudding white clouds, so Dianne paused outside at the south end of the building by the library's entrance to take stock of the imposing structure.

Obviously the town's pride and its showcase for future growth, the mostly unadorned Municipal Building looked like three huge, rectangular, connected packing boxes, its south and north wings slightly smaller in height, width, and length. The central entrance of the south wing that Dianne faced was flanked on both sides by three thin, recessed rectangles with windows positioned on the first and second floors. That entrance was reached by a five-foot-deep porch with raised arms like an easy chair, and two stairs, all inside a shallow stone portico topped by two smaller windows. The facade of the building was a finished, smooth, beige stone that Dianne could not identify. "LIBRARY" was chiseled in Roman letters above the entrance, and the entire building wore a necklace of half-dead small shrubs and hackberry bushes. Dianne surmised it was relatively new because the building bore none of the cracks, discolorations, and deformities of weather or time.

Quietly singing, "birds do it, bees do it, even educated fleas do it" in her better-than-average alto voice, the reporter stepped inside the building to find a flight of steps that rose to an open wooden door with "LIBRARY" carved above it and a second flight of steps that lead down to another wooden door with an inset opaque glass pane and "COUNTY CLERK" painted on it. She walked up the steps singing, "let's do it, let's fall in love" and through the doorway to the library.

Savage stopped in the entrance, overwhelmed by the familiar and welcome vanilla smell of pulp, ink on paper, and polished wood, and the hushed silence that so characterized libraries which had filled her childhood as a single and somewhat pampered child with at least a weekly visit to "the shelves" with her mother or father. It was there she had first lost herself in the fantastic worlds of H. G. Wells' suspenseful "The Time Machine" and "War of the Worlds," of Jules Verne's wild adventure in "20,000 Leagues Under the Sea," of Frank Baum's dark Oz books (her favorite was the Tin Man), Arthur Conan Doyle's logical detective, Sherlock Holmes, and Lewis Carrol's surrealistic "Alice in Wonderland." She had even dressed as the Mad Hatter for Halloween one year before the tragedy.

The reporter was also flooded with fond memories of too brief lazy Sunday afternoons spent reading "Mutt and Jeff," "Barney Google," "The Katzenjammer Kids," "The Gumps," "Tarzan," and many other comic strips all in marvelous color in the funny pages of her father's newspapers— he had bought three different ones every week—strewn around the living room floor, of late afternoons playing with color splashed illustrated blocks, board games about baseball, cutout dolls, train puzzles, and reading picture books about Santa Claus and fairy tales with her parents.

On the third "may I help you?" the reporter's warm reverie was interrupted by the voice of a dour female librarian standing behind a large, dark wooden desk to the left of the doorway. A heating vent in the polished floor sighed in the quiet. The old woman in a worn, forest green floral dress and gold-rimmed Pinz-Nez glasses was staring at the reporter's pants with open disapproval and suspicion.

"I said, may I help you?" she said dryly as she closed the cover on a book. "I'm Mrs. Clive Staples, the Head Librarian."

"Oh, dear, I am so sorry," Dianne apologized. "This is my first time here, and I was just, uh, looking over your wonderful library for a minute."

"Are you looking for anything in particular?"

"Yes. Yes, Mrs. Staples. I'm looking for your section of periodicals; newspapers in particular, and any history of Light's End that you might have, ma'am."

"The periodicals section is on the left wall at the back of the library," answered the woman without looking at Dianne. She removed a black covered book from a stack to her left, opened its cover, removed a rubber stamp from where she'd inked it on an ink pad, and *thup* stamped the book. "Each of our bookshelves is numbered as well as alphabetized; you'll find a brief history of our town on row six, shelf L through N. But I'm afraid that you can't check out any book unless you have a library card."

"Thank you very much for your help; I'll be taking notes here," Dianne said, smiled, and held up her little notebook as she moved toward the aisle between the fourth and fifth rows of bookcases.

Book-filled wood shelving stood on the east and west walls from floor to ceiling, and in eight rows down the length of the building at shoulder height, those bookcases against the library walls broken occasionally by several doors that Dianne guessed opened on offices, restrooms, or meeting areas. As far as she could see, the library was empty outside of herself, the librarian, and a young mother squatting by the side of her redheaded five or six-year-old son, both engaged in looking at a picture book open on the woman's left thigh. When the reporter reached the middle of the aisle, she stopped, turned to her right, and began searching titles in the silence like a held breath by running a finger over the multicolored spines of the books.

It was a moment's work before she found an oversized, thin volume titled "The Early History of Light's End, Maine" with no author credited on the cover. When she opened it, she found forty or fifty typewritten pages with no copyright notice or publisher information. She took the volume from the shelf and moved to the back of the library where she had seen several small tables and chairs standing against the north wall. She sat down, took off her light green cloche hat, lay in on the table, placed her notebook and pencil on the reading table, and opened the obviously unpublished manuscript.

Savage opened it not because she had a compelling interest in or a need to know the town's outré history. She had done that research in Bangor at the state historical society. She began scanning sections of the typewritten manuscript to reinforce her "cover" as a writer gathering information for a book. Although that pretense would erode into suspicion when the first of her articles exposing the flagrant corruption and crime in Bishop's Alley was published, it was necessary to maintain that deception as long as was possible.

The reporter cleared her throat *harrumph* glanced up from the book, and startled.

Impossibly, a grossly fat man sat at the last reading table to her right. She erased her initially surprised expression, smiled, and quickly looked down at her book. As she did so, Dianne reasoned he must have been in a restroom or office to have appeared so suddenly, and her racing heart calmed. She returned to her book, carefully turning pages as if she were actually reading them, and occasionally jotting nonsense sentences on her notepad.

Dianne looked up again.

The Fat Man had yellow teeth and a face full of stubble and distaste and a look of slightly hidden superiority at the edge of the cut of his mouth. His worn and slightly stained short-sleeved shirt and pants were disheveled, as if he'd dressed in the dark. His red hair was in the slow process of balding, and his breathing was noticeably labored. A great, raw, ham of a hand rose and rubbed the red slit that was his left eye.

He was leering at her.

Her heart pounding, Savage looked down at her book. She told herself that he was obviously a bum, and probably a harmless one. She told herself that he was just a man, and she'd learned about men years ago, and had never met one she couldn't handle. She was a committed virgin, although not inexperienced in sexual matters. But she felt his eyes on her, and although she had removed nothing, she knew that she was naked to him.

She looked up.

The Fat Man smirked like a cat that has eaten a canary and winked and ran his left hand through the fringe of his red hair and over a hidden anomaly there.

Her jaw was rigid, and her teeth clenched as she closed the book and picked it up, picked up her notepad, pencil, and hat, and casually walked to the aisle next to her, the heels of her shoes *click click click* loud in the silence of the library. When out of his sight down the aisle, she quickened her pace, and replaced the book in its proper place in a bookshelf. Then Dianne walked to the south end of the aisle. The librarian didn't even look up from stamping a book as the reporter first passed in front of her desk, and then back down the west wall to the section for newspapers and magazines, refusing to be intimidated by the bum or stupid in ignoring a possible threat.

She met with immediate disappointment. The only newspaper hanging from the rack of wooden poles against the wall was one they received at the Bangor newspaper where she worked. It was *The Citadel*, the town's afternoon newspaper, and she had exhausted that disreputable source before she had even arrived in Light's End. As an even further disappointment, this library, as was true with most, carried no pulp magazines (her only market for her fiction) and only a few 'slick' titles including "Good Housekeeping" and the relatively new publication, a news magazine titled "Time."

Frustrated, Dianne sat down at the nearest reading table, and rested her right cheek on the palm of her right hand. She bit the fingernail of the first digit of her right hand. It had been a day of failures and no time remained to do any real work. She rose to retrace her steps back to the librarian's desk and nervously surveyed the room. The woman and her child and, thankfully, The Fat Man, were gone.

As Dianne walked along the west wall, she memorized the several brown, wooden doors that broke up the otherwise unbroken line of bookshelves. All had inset opaque glass windows; the lettering on one indicated an office, and one a restroom. But the third door brought her to a dead stop. The lettering on the glass read: Special Collections.

Savage tried the doorknob. It was locked. She rattled the doorknob. It was definitely locked. That left her no option but to ask the librarian for entrance.

"I'm afraid that's not possible," said Mrs. Staples with finality. She took a book from a stack on her left, and opened the cover. "The books and manuscripts in that room are rare and valuable, and one must be on a list of approved scholars."

"How can I get on the list, Mrs. Staples? I'm only going to be in town two weeks."

"A Board of Trustees decides that. You would have to go before that board, and I'm afraid they only meet once a quarter."

"Could I call one of the trustees?"

The pregnant silence and the librarian's look of derision felt like a physical blow. Diane could see Mrs. Staples' jaw tighten as she glared at her and, Dianne guessed, mulled over how to get rid of the annoyance in pants that had questioned her authority and would not leave her alone. The old woman took her rubber stamp and *thud* struck her open book.

"What is your name, young lady?" she asked, her voice icy and inflectionless.

"My name is Dianne Savage, Mrs. Staples," the reporter answered without hesitation.

"I..." she said with authority and as if she were pronouncing a punishment, "I will call the President of the Board of Trustees, Jake Horne, and let you know his decision, but I wouldn't get your hopes too high." She smiled like a crocodile. "They have never made an exception to the rules. Just stop by the library next week."

"Thank you so much," Dianne acquiesced as she turned quickly and walked towards the open doorway. "You might also ask them to do something about that filthy bum who hangs around and undresses your women patrons with his dirty little eyes."

She did not see but felt unholy fire in the librarian's eyes on her back as she left.

Dianne had decided to buy groceries and return to her apartment to prepare supper and review her existing notes on Bishop's Alley in preparation for a trip to the infamous red-light district on Saturday. The short walk to the Standard Grocery Store on First Street had no unexpected consequences. There, because of her apartment's limited kitchen, she bought prepackaged and canned items: a box of Post Grape Nuts cereal, a can of Campbell's Tomato Soup, and two cans of Libby's Evaporated Milk. To this, she added Heinz Tomato Ketchup, one pound of hamburger wrapped in white butcher paper, two tins of Armour Star Ham, Peter Pan Peanut Butter, two tins of Underwood Deviled Ham, and a can opener.

Nor did she receive the same disdain as on her earlier visit to the store from the sallow clerk who added up her purchases, took her money, and sacked her groceries in silence; she had forgotten to bring her knapsack. He had done all of this with indifference, not even offering to lift the two sacks to deposit them in her arms, so she tossed her notebook and pencil in one sack, wrapped an arm around each, lifted them, and turned away.

With a gasp, she dropped *thud* the sacks on the counter.

The two hulking policemen who had nearly beaten the construction worker to death with their fists and boots were leaning, one on each side, against the doorjamb of the entrance and exit to the grocery store. One was cleaning a dirty yellow fingernail with a pen knife. The other cop was picking his uneven teeth with the edge of an open matchbook cover. Both policemen were grinning like the Cheshire Cat from "Alice In Wonderland" and looking directly at her. When she had dropped the sacks, the toothpick cop tipped his hat.

"Is there another exit from the store?" Dianne asked the clerk, trying to mask the nervousness in her voice.

"Not for the public," said the clerk, now also grinning. "What's wrong?"

The reporter sneered at him, looked at the policeman, and then back at the store behind her. Then, mustering her courage, she took a deep breath, held it, picked up the sacks, and walked towards the door, her eyes never falling on the cops.

The pen knife moved, the matchbook moved, and their lizard eyes followed her progress towards them. They grinned.

Dianne walked between them, her shoulders held back, her face unflinching and forward. The cop to her right removed his toothpick and said: "As above, so below."

Then Dianne was beyond them and out of the door, then around the corner of the grocery store, where she released her breath.

Dianne had several unpleasant options that she mulled over that afternoon: either the policemen kept surveillance on strangers like her in town, they were simply being obnoxious and man-stupid with a woman, or they had found out about her connection with the construction worker they had beaten. But she refused to be paranoid; no hard evidence really supported that counterproductive, crippling attitude. So Savage went about the daily routines of life in her temporary home. While putting her hamburger in the freezer of the refrigerator, she was at least pleased that the ice man had stocked it while she had been in town.

After storing her groceries in the kitchen cabinets, Savage settled into the room's one chair to finish reading the issue of *College Humor* she had brought with her from Bangor. Rising, she then prepared and ate her evening meal, washed the soiled dishes and pans, and turned to her journal to review what she had learned about the notorious prostitute, violence, and dope-saturated Bishop's Alley before coming to Light's End.

The reporter had kept her journal — a simple, thick notebook — for many years as part of her employment at the newspaper. It was there that she gathered facts and opinions that would later be used in the articles, and, occasionally, fiction that she wrote.

She read:

1910. V. T. Bishop, lawyer, bought land west of August Street and the city. Built clapboard bars, dance halls, whore houses both sides of a dirt road. Open all hours of every day. First was Blue Heaven; "Tangle Eye" Elliott, manager, relative to one of town's founders, hired 'dime-a-dance' girls. Danced to a tinny Victrola phonograph on dirt floor, some making extra money as prostitutes, also picked pockets or set-up drunken customers for shakedowns as reported in *The Citadel* newspaper. Bishop also built shacks for employees and their 'customers' next to the saloon. When it rained, mud was so deep girls danced in boots, but it flourished.

The Palace was next, seven months later on the north side of road, "sophisticated" sin, live music, behind a new boardwalk. Customers guzzle "'ho-made Jake that give you Jake-Leg" and whiz-bang (cocaine). "Red" played saxophone, "Honey Girls" dance; also after flicker—State Theater downtown. From *Citadel*: "Patrons cower in dark until neighbors sneak out for fear of being seen." Jess Hayes, proprietor, called King of Underworld, wore diamonds, carried money, murdered April 13, this year, by Tom "Black Murphy" Calvert.

On south side, Blue Heaven, 49'er Dance Hall, Bucket o' Blood, Mother Murphy's. On north, The Palace, The Big Sea, The Kentucky Rooms. Bootlegging, dope, rage, hijacking murder. Outraged town slop whitewash across August Street where town stops and Alley begins. Mortuary service/furniture store located just on right side of white line.

Elliott eventually killed Red over girl. Tangle-Eye fled, never seen again.

Fifty-six night clubs in vicinity.

Dianne laid her journal on the top of the apartment's chest of drawers, went to the refrigerator in the kitchen for ice, poured and drank a glass of cold water and went to bed.

The bus pulled slowly into the breezeway and stopped with a squeal of brakes, and the driver opened the vehicle's rusty doors with the thrust of a metal handle by his seat.

"Light's End," he announced without turning his head. "Everyone off." Dianne was the only passenger who rose from her seat and walked to the front of the bus.

"Our guys will unload your luggage," continued the driver as he turned in his seat to face her.

His bearded face shown like the sun.

"Do ya want it carried to the Station or the Cafe, Miss?"

"The Cafe," she answered.

Then Savage woke up.

Chapter Three

On Friday morning, October 12th, at 9:00 am, Savage picked up her cobalt black leather Eastman Kodak No. 2 Hawk-Eye Special camera from her bed, opened its back, loaded one of two 120 exposure film packs she had brought with her, and sealed the camera. It joined the little bundle in her knapsack of dirty clothes she planned on dropping off at the Seminole Cleaners on her way back to the Van Sanford Apartments later in the day. The otherwise cerulean blue sky seen outside the window facing the back of the complex was heavily spotted with dirty, gray clouds that threatened rain. She hunched her shoulders in resignation to what was beyond her control, and left her apartment dressed in her last clean blouse — white, short-sleeved and cotton — and clean, blue dungarees. Her green cloche hat covered most of her red curls.

The folded paper pinned over her heart on her blouse read: *I will instruct you and teach you in the way you should go, I will counsel you and watch over you. Psalm 32:8*

It was an uneventful morning that had been consumed with the daily routines of personal hygiene and preparing and eating breakfast. There had been no visible police outside her window before she left her apartment, and she was mentally prepared to write off that earlier fear of threat to herself as unfounded as she walked down the first floor hall at to the main entrance of the apartment complex and the stairwells that led down to the basement and up to the second floor. She began to descend; *click click click* the sound of the heels of her shoes like little exploding firecrackers. Her hope was that she could talk at least briefly with Margo Willson about the corruption in Bishop's Alley.

As she descended, she saw Gene Sorenson entering the laundry room. Dianne quickened her descent, and, raising her right arm in greeting, called out, "Mr. Sorenson!" but he was through the doorway before her words could reach him.

The reporter reached the bottom of the stairwell and walked to the laundry room. As she entered it, she called again, "Mr. Sorenson; good morning!"

The gloomy, grey room was empty.

The room was utterly silent and impossibly empty. The reporter again surveyed it slowly and carefully. The two, large, commercial sinks stood against the opposite wall as before and the incongruous door hinged to the floor had not been removed. The room was an otherwise bare and inexplicably empty cement box, and Dianne leaned against the doorjamb, completely befuddled. Had she not seen Sorenson entering? Was her imagination running away with her; a mind that had been trained for observation? She shook her head, straightened, turned, began to walk to the door of Margo Willson's apartment, and stopped. She turned back and looked at the door in the floor, her reporter's insatiable curiosity strong. She looked into the laundry room to her left, then to her right. She turned slightly, and looked behind her back towards the stairwell. No one was near. Then the reporter entered the laundry and walked to the door in the floor.

Savage knelt, placed her hand on its elaborate glass onion knob, and hesitated. It felt warm, or was she sweating? She expected to see concrete beneath the door. But was it instead an entrance to a clammy, hidden chamber where the Sorensons tortured writhing sex slaves, or an unspeakable entrance to the bowels of Hell? Had she stumbled onto a black hole to another dimension, crawling with slobbering horrors, or a warp in time that would carry her back to the crucifixion of Christ? Would she uncover an unholy secret of the created universe that had baffled the human mind for untold centuries?

She thought: *I've been reading too much "Amazing Stories" and "Weird Tales."* Savage opened the door on the concrete floor onto a concrete floor. She carefully let it slowly fall back to the floor as she chastised herself for her overactive imagination. Even though something unanswered still gnawed at her sense of order, she concluded she surely could not have seen Sorenson.

Dianne left the laundry still bewildered and a little ashamed of herself, walked to the basement apartment, and knocked *thak thak thak* on Margo Willson's door. It opened and Margo stood, indifferent and a little unfocused and haggard, as diapered but otherwise undressed baby Veyda crawled on the floor behind her. "Oh," she said, "it's you; the new gal from upstairs."

"Good morning, Miss Willson," said Dianne. "I'd hoped to catch you before you went to work so that I might ask a few questions. But if this is a bad time..."

"It is a bad time," she grumbled, unconsciously twisting a strand of her auburn hair between the thumb and index finger of her left hand. "A bad time that I'll work myself through, Miss...?"

"Savage. Dianne Savage. From upstate. Bangor."

"Miss Savage. But I guess it's as good a time as any if you can watch Baby Veyda for me while I get ready?"

"Oh, I love children! I'd be happy to, Miss Wilson," she answered and unconsciously bit the ragged fingernail of the first digit of her right hand.

"Then, please come in," offered Margo with a sweep of her left arm, visually signaling her welcome as she stepped back from and to one side of the door.

"You have a lovely apartment," said Dianne politely in recognition of and respect for their mutual femininity as she entered. "Just lovely."

"Let's not start off with a lie, okay, even if it's a sweet one. I get enough of that where I work," said Margo with bleak weariness. She moved to a small, cluttered kitchen table and sat in front of a number of little jars and containers that obviously held cosmetics as the reporter squatted next to the baby, who met Dianne with curiosity laced with suspicion and reservation, as if Veyda were studying a bug under a microscope.

"I understand completely, Miss Willson. You work down at Bishop's Alley?"

There was a moment of stony silence as the young woman walked to her kitchen table and sat down. "Who told you that," she said (not asked, defensive but unafraid).

"The apartment manager," answered Dianne as she gently stroked Veyda's cheek. "Gene Sorenson."

"Oh. I do work at The Palace dance hall in the Alley. They got a crummy little four piece band, and me and the other girls who work there stand inside a railing around the dance floor while men wait on the other side. One of us girls picks a customer and he pays twenty-five cents for a quick dance, and we keep ten cents. That's it. Nothing else."

"Who is the manager there, Miss Willson?"

"Ruby Scott. She came up from Mexico without a lot of noise after her husband died of cancer. She had arrived with five dollars in her purse, the clothes on her back, and a cancelled train ticket. At least, that's the way she tells it. She sewed cheap dresses during the day and started out as one of the dancers at The Palace at night. Then she opened a hamburger shack called the Red Burger in front of one of Bishop's lousy, dirty rent houses where she lived at the far west end of Bishop's Alley, and lost her shirt on that."

"She sounds like a tough cookie," said Dianne, as she picked up a still reluctant Veyda from the floor. The baby immediately pointed a chubby arm at the door and said, "Go."

"Where do you want to go, buddy?" asked Dianne of Veyda, smiling.

"She wants to go to the park," interjected Margo, picking up a tube of red lipstick from the table. "Ruby's a man in a woman's body. So she made her home a beer garden with a bar in the living room and made money. When The Palace's first manager was brutally murdered, Ruby was hired to replace him as much to get her to shut down the competition as because she knew how to run a joint. She even wrote a song, called "Bishop's Alley Blues," that everyone tries to sing down there. She wears riding pants, boots, carries a gun, and her voice is deep as a man's. The cops, who are all on the take, leave her alone.

"Spanish Blackie, her lover, is a Negro Mexican who handles a stiletto like it's a sixth finger. He runs the gamblin' games in a back room where he separates 'fools' from their paycheck. And that's about all I know about The Palace or Bishop's Alley, except to mind my own business and watch my back."

"The newspaper says prostitution, dope, and even murders happen down there, Miss Willson," said Dianne. "Don't you get scared?"

Margo put down her lipstick. "I mind my own business and watch my back," she repeated with ice lacing each word. "And it's Mrs. Willson."

"Oh! Uh, well, I... uh, Mr. Sorenson said..." The baby pointed her arm at the apartment door and said, "Go."

"My husband was recently killed in an accident working on the storm drain project here, Miss Savage, leaving me penniless and with no other choice but to dance at the Alley until I can earn enough to get myself and my baby back home."

"Oh, dear," said Dianne, placing Veyda gingerly back on the floor and patting *thaf thaf thaf* the bottom of her diaper. "I had no idea. Please accept my apologies..."

"You had no way of knowing, and it's time for me to dress and take Veyda up to the Sorenson's—who watch her for me. Don't mean to be rude, but..."

"Don't let the door hit me where the sun don't shine," grinned Dianne. "Gotcha. I am truly sorry and hope we can get to know one another better."

Margo stood up and looked the reporter, unflinching, squarely in her blue-green eyes. Without smiling, she said, "No offense taken, honey. Any friend in a storm."

The door did not hit Dianne as it closed behind her.

Unsoiled by the human refuse of sordid clam bakes, midnight drunken swimming parties, or illicit debauchery, or even the ocean's refuse of dead flotsam: seaweed, jellyfish turned to goo, and bleached shells of hermit crabs left behind by the slight, sluggish swell and sough of the filthy waters of Abomination Day, Savage still sensed that the yellow sand, the crust of which crunched beneath her shoes, was somehow unrelentingly unclean. The unsanitary stink of it was palpable even in the stagnant, unmoving air. The reporter covered her nose and her mouth with the palm of her right hand. She squinted east with watering eyes at the short, narrow, railed pier that stretched before her from the empty beach that the people of Light's End had ignored, or even pretended didn't exist, to the shoreline of the bay.

Although it was October and twilight in Maine, the severe, short-sleeved, unadorned, knee-length black dress that she wore to funerals clung to her because of the hot sheen of sweat between it and her flesh. She wore no coat or hat.

Above her an under-lit, unbroken, grey blanket of clouds, like the bloated underbelly of a dead fish, roiled and rolled in frustration and threatened in deep rumbling anger to spit freezing rain and lightning.

In the otherwise eerie silence and to her distant left squatted the wild throw of stone that was Elliott's Head cliff; at its base, the legendary mouth of Caleb Elliott's cave that was both nursery and tomb for his unholy offspring with a naiad. It remained forever clogged with a motionless, ragged flow of dirt, boulders and debris that fell down and into the bay. To her right, the thin, yellow, dirty beach curved beyond her sight into oblivion.

Dianne stepped onto the deserted pier.

It was completely irrational for her to be there or to do so. There was no earthly reason for a pier that looked like it had been built yesterday to stretch into the fetid, dead waters of the bay where no ship had ever docked, no commercial or casual fisherman had ever thrown a line, in which no sane person had ever swum out and back, and on whose sunken piles no seagull had ever roosted. Indeed, it had illogically looked worm-eaten and rotten from a distance, and there was no reason for her to walk out over the bay on it.

She took a second step. Thunder rolled.

She took a third, and fourth, and fifth step.

Savage stood at the end of the bleak pier and looked ten feet down at the sluggish morass that was the dead waters of Abomination Bay, forever denied most of the natural egress and exit of water from the Atlantic by Abomination Reef. Even at high tide the majority of the jagged reef of naked stone crouched just beneath the lapping waves a thousand feet or so beyond the pier, the visible sky above the ocean looking like a dead, half-eaten rat black on the horizon.

She looked down at the dirty mirror of copper water that belched a sudden cluster of bubbles. She looked down at the dirty water that belched a second time as a black mass rolled up just beneath the surface, and belched a larger cluster of bubbles again. She looked down as the mass rolled up and broke the mirrored surface.

She looked down and opened her mouth to scream.

And sat up in bed.

Saturday, October 13. It was colder than yesterday as Dianne walked briskly down First Street, already noisy with the *hurrrrmm* of motor vehicles and *clop clop clop* of horse drawn carriages towards Ferry where she would turn north to downtown Light's End. She was approaching the Seminole Laundry on the corner of First and Wells — a beige brick, rectangular building with its red adobe tile roof extended to create a covered drive-through for customers — when she decided on a change of plans. She crossed First Street to the northwest corner of Wells, and then crossed Wells to the laundry to drop off her little bundle of dirty clothes with the hope that they might be cleaned by the time she returned to her apartment late in the afternoon.

The slight woman behind a long, wide desk who greeted her with a tepid smile was easily in her mid- to late fifties, and of American Indian descent. Her high cheekbones, black hair, and copper skin added to her dignity and beauty. Dianne noticed she wore the same odd cluster of crosses that formed a diamond shape on her lapel as did Sorenson; the woman said, "Good morning. May I help you?"

Behind the laundry woman snaked a long, suspended, motionless conveyer full of hanging clothing of all colors, fabrics, and styles. On the desk sat a pumpkin and a necklace of fall leaves as decoration, and a large glass jar with some money inside; a paper card leaning against it read: Please give First Church of Tenebrae.

The store was very hot from the tubs and commercial presses, probably located behind that conveyer, that were used to clean clothing. So Dianne made short work of emptying the dirty clothes from her knapsack onto the desk, and then dropping a few coins into the jar. She noticed the woman staring at the camera in her knapsack.

"Thank you for the donation," said the woman. "This should be ready by four or five this afternoon. I hope you don't mind my asking, but are you new to Light's End, Miss? I couldn't help but notice your camera."

"Yes, I'm from Bangor," Dianne responded as she closed up and wiggled back into her knapsack. "I thought I'd take a walk downtown this morning to see your retail district, take some pictures, and maybe do a little shopping."

"That's wonderful," said the woman as she sorted the reporter's clothes on the desk. "Keep your eye out for my son while you do, and please tell him I said hello; I don't see as much of him as I'd like nowadays."

"And where might I see him, Mrs...?"

"Seminole. My name is Mary Seminole, and his name is Joe. I like to send pretty girls his way; he's a bit shy, and still single, I might mention. He'll be selling popcorn outside of the Rex Theater on August Street by the time you get there, I'd imagine."

"Your name is Seminole? Like the Seminole on the metal sign outside?" asked Dianne, a bit puzzled.

"Why, yes. My husband and I own the laundry. I can see that you thought I was just a clerk here."

"Oh, n-no, n-no," Dianne stuttered, but could not hide the slight crimson color creeping into her otherwise unrouged cheeks. "A bag of fresh popcorn might just hit the spot. I'll make sure to keep an eye out for Joe, Mrs. Seminole, and I'll see you later this afternoon."

Savage was halfway down the north side of red-bricked Ferry Street, ignoring the businesses she passed, before she stopped in front of the Owl Drug Store. A few grey clouds scudded above, and Ferry Street was vibrant with a cacophony of sounds, smells, cars, trucks, and an occasional horse-drawn vehicle, most in motion, many parked. The sidewalks were a bustling jumble of men, many in work clothes, women, and a few children.

Across the street from the reporter stood the large two-story, Grisso Hotel next to the incongruous Pat's Cafe built of natural stone, and then the red bricked Maritime Supplies on the corner of August Street and Ferry. A huge, sign painted in orange letters on the side of the second story of the Maritime building read: Grand Pool Hall.

Even though the light wasn't the best, the reporter shook out of her knapsack, sat it on the sidewalk, opened it, and removed her camera. She leaned against the northeast edge of Owl Drug Store to steady her hand, and began to take photographs of the hotel, cafe, and Supply Company any time there was a lull in traffic. It was the work of only moments before she knelt to close her knapsack, and rose, her camera still in hand, when the Fat Man from the library lumbered out of the entrance of the Crawford Hotel.

She covered her mouth involuntarily with her free hand, and quickly stepped back and around the corner of the drug store, pressing herself against the wall, a response more defensive, female, and animal than one made out of conscious fear, as the Fat Man shuffled to the passenger side of a luxurious 1925 Buick Illustration automobile double parked in the street. Noticably unkempt and dirty even at her distance from him, the Fat Man opened the Buick's door with the body language of familiarity and authority (uncharacteristic of a bum), sat, and closed the door, talking to the driver as he did so. The automobile pulled into traffic, heading north.

Well, how about that, said Dianne inside her head. *How does that fit into anything?* She laid her camera carefully on the sidewalk, shrugged into her knapsack, picked up her camera, and walked to the corner of Ferry and August Street, mulling over the already growing number of ineffable, minor mysteries she could not yet unravel.

On the corner of Ferry and August, Savage leaned against the wall of the City Drug Store and took five photographs in rapid succession of the northeast block of Light's End's main retail district that descended to the train depot at its mouth. Her photographs included Dolittle Sundries, M & K Cafe, State Theater, Majestic Cafe, Rex Theater, and three other businesses that were at too great a distance for her to read their signs.

On the northwest corner of Ferry and August, Savage leaned against the wall of the Commercial Hotel. August Street stretched down to the end of the hard-edged town, the train depot. The sun was momentarily obscured by gray clouds that cast shadows into the street cobbled with red brick and lined on either side by buildings further shaded by metal awnings. A line of parked cars down the center of August split it into two busy avenues. At the end of the street, the adobe train depot roofed with red tile sat on the Pishon River that emptied into the harbor.

She lowered her camera and looked at the young man in a beige suit who stood straight and tall next to a popcorn wagon in front of the Rex Theater; certainly it was Joe Seminole. The movie house behind him had been converted from a brick building not originally built to be a theater. It had the recessed entrance, freestanding ticket booth, and theater posters mounted to walls that were common to almost all movie houses. But there was neither a large marquee announcing the movie nor the hundreds of blinking marquee lights that glamorized most theaters. Instead, the Rex had a flat-topped metal awning supported by five wooden posts and extending over the sidewalk and the two businesses adjacent to it and, at a 45 degree angle to the face of the building, a small "REX" sign over a tiny marquee below with changeable lettering. The two sets of two windows on either side of the sign and marquee looked like the common windows in a family home.

During a lull in traffic, Dianne crossed the street to lean against a wall of the two-story Commercial Hotel on the northeast side of Ferry. Again in quick succession, the reporter snapped five additional photographs of the southeast side of August that included Maritime Supplies, The New York Store, Dunlap's Department Store, Phillips Pawn Shop, The Citadel newspaper, and several other building too distant for her to identify. Then she crossed the street and walked to the Rex Theater and its popcorn wagon. As she approached, she heard: "Hot, fresh, and delicious popcorn," shouted with the feigned enthusiasm of a circus barker by the assumed Joe Seminole to the people approaching from the west and above the low noise of the sidewalks and street. "Only one nickel a bag! Get it here! Hot! Fresh! Delicious! Eat it here, enjoy it at the exciting flicker inside, or take it home!"

"I'll take one," said Savage, and Seminole turned to face her. He had the same high cheekbones, black hair, and rich bronze skin as his mother, a strong, masculine jaw line, and deep brown eyes in a youthful and strong face that seemed to sparkle with mischievousness.

"Well, well, well, it's always a pleasure to serve a beautiful lady," he said and smiled with his entire face. "And pants, no less! You a Suffragette?"

"Well, I'd say I'm suffering from that last comment," Dianne said, as she pulled a nickel from her pants pocket and handed it to him. "Are you, by any chance, that shy young man, Joe Seminole?"

"Shy young... ?! Who told?!" he asked and handed her a paper sack full of popcorn.

"A little bird at Seminole Laundry."

"Ah. That beautiful little dove still thinks I'm three years old. As you can see," he said, spinning around, "I'm a growed up man with all my teeth and hair, and lots of prospects, thank you very much. And who wants to know?"

"My name is Dianne Savage, and 'lots of prospects'? You're a twenty-something year old man selling popcorn at a movie house."

"Well, Dianne Savage, pleased to meet ya. I'm actually the Assistant Manager of the Rex Theater, and that means that I do the work of ten employees, especially when one doesn't show up, and everything the Manager is supposed to do and doesn't. And as for prospects, I'll own this theater some day, and rename it the 'Seminole'!"

"Well, you're cocky, I'll give you that," grinned Savage, and pushed a red curl back under her cloche hat.

"You're new to our wonderful little town, Ms. Savage?" he asked, and Dianne noticed that his face made dimples when he smiled broadly. "Not many of the locals take photographs of downtown businesses around here."

"Very good deduction. Yes, Mr. Seminole, I am visiting from Bangor. I'm collecting research for use in a book I'm writing on small towns in Maine."

"Here's a small town fact for you. Everyone calls me Joe, not Mr. Seminole. And may I offer my services; I'd love to give you a tour of Light's End, Dianne."

"Here's a fact for you, Joe. Call me Miss Savage. And I don't know you from Adam. So why should I trust you for anything beyond a nickel bag of popcorn?"

"Correction. The best nickel bag of popcorn in town! You should trust me because my mother thinks I'm peachy, and mothers don't lie, because I have a star for perfect attendance in High School, and I have an authentic certificate from Little Orphan Annie that says I'm a swell guy!"

"I'll think about it, Joe," she said with an unconscious lilt in her voice.

"At least come back for the show! It's a great one. Now showing!" he added with a grand flourish of his bronze hand and arm, "'Tarzan the Mighty,' starring Frank Merrill, Natalie Kingston, and Bobby Nelson! Big stars all!" And Joe threw back his head, opened his mouth for a silent yodel, and pounded his chest in imitation of the Ape Man.

"Despite that silly display of male chutzpah, I'll still think about it, Joe Seminole," Dianne responded, and turned on her heels and walked away, feeling his eyes following her as she wound her way through the agitation of citizens of Light's End down August Street.

On the northwest corner of Ferry and August streets, the reporter leaned against a light pole, and took five exposures of the second block of businesses on the southwest side of the town, freezing in time and immortalizing forever the people and vehicles captured by each picture.

"Are you…that shy…Joe Seminole?"

This included City Drug, C. R. Anthony's (with Crandall's Art School upstairs), The Vogue dress shop (with Cecil's Boot Shop upstairs), T. J. Collins — Dentist, the Liberty Theater, Jones Drug Store, and several other businesses too distant to discern.

She recognized no one who passed her on the sidewalk, as was to be expected, the morning breeze that carried the faint salty smell of the ocean and beach had stiffened as she took the final picture, and the temperature had fallen enough that she caught herself occasionally shivering. So she decided to stop in at the K. C. Store on the side of the block where she stood to buy a jacket before taking her next set of photographs.

She chided herself for this unanticipated and foolish oversight when planning her trip because buying a coat would deplete her funds much more quickly than she had planned. So, as she walked into the shop, Savage resolved to stop by the telegraph office on the way back to the Van Sanford apartments to send a cryptic request to her editor for more money.

As she entered the K. C. Store, she saw that multicolored piles of merchandise were stacked on flat tables and in shelves along walls bare of advertising rather than attractively displayed like in the bigger Bangor shops, and Dianne walked to the men's clothing section as soon as she saw it. There, she made short work of finding the smallest men's brown leather flight jacket; the price of men's clothing was always unjustly less than women's and the reporter, for her purpose, cared nothing about fashion.

After paying a clerk, she removed her knapsack, donned the jacket, replaced her knapsack, and left the store, still carrying her camera. She walked west to the corner of Wells and Ferry, and took five photographs of the second block on the southwest side of downtown Light's End. In addition to continuing her charade of interest in the businesses to reinforce her facade as a novelist, her interest in the Williams Cafe across August Street was sincere; her stomach was growling. So she crossed the busy street in mid-block, and entered the small eatery.

The cafe was long and narrow with a high stamped tin ceiling, packed with men — most in work clothes, not even removing their caps or hats, and most smoking cigarettes before, during, and after their meal — women, children, and harried waitresses. The eatery was raucous with the low murmur of human voices, the shouts of waitresses, the clink of utensils, glasses and dishes, and pungent with the warm smell of fried foods, especially fish, hamburger, potatoes, and chowder. A passing waitress dropped a menu on the table in front of Dianne, apologizing for any delay and promising to return shortly, which she did.

The chowder with crackers and coffee the reporter ordered came quickly, obviously precooked in volume in anticipation of the regular crowd of hungry customers for lunch.

As Savage ate, she noticed a plaque on the wall with a curious inscription. It read: The KNOCKERS meet here Wednesday. Above this was that curious diamond shaped cluster of little crosses that her apartment manager had worn on his shirt and that she'd noticed at the Seminole Laundry. Dianne stopped a waitress who was walking by with a line of plates balanced on her left arm and, pointing at the sign, asked: "Excuse me, miss. What's that all about?'

"Men's club," answered the woman, barely pausing and perturbed at the interruption. "Civic club. As above, so below." And she was gone.

Savage made a mental note to ask Sorenson about the offensive name and the purpose of the group, rose from her table, paid her check, and walked out onto the sidewalk.

Back at the southwest corner, the reporter took photographs of the opposite side of the block east of her, paying no attention to the names or locations of the businesses. Then she turned west and took five photographs of the block west and opposite where she stood. She crossed the street, and walked west up the last block of downtown to the northwest corner of Dunlevy and August Street.

She had anticipated and glamorized the notorious red-light district of Light's End in her mind to the extent that Bishop's Alley was a surprising disappointment.

"Damn," Savage whispered to herself, and immediately berated herself for cursing.

The road before her was unpaved, rutted, and filthy with trash and empty bottles, sparsely populated with automobiles and trucks parked in front of what could only be described as squalid shacks of varying sizes. At its mouth stood several retail businesses that seemed out-of-place — Sutherland Lumber, a new and used furniture store, a hamburger joint, and a barber shop — before the bars and dance halls multiplied like rats on both sides of the road, and a few men, young and mostly in work clothes and hats and caps, smoking cigarettes, were randomly scattered down the dirty boardwalks; a few staggered, a few lay slumped by the doors of the bars.

The signs that Savage could read were clumsily hand-painted on the sides of the seedy shacks or on lumber protruding above doorways. Lines of what looked like cheap Christmas lights were strung both across the street and down and above the boardwalks from the stunted, wooden light poles that dotted both sides of August Street.

From the vacant lot where she stood, Dianne could not see the sign for The Palace where Margo Willson danced. So she steadied her camera as best she could, took a deep breath, and took five photographs. She walked across the street to the southwest corner of Dunlevy and August next to the Light's End Municipal Building and Library, and snapped five more photographs of the foul-smelling red-light district.

It was unspoken but assumed by decent people that a respectable, young, unattended woman would not be caught dead in Bishop's Alley, day or night, so it had taken every ounce of the reporter's will power not to walk into the Alley to begin her investigation, therefore taking the chance of blowing her cover as a casual observer. She shrugged out of her knapsack, opened it, placed her camera inside, closed and wiggled back into the knapsack, and began walking south on Dunlevy back to her apartment. The clouds above her were a thick, rolling, tattered blanket of iron gray beneath which a dirty splatter of damp ducks hung and then swirled and hung again in the bleak October sky.

Dianne awoke in her apartment on Saturday at 9:00A.M.to a slow, drenching rain and its low, unending sigh; cold tears that distorted reality wept on the window facing the parking lot. Frowsy and grumpy, she resigned herself that her first trip into Bishop's Alley was probably not going to happen on such a dreary day, so she went through her morning hygiene ritual including a long, hot bath, dressing in the clean clothes she had picked up yesterday from the Seminole Laundry, preparing and eating toast and eggs for breakfast, cleaning the dishes, and then curling up on her bed to read her Bible.

She read for a little more than an hour, occasionally checking to see if the rain had stopped, then put her Bible aside and rose to pace around the room in an effort to dispel the pent-up energy that had made her a successful, driven reporter. As she paced, the idea struck her that she could possibly talk to Sorenson about the Knockers or chat with Margo Willson. She picked up her pencil and note pad and left her apartment.

Savage's knock on the office door of the Van Sanford apartments was met with a woman's voice: "Come in; it's not locked." As the reporter entered, a middle-aged, brown-haired woman in a modest plaid blouse behind Sorenson's desk looked up from a stack of papers, and Dianne was met with an open and pleasant smile and a friendly greeting.

"Hello; I'm Judy Sorenson. May I help you, Miss?"

"Oh, hello, Mrs. Sorenson. I'm Dianne Savage, your new renter just a door or so down the hall. I was looking for Mr. Sorenson."

"Gene's out, but maybe I could help?" asked Judy, as she laid the pencil she had been using on the papers before her down on the desk. She waved for the reporter to come closer. "Pull up a chair, Miss Savage. Would you like a cup of coffee?"

"Oh, yes, thank you. Black, a little cream, and no sugar, if that's ok?" Dianne pulled a chair in front of Sorenson's desk and sat; the apartment manager's wife extended an empty cup to her, and picked up a half-filled carafe of coffee from the desk. "I was just curious about some things I've run into while walking around your town, Mrs. Sorenson."

"Please call me Judy, and ask away," responded the woman as she filled Dianne's cup. "I'm no historian, but I hear gossip around this little berg."

"Judy. I notice that your husband is a member of something called the 'Knockers'...?"

"You mean the 'Sophist's Club.' But you are right that everyone seems to call them 'Knockers.' That," said Judy, holding one hand parallel to her body and rapping her knuckles into its palm, "is because of their secret greeting. See? Knocking? Not much of a cryptic secret. I'm a member of their women's auxiliary, the 'Daughters of the Star,' and we have a secret greeting too! It's nothing sinister or nasty, dear. The Sophists and the Star are both civic organizations. We meet to eat lunch together once a week. We raise money for scholarships and to buy eyeglasses for people who can't afford them and baseball uniforms for the school team by holding dances and pancake breakfasts and other fund raisers. It's just a way to have a little fun. It has nothing to do with these," she said, pointing at her breasts and smiling. "Anything else?"

"I noticed that the Knoc....," stumbled the reporter, then caught her mistake and continued. "... the Sophist's Club and the Church of Tenebrae use the same diamond-shaped cluster of tiny crosses as some kind of identifying symbol, Judy. I've never seen it before. Do you know what the symbol means and why they use it?"

"Why, yes, that's right! How very observant of you. I do know that because both Gene and I are members of the Tenebrae Church, although we don't go as much as we should. But I must confess that I never thought about the little cluster."

"You go just on Christmas and Easter and maybe Mother's Day, like a lot of folks?" Dianne smiled, and pushed a red curl back into place.

Her antiseptic smile and question won Savage a cool, puzzled look from Judy.

"Just about everyone in Light's End goes to the Church of Tenebrae, Dianne," she said, opened a drawer in her desk, and began to rummage through its contents. "I'm certain someone can answer your question, but I have a little something that might satisfy your curio... here it is!" She held up a thin brochure. "This will tell you about the church. It's yours."

Dianne took the brochure, and sat her empty coffee cup down on the table. She opened the pamphlet for a quick glance, then closed it.

"Thank you so much for your help," said the reporter as she rose from her chair. "I will certainly read this, and I hope you have a wonderful day."

"Good day to you as well," chirped Judy. "It was nice to meet you."

Savage stood at the main entrance of the Van Sanford Apartments and watched the somber rain crying. An occasional low growl of thunder without lightning rolled under the gray clouds and joined the melancholy sigh of the rain. She sat down on a dry patch on the porch to the left of the doorway, stretched out her legs, and read the pamphlet. On its cover was a picture of the church; a large version of the cluster of crosses hung above its entrance. In addition to the usual information about location, worship times, and special services, she read:

"Tenants of the Church of Tenebrae:

"1) There is no God; 2) Love yourself; 3) Deny yourself nothing; 4) Truth is relative to need; 5) Nothing is sacred or forbidden; 6) Eliminate whatever threatens your welfare; 7) If two agree, sex is free (of stricture); 8) Take what you must; 9) Embrace Enlightened Self-interest; 10) Hide openly.

"All of the tenants are contained in: Love yourself and do what you want."

Dianne was more than puzzled about an outrageous list that seemed to promote atheism and humanism published in a brochure for a church. But it was not the only surprise.

At the top of the list of church staff members, under the title "First DemiUrge," was printed "Jake Horne."

Savage stood impatiently at the checkout counter at the Standard Grocery Store with her groceries, placing each item in her knapsack after it was rung up on the cash register. According to her wrist watch, the rain had finally ended at 3:45 P.M. that afternoon, and she had felt her time best used by stocking up on food since almost all of the stores would be closed on Sunday due to Maine's Blue Law. She had spent her time after talking with Sorenson by knocking on Margo Willson's door (no one answered), then preparing and eating lunch, reading her Bible again, and uncharacteristically napping.

It had certainly been a day of enigmatic surprises and questions, but nothing unusual had transpired during her trip to the store, or during her choosing her items. Before the last item was processed, she picked up a copy of the current *Citadel* newspaper from a stack on the counter, and added it to her purchases. Although she had no faith in the accuracy of the Light's End daily newspaper, it would at least help fill the hours until it was time for sleep.

As she was walking back to her apartment on the north side of First Street, she changed her mind about preparing supper for herself, and stopped at the tiny Harley's Drive In hamburger joint across from the Van Sanford, and ordered a cheeseburger, french fries, and tea. She sat on one of the wooden, yellow picnic tables on the east side of the common hamburger joint, ignoring the remaining raindrops there, and opened her copy of *The Citadel* as she waited for her order.

Savage scanned the headlines on the first page of *The Citadel*; all were of the mundane activities and conflicts usual for a small town newspaper. She opened the newspaper. The headline of the major story on page three caught her attention. It read: Vagrant Decapitated in Train Mishap.

As she read, she choked back a gasp, her eyes welled up with tears, and she dropped the newspaper on the top of the bench, forgotten.

The vagrant had been Vernon Thomas.

CHAPTER FOUR

Wearing her green cloche hat and the only dress she had brought with her, Dianne Savage left the Van Sanford promptly at 9:35 A.M .on Sunday morning, October 15. Though the sky was a clear, cerulean blue, it was cold as the reporter briskly walked the three blocks south down Angell Street to a modest Craftsman house with a little, metal yard sign that read: Light's End Baptist. There was neither steeple nor cross nor any other icon that identified it as a church.

Clutching her rolled up copy of *The Citadel* that listed the location and worship times of the town's churches in her left hand (only two were Christian), the reporter pulled her new brown leather jacket tight across her torso as she ascended a short flight of steps to the house's covered porch and front door. On that door was posted a handwritten note on typewriter paper that read: "All are WELCOME in God's house." Through that door came the muffled refrain of a handful of untrained voices singing the traditional hymn "Great Is Thy Faithfulness."

The best "legman" and newshound at the Bangor Daily opened the door.

Dianne counted eleven men, women, and children (most of whom were held in laps; one sat at an adult's feet) and, among them, two surprises. The tiny congregation was holding hymnals and singing, sitting on a worn couch or one of several common house chairs or metal, folding chairs, facing a balding young man probably in his mid- to late thirties. Two surprises in the worshipers were Margo Willson and Veyda, asleep in her mother's arms.

Dressed in a simple blue shirt and gray trousers, the pastor stood by a tired, overstuffed brown chair helping his congregation sing by indicating the song's strong rhythm with the intricate patterns formed by his right hand in the air. Savage walked to one of two vacant folding chairs and sat and was recognized by the pastor with a nod of his head. The woman sitting next to her offered her a hymnal that Dianne waved off with a smile; she knew the words to the song, and joined in the spirited but unpolished singing.

After the hymn, the pastor offered a brief prayer, and all sang "Holy,

43

Holy, Holy" before he began a carefully crafted, half-hour sermon on the glory of their eternal creator God. Then the service was concluded by singing "It Is Well With My Soul" and a prayer.

With the exception of one couple who exited with a polite smile and a farewell wave, the congregation formed a line to greet Dianne and enthusiastically introduce themselves. The first were Rebecca and Joshua Nantier who introduced themselves, their eight-year-old son, Schlomo, and his three-year-old brother, Kenneth, before inviting her back next week.

A grumpy and half-awake Veyda yawned as her mother offered her left when Savage extended his own right hand. "You still look a little surprised, Miss Savage. I know what you were thinking the other day too. I told you I only dance. That's all I do. So maybe now we can start on a new foot?"

"Oh, dear, oh, my," Dianne acquiesced and lowered her head to hide the scarlet in her cheeks. "I am so sorry, Mrs. Willson. I... I am ashamed of myself."

"Forgiven and forgotten," Margo said with the faintest of smiles. "I've got to get 'Little Miss Wiggle Worm' back home now, but do stop by again, and we'll talk."

"Bye bye," added Veyda and waved, and they were gone to be replaced by the apt pastor and a woman that Dianne supposed was his wife.

"Welcome to our little home church! I'm Darren Miller, the pastor here, and this is my wife, Paula. It is my tradition to ask visitors to chat for a moment before they leave. Do you have the time, Miss...?"

"Of course! I'm Dianne Savage, and I am a 'Miss.' But please call me Dianne."

"Wonderful! Paula, could you wait... " Miller added, asking his wife to sit with a wave of his hand. "I won't keep you long. My little office is right through that doorway."

"I enjoyed your service," said Savage as they walked to and through the doorway. "It is all about grace, isn't it? Although, I must admit I was a little surprised at the small number of people today, Reverend. And, well, your church is a house!"

"Please, this is way too small a church for 'Reverend,' Miss Savage. Call me Darren." Before sitting he moved to, then behind, a small desk in a room that looked like a modest den. With a gesture of his hand and a smile, he indicated a chair for Dianne. "In fact, Paula and I live here. We are missionaries to Light's End. Make yourself comfortable. Are you moving to this isolated little hole-in-the-wall?"

"Oh, no; I'm just visiting from Bangor for a few weeks, and found your church in the newspaper... that I just remembered leaving on the floor next to my chair!"

"Just visiting?" Miller's hopeful anticipation of a new member vanished from his face as he opened a drawer in the desk below her field of vision, removed something, and placed it in his lap. He failed to mask the wary timbre of his voice as he continued. "Well, it is always wonderful to meet a sister in Christ even if you won't be doubling the size of my congregation. As for the small size of our church, most everyone in Light's End goes to the Church of Tenebrae."

"I'd never heard of that church before coming here, Darren. And I must admit, I read their pamphlet and can't image it's a Christian denomination."

"Two-thirds pagan and the rest a cherry-picking of what they like in philosophy, science, and atheism, I'm afraid. But don't be deceived; it is very powerful here. I try to stay away from it. But, of course, I can't, but you can, and that's what I'd advise.

"I hope to see you here for as long as you are visiting, Miss Savage, and don't hesitate to ask if you need help with anything. I'll leave you with a simple word of advice. In Light's End, if something walks like a duck and quacks like a duck, it may be a snake."

"Thank you so much," Dianne said as she rose from her chair. "I won't keep you from your Sunday lunch. I'll try my best to be here, God willing, next Sunday."

As she left the sparsely furnished room, Darren took the loaded revolver off of his lap, put it back in the desk drawer, and closed it quietly.

"Well, I must admit I was surprised," said Dianne who was sitting on the smooth, brown vinyl bench of one of more than two dozen booths and freestanding tables at the Majestic Cafe on August Street. She sipped her coffee.

"I didn't expect a knock on my door on a Sunday, or on any day, actually, much less an invitation for pie and coffee."

"Then my guess that a young, single, woman in an aberrant town wouldn't be interested in talking to a creepy old man alone in her room was right," grinned Charles Walton whose soft spoken words were somewhat muffled by the sounds of silverware clinking, the *hurrrrmmmm* of heaters stirring the air, and the undulating murmur of the sparse group eating at the small cafe. Dianne studied the old, rectangular face of Walton with mild amusement — his hair cropped almost to baldness and several days, growth of blond stubble adding a male ruggedness to his jaw that was a bit diminished by the glasses on his aquiline nose.

"So, we meet again," the newshound said, glibly.

"It's rare to meet anyone," he continued, unconsciously touching the black rim of his glasses with the tip of his right forefinger, "interested in history, much less a beautiful young woman. So, what do you want to know about our queer little jerkwater town's past."

"Tell me about Caleb Elliott who founded Light's End and fathered the 'giant, pustulant maggot that lives in the well in a cave under Elliott's Head cliff and tears the flesh of men apart like cotton batting.' Or how about your lighthouse 'destroyed by the hand of God because of the demonic abominations performed in its bowels.' Or Shelley Azreal who slept with a monster from outer space. You choose, Mr. Walton."

"Please, call me Chuck." There was an extended moment of wary silence as Walton tried to discern if Dianne were being serious or caustic. Then he smiled and said:

"My two areas of study when I was a professor ten thousand years ago were local legends and theology, so all three of your questions are right up my alley, so to speak.

"First up, Caleb Elliott fathered a grossly deformed son by a prostitute in England, and fled with him to America. Caleb established a little trading post at the foot of what is now called Elliott's Head cliff, and hid his ugly child, partially out of shame, and partially so as not to scare off trade, in a small cave behind his deplorable shack. But not in a well. There was no well. To protect himself from the Abenakis Indians who were threatening to kill him, he told them that his son had been fathered on an ocean god who lived in what we now call Abomination Bay. They were appropriately awed, and 'the Godman,' as the Indians then called Caleb, flourished on the trade he conducted with them.

"Flourished, that is, until a murdering conman and thief named Ezekiel Azreal and his illegitimate son, Hiram Percy, tried to steal everything Caleb owned. Ezekiel killed Caleb, and Caleb's deformed son killed Ezekiel." Walton unconsciously touched the rim of his glasses with the tip of his right forefinger. "Hiram tried to cover up the murder and robbery by blowing up the entrance to the cave and spreading the monster story Caleb had concocted to anyone who would listen. That's the truth and nothing but the truth."

"Since this happened so long ago, Chuck, how do you know all of this?"

"It comes from a deathbed confession written by Hiram and preserved in the special collections room at our town library. As for the black lighthouse built by Jeroboam Azreal, it was where the Tenebrae Church first met, and was shaken apart by an earthquake. The legend was started by townspeople who feared and hated the Azrealites and their cult. As for

Shelley Azreal, same as Caleb. Her father attributed her birth defect to some sin against 'God.' There was no monster or shining angel from outer space, just a boy who got too friendly with his sad little daughter and paid for it with a bullet from Shelley's father.

"All the rest in each story is exaggeration in an effort to escape the sameness and boredom of mundane lives, or from feelings of unfounded guilt, or an attempt to hide what actually happened, married with the almost inherent belief that the consequences of sin include birth defects, personal calamities, and natural disasters. Hogwash, of course, completely discounted by science. Add to that the fact that, like nature, all human beings hate a vacuum and would rather believe an absurdity than to live with an unanswered question, and you have the recipe for all legends all over the world."

"Your answers sound reasonable to me, so far, Chuck, but I couldn't help but notice that every time you said God you seemed to put quotes around it. I thought you said you were a professor of theology?"

"Yours is an understandable and common misconception," said Walton with what Dianne took as a condescending grin. "Just because I study theology doesn't mean I believe a god or gods or even the 'supernatural' exists. If I had to characterize myself, I'd call myself an agnostic. A better term would be a seeker and amused skeptic. So it shouldn't surprise you to see me at a Baptist Church or at the Tenebrae gathering."

"Well, it should surprise you to see me at a Tenebrae meeting, but that's a discussion for another place and another time, perhaps. If you'll excuse the observation, if theology is the study of God, isn't a theologian who doesn't believe in God sort of like an automobile mechanic who doesn't believe in automobiles?"

"Interesting idea, but I'm afraid your analogy is flawed. A car is a material thing that can be touched, heard, felt, tasted, and seen. God is not a material thing."

"True," said Dianne, warming to the challenge, "so I'll change my picture. Does an automobile mechanic believe someone built the car he can see, feel, hear, taste and smell?"

"Of course," confirmed Walton.

"I can certainly see, feel, hear, taste and smell the material world that God created."

"Ah," said Walton, rubbing his chin. "An interesting thought. But do you think now is the time and place to debate it, my dear?"

"Agreed. Then for now, tell me about your smarmy little Bishop's Alley."

"It is a physically dirty and dangerous place where people escape their mundane lives. On my last visit, I noticed a sign posted at Mother Murphy's, one of the saloons, which reads, 'No Knives or Firearms Allowed.' I think the sign speaks volumes about what kind of people go to the Alley. They are tough people living marginal lives. Some would loan you their last quarter or bash in your skull with the butt of a gun with equal indifference, depending on their mood at the moment and the amount of hooch or whiz-bang in their blood. Most are workers on the water and storm drain project, and are young and unmarried, or reluctant to bring their families to Light's End to face such frankly rough, occasionally violent, lives. They break their backs in twelve hour shifts and rent a room for eight hour stretches. Because of a shortage of rooms, three different men may sleep in one room at different times. And because of their loneliness, the dregs of the earth feed on them at Bishop's Alley for easy money: bootleggers, dope peddlers, hijackers, thieves, conmen, prostitutes."

"You have gone there?" asked Dianne with mild but real surprise.

"I have. Nor am I the only 'decent' citizen on this side of the whitewashed line that separates the polite society of Light's End from its red light district. A minority of its customers are men and a handful of women who sneak into Bishop's Alley to escape the crushing boredom of their lives, or broken and unhappy marriages, or frigid wives or uninterested husbands, or shattered goals and dreams, or the stress of jobs they hate, or simply to escape the most basic and most denied fear of every human being, the great unknown of death. You'll notice the important repetition of the word 'escape.'

"For ten cents, a man can dance with a girl who would normally never touch him, and more than likely, will also pick his pocket or maneuver him over to a boyfriend who shakes him down for a lot more than a dime. The red-brown mud on the dirt floors is sometimes so deep that the girls dance in boots. Some of the saloons don't even have a roof. It's in a back room where someone with the foolish inclination can gamble his paycheck away or escape into a nightmare of alcohol or whiz-bang induced hallucination."

Walton unconsciously touched the rim of his glasses with the tip of his right forefinger, then raised his cup of coffee to drink.

"Tell me about the Church of Tenebrae," asked the reporter. "That's a weird name for a church since Tenebrae means 'gathering darkness.' What's it all about, Chuck? Do you know their tenants?"

"I do. If you casually visited one of their services on the corner of Ash and Ebaugh, it would probably feel like you were attending a motivational seminar on prosperity. If you were to join, it would most likely feel like joining a country club that only requires a little money and a little time to be a member and nothing else, just like most churches. And also like most of the members of most churches, they don't waste time in learning or questioning or even reading the aberrant and slightly occult doctrine of the Azrealites."

"Yuck," Dianne said.

"At least they openly embrace selfishness. If you became one of the tiny handful who actually take the Azrealites seriously — members are called Azrealites after the family that co-founded Light's End, the Azreals — you'd discover you'd be required to move up through a series of preliminary levels to learn the arcane, core beliefs of the church. These secret beliefs are a dirty little hodgepodge of archaic, occult perversions cherry-picked from a large number of pagan and even Satanic cults from around the world, and are not to be shared with anyone outside the church. They are principally concerned with power, death, and sex. And if you reached the level of DemiUrge, which is equivalent to what other churches call a deacon or elder, you would participate in their ultimate, black ceremony they hold on each Halloween night called 'The Goat With No Horns.'"

"What on earth is that?"

"Depending on whom you ask, it is either a ceremony at which a newborn goat is symbolically sacrificed as an ancient and nascent celebration of the First Incarnation of The One, or at which they slit the throat of a human baby. Either way, they then throw the bloody corpse into the well in Elliott's Head cave that doesn't exist to feed the maggot that doesn't live in that well that doesn't exist.

"In some way that remains unclear to me, the Azrealites are to father the Great DemiUrge of the Third Sixes and wed science and the supernatural and breathe new life into the dry bones that 'will destroy most human beings and shake the world to its knees.'"

"The Three Sixes?'

"'The One, perfect, beautiful and full of power, who bought free will for us and paid for it with his life, and the Mother and Son of Tenebrae.' I have no idea what that ugly, outré statement of faith really means.

"You see, despite their denial in public that there is even a god or a supernatural realm, the higher levels are all full of violent, nasty, occult nonsense."

"What does that little diamond shaped cluster of crosses mean, Mr. Walton?"

"Frankly, I don't know. I'm not exactly a member of the inner circle of the Azrealites. But I do know it's a corruption of a symbol of the Knights Templar used in the Middle Ages. I also don't know why most of the members chew that horrible smelling gum that made you wrinkle up your nose in the Mermaid Cafe when we first met. The waitress chews it. It is called Asafoetida, and was supposedly used by witches to call up demons. They don't believe in gods or devils, so it doesn't seem to fit. Nor does the weird little anomaly branded under their hair when they are initiated into the Tenebrae Church."

"You are kidding," Dianne said, adding emphasis to each word as she leaned across the table and roping her coffee in the palms of her hands. "What is it?"

"Three numbers," said Walton, and leaned across the table to meet her enthusiasm.

"Six. Six. Six."

Early in her career, Jim Copeland, the managing editor of the *Bangor Daily Register* paper, had taught Dianne to keep a detailed journal in which she included first impressions, facts she'd learned while researching a story, quotes, random thoughts and opinions, and any thing that might strike her as even possibly of use as a journalist with the promise that, from this rich field of observations, she would harvest many a story. The reporter had done so for years, cataloging her journals by writing the cumulative beginning and ending date of her entries on each of their beige covers. In the quiet of that night, Dianne wrote in her journal:

It is possible that the Azrealites of the Church of Tenebrae in Light's End are devil worshippers, although I have no concrete evidence yet, and that their church is an intentional mockery and perverse imitation of Christian churches. I am certain that the headquarters of this cult that is sparsely scattered across the world is here in Light's End, although I have found no formal offices. The town itself is picturesque on the surface, and diseased beneath; the outskirts are heavily wooded, its two rivers, the Gihon and the Pishon, babble and sparkle in the sunshine as they run to the ocean, and the town is isolated from the world by lack of highways into and out of the place: there is only one. Their Abomination Bay is aptly named and so polluted and nasty that even seagulls cannot "dock."

But charming as this town of about 8,000 appears to the casual eye, it shuns Christians and Jews like the plague as it enthusiastically embraces every aberrant philosophy and cult imaginable, the more weird the better. I also believe it hides something under a cliff that overlooks Abomination Bay that they've named "Elliott's Head" and that they've obscured it with silly legends. It is certain that Light's End is the home of the "DemiUrge," the founder or the head of this cult. I believe that Azrealite pilgrims from across the world secretly travel here annually on the occasion of a weird festival cloaked as a citywide Halloween carnival that is something much darker and an absolute horror.

I must note they tolerate two, tiny Christian churches here so that they can brag about being 'opened-minded' and tolerant, but my best guess is that there are no more than fifteen or twenty Christians in Light's End. There is neither a synagogue nor mosque.

Although no one will say it, I suspect that a man named Jake Horne may be this Azrealite DemiUrge; he seems to have his literally dirty hands in everything in Light's End, although he holds no important, official position or office in town that I can discern.

The town gossip, Chuck Walton, told me that Elliott's Head is honeycombed with caves and tunnels that all lead to "The Tomb of the Worm" that is also called "The Tomb of the One" in the largest cavern. The man-made well in the northeast corner of this cavern was supposedly sunk by the town's founder, Caleb Elliott, and is a faćade, no more than five or six feet deep. It is whispered that the ebon well is an edifice where Azrealites worship "The One," although how they could get into this sealed cavern is a mystery I intend to unravel. The Worm is the son of Caleb Elliott by a naiad he found in a nest of mermaids below Abomination Reef at the mouth of the bay. What a crock. This monster is sacred, in some way related to the supernatural "One" they deny even exists if asked, and the well is still the Sanctuary of the Worm to this day; it is the befouled altar at which these devils worship.

The mouth of this cavern was sealed with dynamite by Hiram Percy a long time ago, and remains so. This sealed mouth, a frozen waterfall of rock and debris, faces the rising and sinking sun on the far horizon of Abomination Bay. Hiram dynamited the cavern to kill The Worm; the bones of both Caleb and Hiram's father, Ezekiel, are buried there. The Worm, of course, is still alive and hungry.

At a later date, a lighthouse they called "The Watch" was built of local stone on the crown of the otherwise bleak cliffs. It was shaken to pieces in an earthquake or a storm or something; I'm not clear yet of this piece of Light's End melodrama. I have not yet been to the ruins of this lighthouse, that is now, I'm told by Walton, a random throw of rough cut stones hidden mostly by weeds. I will check it out soon. It is all hogwash, of course.

On All Hallows Eve each year, when "The Feasting" Halloween party is in full swing in downtown Light's End, the DemiUrge of the One presides over a bizarre ceremony that takes place as the shadows lengthen. It seems their ultimate esoteric mission is to bring back "The One" into the material universe, i.e. Earth. I don't know who or what "The One" is, and, although what information I have leaves many unanswered questions, I will find the answers.

Acolytes dress in soiled white robes with an odd, diamond-shaped emblem stitched or printed over the heart. I would learn later that this symbol is composed of tightly intertwined crosses of differing sizes; its origin lies with the Templars. Here is my sketch of this Azrealites symbol:

Dianne put her pencil down, closed the book, and went to bed.

Early Monday morning after her hygiene ritual, a Spartan breakfast, and the cleaning of the apartment's kitchen, Dianne sat down at the small, wooden, kitchen table and wrote the initial draft, in longhand, of her first article on Light's End and Bishop's Alley for the *Bangor Daily Register*. It took two hours to do so. She set the story aside and read her Bible for an hour while lying on her unmade bed, and prayed. It was 11:33 A.M. when the reporter then finished the second draft of her article, also in longhand, and folded and put it in an off-white envelope addressed to Larry Allison in Bangor.

"Huuuuuh!" she yawned.

She wondered what headline "Allison" would write for the story and if it would make the first page of the newspaper.

She leisurely dressed in her typical, boyish style, donned her pale green cloche hat, and pinned the little piece of folded paper to her blouse as she did every day except on Sundays. It read: *There is no fear in love; but perfect love casteth out fear... 1 John 4:18.*

The newshound put on her new coat and left the Van Sanford Apartments without her characteristic knapsack. The grey sky was still muddy with low clouds, and it was quite chilly. As she walked, Dianne noticed a small crew of men stringing orange and yellow Halloween decorations on light poles. But Savage was thinking of the Rex Theater and Joe Seminole, not of witches and goblins and things that go bump in the night.

Dianne briskly walked the several blocks east down First Street, then north on Dunlevy Avenue, until she reached the Light's End Post Office. As she did so, she quietly and alternately sang or hummed the popular song "Together."

After the reporter deposited her letter in the large slot marked "Outgoing"

"...shaken to pieces in ...a storm..."

in a marble wall, Savage left the Post Office to return to her apartment. She was in no hurry, so she stopped in front of Clausing's Feed and Seed to look at the new Halloween display in one of its large display windows. In one corner of the display sat a bale of hay under a hanging, yellow moon, scattered fall leaves, gourds, an orange pumpkin, and a weird, cloth doll — an obscenity of spider's legs writhing around the bloated cotton head and gnashing razor teeth of a gigantic pustulant maggot — Caleb Elliott's monstrous son sired on a demigod.

She squatted in front of the window for a better view of the aberrant doll, wondering what possible thought went behind creating such a hideous thing for children and displaying it. Surely, it was too frightening for use for any child, even the offspring of one of the elders of the Tenebrae Church. And why put it in the window of a retail business as a Halloween decoration? Was the damnable thing supposed to leave quarters under pillows for lost teeth, or carry a bag of toys to excited children, or hide eggs on a lawn?

As she leaned back slightly on her heels, a reflection in the glass came into clear focus. It was the ghostly image of a man standing across the street from her, leaning against a building, his hands deep in the front pockets of his blue uniform.

It was one of the two thugs who had brutally beaten Thomas.

Dianne's blood froze in her veins as she stumbled back on her heels and almost fell to the sidewalk, the cop's image in the window instantly erased by her changed position.

She forced herself to casually stand up straight. Fighting back panic, she then turned from the window and began to walk away. Out of the corner of her left eye, she saw the policeman leering at her, and choked back a gasp. His expression was not of disdain, sour humor, fained indifference, or even the threat of physical violence.

It was the leer of naked lust.

He did not move.

When he was out of the possible range of sight, Dianne ran.

It was early Monday evening when Savage, her self-confidence still shaken, looked at the rather plain Rex Theater across the street from her with a jaundiced eye; it wasn't much compared to the elaborate Vaudeville and movie theaters in Bangor. She thought: *I guess that's to be expected in a raw-edged, unsophisticated, backwater berg like this little yellow 'jewel' of the Atlantic.* But she had found the show times for the movies in *The*

Citadel, and going to a flicker seemed better than sitting around her apartment worrying about a rogue policeman.

The reporter was both disappointed and somewhat relieved that she did not see Seminole or his popcorn cart in front of the theater; her emotions about the flamboyant assistant manager of the theater were confused, at best. She had to admit to herself that she'd chosen to come to the Rex instead of the other theaters in downtown Light's End on the off chance that Seminole would be there, but...

Dianne glanced east down the sidewalk busy with late shoppers and sniffed the mundane smell of oysters, clam chowder, fried fish, and boiled potatoes that drifted from the Majestic Cafe next door to the Rex. She made a mental note to herself that she might eat there after the movie if the little eatery was still open. Savage then looked first at the adobe train depot at the end of the bricked street, and then back up the opposite side of August Street before crossing to stand under the Rex's tawdry marquee.

The young girl inside the glass enclosed ticket booth chewed bubble gum, popped it, and ignored her as Savage reached into the right front pocket of her dungarees, removed, and then placed two coins on the counter. Dianne accepted her ticket, and walked inside.

The lobby of the theater was full of the drowsy, timeless smells of candy, salt, butter, popcorn, hot dogs and soda pop. The air was cool and embracing. Savage walked to a swinging door with a porthole in the center that separated the lobby from the auditorium, and pushed it open. The white light of the lobby tittered away behind her.

As she moved to a row of unadorned, wooden seats with the muted sound of the lobby doors swinging in diminishing arcs behind her, a cone of diffused light blinked on above and behind the reporter in the darkness and pooled on a huge, white screen above a narrow stage.

Unseen fans sighed cool in the darkness and Dianne noted only a few people scattered around the theater. She studied with distaste the carpeted floor littered with sticky candy wrappers as she chose a seat and sat. She placed her hands in her lap and drifted away in thought of Seminole and of school hay rides and dances in her past, of beaus that had unsuccessfully called at her door, of the possibility of her own wedding someday, and baby showers, and of long nights that now slipped imperceptibly into a weary, yearning loneliness until those dreams were realized.

Savage looked up on the screen at a distant, near-naked savage swinging between trees. He grew big as he dropped effortlessly onto a huge tree limb, threw back his tousled head, threw out his massive chest, and yodeled without sound.

Something on the edge of Savage's vision began to crab sideways down the row of seats towards her. She did not turn her head as it passed the third, the fifth and then the seventh seat, and Dianne's uneasiness that he or she would sit next to the reporter and invade her privacy grew.

It sat. Dianne put her right hand over her mouth to hide her smile.

It was Joe Seminole dressed in slacks, a long-sleeved white shirt under a gray vest, and a tweed Pub cap.

"May I?" he asked, indicating he wished to sit next to her with a wave of his open-palmed hand even though he was already seated.

"It's a free country, Mr. Seminole," said Dianne and bit the fingernail of the first digit of her right hand.

"Well," he grinned, removing his cap. "I wasn't sure I would see you again. I'm glad you choose to come see me... or Tarzan the half-naked Ape Man."

"I came to see the movie," she said, subconsciously giving in to the inevitable male and female dance of fertility and mortality that women instinctively understand: that to give is to begin to die, that to withhold is to never live.

Half-way through the flicker, Seminole put his hand over her right hand resting on the arm of the theater chair. Without even glancing at him, she removed her hand.

"We are relatively new to Light's End from Oklahoma," said Seminole, starring at the half-eaten blueberry pie sitting next to his half-empty coffee cup sitting on a table at the Majestic Cafe.

"My father took the last name of Seminole after our tribe, the Seminole Indians, and the town we lived in there. They struck a huge amount of oil in Seminole—it's a boom town right now—and unlike many of our tribe who sold their land outright to oil men, my father traded our mineral rights in exchange for a percentage of the oil drilled there. Frankly, it has made us quite wealthy, and since my father never cared for the town, we moved to Maine and collect our royalty checks at the post office every month."

"And bought the Seminole Laundry," added Dianne.

"And the Seminole Bakery, the Seminole Maid Dairy, and Seminole Motors, among a few others. And someday, I'll buy the smarmy little, second-rate Rex Theater where we met, remodel it into a first-rate movie theater, and rename it the Seminole Theater."

"With the money from your family's oil in Oklahoma," added the reporter, taking a bite of her own half-eaten cherry pie. She knew from his adamantine expression of suppressed anger that she had misspoken before the words had even faded into the muffled sounds of silverware on plates, orders shouted by waitresses to unseen cooks, and conversations in the restaurant.

"Noooo," he said coolly with the subtle effluvia of restrained anger at her affront. "I am my own man, Ms. Savage, and will make the money to buy the theater myself. You might not have noticed, but I'm a fully grown, independent man."

"I'm sorry, Joe; I didn't mean to impugn your masculinity. Really." Dianne leaned slightly forward across the table in a subconscious, physical affirmation of her sincerity. "I completely understand a person wanting to stand on his or her own feet. I've done so myself. My mother and father were killed in an accident when I was thirteen, and I grew up in an orphanage in Bangor. I began making money throwing newspapers when I was thirteen, then clerking at a variety store, then writing obituaries for a newspaper, then writing essays for 'literary' magazines and advertising copy for an agency when I was fifteen or so. I've been able to eke out a very modest living with my writing ever since."

"Then we both insulted each other out of ignorance of the other's life. That," said Joe, his strained expression relaxing as he ran his fingers through the black hair at the back of his head, "is easily forgiven, and a problem solved. Tell me all about yourself, Ms. Savage."

So they spoke at length of their lives as they finished their pie, and drank their coffee, and danced, without moving, the first tentative steps of courtship that are full of ineffable excitement and nervous uncertainty. Half-way through their conversation, Seminole put his right over her right hand resting on the table. Without even glancing at it, Dianne did not remove her hand.

Later that night, through a chilly, otherwise soundless, starless night, Joe drove her back to the Van Sanford Apartments to the *hurrrrrmmmm* of his tires on the cobbled streets in his new, 1928 Model-A Ford Four door Leatherback automobile.

The only thing unexpected in her apartment was an ice pick left by the company that restocked her ice box. It lay on the counter of her little kitchen and on each of four sides of its rectangular wooden handle was printed: 1) Phone 1000; 2) Buy a Coolerator; 3) The Air Conditioned Refrigerator, and 4) Seminole Ice Company.

The newshound smiled.

CHAPTER FIVE

Early Tuesday morning, October 16th, after hygiene, breakfast, and cleaning the kitchen, Dianne sat down at her kitchen table and wrote the initial draft in longhand of her second article on Light's End for her newspaper. She put the story aside for meditation and prayer for half an hour while lying on her bed. It was 11:15A.M.when the reporter then finished the second draft of her article, folded and put it in an envelope addressed to Bangor.

She wondered what headline Allison would write and if her article would make the first page of the newspaper.

She dressed in her blue dungarees, a white blouse, and cloche hat, and pinned a piece of folded paper to her blouse. It read: *We love Him because He first loved us... 1 John 4:9-10*

Savage donned her coat and left the Van Sanford with her letter and without her knapsack. The sky was spotted with scattered, diluted clouds like the suds in dirty dishwater, and it was as chilly as yesterday. As she walked the several blocks to the Post Office, Dianne was thinking with fondness and some reservation of Joe Seminole.

After the reporter mailed her letter, Savage left the Post Office, stopping again in front of Clausing's Feed to look at the Halloween window display. In addition to the bale of hay, yellow moon, scattered leaves, gourds, and pumpkins, stood a cardboard cutout of a witch with a broom, wearing a peaked, black hat and black clothing. The weird, cloth obscenity of spider's legs and gnashing razor teeth was still there in its corner.

She again squatted in front of the window with a modicum of fear at what she would see, but there was no reflection on the glass of a man standing across the street. She congratulated herself for her courage, sighed with relief, and rose.

The reporter walked to her grocery store, and bought a copy of the *Bangor Daily Register* and *The Citadel* newspaper. Her article had not been published.

"I'm coming to the Alley with you tonight," said Dianne as an unemotional statement of uncontestable and refutable fact. "No ifs, ands, or buts about it."

"No, you're not," said Margo, as she combed her auburn hair at her tiny, metal kitchen table using a pocket mirror lying flat on its top. Veyda crawled on the floor close to her feet. "With a whole bunch of ifs, ands, and buts."

"Yes. I am," the reporter answered flatly, not really listening to Margo as she looked at the secondhand, shabby furnishings and accessories in Margo's room, thinking *I thought these apartments come furnished.* "With or without you. I'd feel much safer with you there, of course."

"You can be pretty obnoxious, hard-headed, and pushy for someone who's supposed to be a Christian lady," said Margo as she laid her comb next to her mirror and stooped to pick up her baby. Veyda clucked and watched Dianne from the arms of her mother without fear or even interest as someone who was no longer threatening or questionable.

"What's so important to you," added the dancer, "that you'd put yourself in danger?"

"That's me," grinned Savage. "I have a book to write, and it wouldn't be complete without a first-hand visit. And don't you think the immorality, corruption, and crime in that place should be exposed, or is that too much to expect from a Christian lady who is dressed in a flimsy 'flapper' dress who dances there. In fact, since you don't 'do' what the other women do at The Palace, I've been wondering why they even keep you on at the place."

Margo's face flushed pink with an emotional soup of shame and anger as she bounced Veyda on her knee. "They keep me on because I work ten times harder than the other women, and they've got enough girls who 'do' that, as you put it, that one that doesn't do it doesn't matter. And after your exposé puts every man, woman, and child who works there out on the street, maybe you can explain to me how a widowed woman with a baby, who hasn't got enough of an education to count change at the five-and-dime or the money to get herself and her baby back home will make enough money to even buy bread and milk."

"Well, some 'jobs' aren't worth....." Dianne began, and stopped, her own face flushing with shame and her eyes welling with tears as she looked at baby Veyda cooing on the lap of her widowed mother who honorably worked in a Hell hole and lived in a shabby basement on slave-labor wages in her best effort to live out Christ's calling to faithfulness and integrity in what many less mature women would call a hopeless situation, and her heart melted, and she thought *please God forgive me and my fat mouth.*

She said: "I will pay your way home."

"What did you say?" asked the dancer, startled.

Dianne repeated, "I'll pay your way home. Since I've had a little success with my writing, and I don't have many expenses, being single without children and all, I've been able to put a little money back. I'll have to have someone send it to me from Bangor, but I could have enough here to get you home by Monday or Tuesday of next week."

"I couldn't ask you to do that," said Margo, choking back her own emotions, and her own eyes beneath the blue eye shadow welling with tears.

"You didn't ask me to do that, Margo," said Dianne as she moved to the widow's side and put her arm around her shoulder. "That's what 'sisters' do, isn't it? Help one another when they're down and out?"

Baby Veyda laid her tiny, soft hand briefly on Margo's breast as the women shared in that universal and common intimacy of shared gender that is so alien to men that it never enters their minds and therefore separates the genders forever. When the moment's emotional intensity waned to a glowing ember, Margo said:

"The one luxury I allow myself is a cab ride to work, Dianne. The Sorensons watch Veyda for me, so if you can be back here in an hour, it's Bishop's Alley tonight."

"If you don't mind, why don't I stay and play with Veyda while you finish getting ready, Margo. She's such a sweetie, I'd love to spend more time with her."

"That's fine. I just can't believe that tonight I tell them... I quit! I'm going home!"

The knot of angular, squalid buildings continued to grow in the window of the Dixie cab as Margo and Dianne approached the mouth of Bishop's Alley on west August Street. Dianne noted incongruous businesses like Sutherland Lumber, a used furniture store, hamburger stand, and barber shop, all but the Lumber Company looking as if they'd been thrown together in a fit of expedient greed with spit, bailing wire, and used lumber. These legitimate businesses were quickly replaced on the south side of the trampled and rutted dirt street by dance halls and saloons including The Blue Heaven, the 49'er Dance Hall, the Bucket o' Blood, and Mother Murphy's. On the north side, obstinate jazz already thumped in the late afternoon at The Palace where Margo danced that was preceded by Salty Dog's Salon, Fields Barber Shop, Conway's Used Furniture, and Epps Hamburgers. West of The Palace were The Big Sea, The Kentucky Rooms, Wintergarden, Ada's Bar, and other dives. Naked but unlit, green and blue and white Christmas light bulbs that were strung between the buildings and crossed the street swung lazily in a mild, cold, salty breeze, and the ghost of endless nights of low tittering, incontinent and slack singing, foul cursing and whooping helped recreate the bizarre atmosphere of a cheap tawdry carnival.

The cab squealed to a rolling stop in front of The Palace on an otherwise mostly empty road in front of a throw of weathered and worm-eaten planks meant to be a boardwalk just as the sun touched the lip of the horizon in the west smearing the clouds there in subtle, impressionistic yellows, oranges, and reds. The dance hall and its sordid neighbors were worse than the dirtiest derelict tenement that Dianne had seen in the slums of Bangor. She thought *these are not temporary buildings, these are momentary.*

The only thing similar with the unpainted Palace rat trap and its namesake was a roof; many of the other dance halls and a few of the saloons only had a heavy canvas tarp stretched between their walls that were used when it rained or grew cold. The Palace roof was tarnished and battered tin. Its marquee was a panel of plywood with holes cut out of it to spell P-A-L-A-C-E when the light bulbs poking up through those holes were lit. There were no windows, the walls were spotted with scrawled profanity and dirt, and its entrance was a common house door painted red.

As she stepped out of the cab, Dianne was met with the subtle but all permeating smell of stale beer, human sweat, urine and feces.

The cabaret door swung open under Margo's hand onto a dim hall no longer than six feet long and four feet wide. Immediately to their right was a frowzy woman too old to be a dancer or a prostitute wearing a worn and slightly soiled brown dress, smoking a hand-rolled cigarette, and sitting on a stool. Beyond her and also to their right was a second door which Dianne would learn was the entrance to the dance floor. Dianne glanced at a bulky, sallow man in overalls sitting on an armless chair tilted back on its hind legs next to this door who was studying her with the indifference of long dreary hours of meaningless labor and little sleep. He wore a worn, brown, leather holster and a pistol on his hip.

"Evening, Judy," said Margo to the old woman, as she brushed a stray hair back from her own face. "This here is a friend of mine."

"Margo," she responded in a voice rough from long years of booze and smoking as she looked over the reporter like a rancher considering buying a heifer. "Go on in."

The man in the armless chair rapped three times on the door next to him with the back of a hairy fist. The door was opened by someone unseen inside. The thin and inexact music of a saxophone, piano, drums, and a guitar stumbling over a Ragtime tune joined the nasty smell that was even stronger inside The Palace than in the street.

Standing next to a gate in a wooden rail that stood about six feet back from each unpainted exterior wall was a woman or a man with close-cropped, greasy black hair smoking a thin, black cigar and wearing riding pants stuffed into scuffed black boots, a plaid short-sleeved shirt, and a pistol in a holster around her fat waist. She wore a metal coin changer — a series of tin tubes like a Pan pipe — above the holster. On one of the boards framing the gate was a fat round of tickets on a nail. The railing also created a long, rectangular arena like a cattle pen where men and women danced under the harsh light of naked light bulbs hanging from the tin roof to what passed for music on a worm-eaten, pine floor.

"Hello Ruby," said Margo with an indifferent and emotionless courtesy not born of respect but of habit. "This here is Dianne Savage, a friend visiting from out of town."

"Margo," she answered in a voice masculine, deep, somewhat suspicious because it was not gender specific, and rough from long years of smoking as she examined the reporter. Dianne initially thought Ruby's pupils were black and dead until she realized they were dilated because she was doped. "Is she lookin' fer a job?"

"No, no, no," answered Margo as the door closed behind her. "She's just a friend who wants to see where I work, Ruby. That's okay, right?"

As she spoke, Dianne glanced at the hulk of a man leaning on the rail around the dance floor to her left about ten feet from her. The reporter's blood ran cold. It was the second cop that had brutally beaten Thomas; he was out of uniform but also wearing a tan leather holster and pistol on his hip, and was not the cop she'd seen reflected in the window of Clausing's Feed. But her quick glance was met with the indifferent expression of a man who did not recognize her and only momentarily noted her presence because it was his job to do so, so her racing heart slowed as she began to observe the employees and customers of the decadent dump called The Palace.

Directly across the entry gate where she, Margo, and Rudy stood was another closed gate, a closed door in the wall behind it, and a ten or fifteen foot section of the dive isolated by a cross of boards nailed from the rail to the wall to the right and to the left of the door. She would soon learn this was where the dancers waited for men. Apparently every available woman was mechanically and vacuously dancing (not really hearing the music or even feeling the rhythm of it or even the rhythm of the beat of their own hearts) with the five men now on the floor with the hypnotic, grinding, hopelessness of endless and senseless repetition because the isolated section behind them was empty.

"Our shifts are staggered," said Margo. "There will be girls coming in as business picks up and some leaving throughout the night. Come on."

As Ruby opened the gate for them, and Margo and Dianne began to walk across the dance floor, Savage notice that on the left side of the closed gate to the dancer's waiting area and behind the railing stood four musicians, all young black men, bobbing in rhythm to their own music, all wearing the most colorful and flamboyant clothing possible on a pauper's budget. To the left of the musicians was another closed door; Dianne would learn it led to the back room where Spanish Blackie oversaw the gambling that was actually the strongest revenue stream for The Palace.

On the right side of the gate sat a huge, boxy, kerosene stove, one of several around the dance floor, and an aberration that stopped Dianne in her mental tracks as she surveyed The Palace. Next to the stove on an armless chair sat what first appeared to be a dwarf with matted, dirty, black hair hunched forward with his sweating, pimpled face resting on the palms of his hands, and his arms on his knees, leering at the women on the dance floor. Leering at Margo. Leering at her.

"What is that," hissed Dianne to Margo by rolling her eyes in the direction of the stove as they wove their way through the dancers.

"That is Ebenezar Azreal. He's the twisted, perverted little son of the richest and most powerful family in Light's End, supports half the prostitutes and spends half his life in Bishop's Alley. He likes to watch instead of do, and he's every woman's worst nightmare on the worst night of her life. Stay. Away. From. Him."

"Azreal?" asked Dianne as they neared the closed gate. "As in the Azrealites; the Church of Tenebrae?"

"One and the same," said Margo as she swung the gate open by its hinges. "Most Light's Enders are Azrealites, at least in name. Even Ruby and Spanish Blackie. Most wear that diamond shaped pin you've seen, and you may even see some of our customers pull out a little black stone out of their pocket to show to Ruby. Each stone has a weird little name on it that they get when they're initiated into the Tenebrae Church. That means they're members, too, and get a discount. And as far as Ebenezar is concerned, you're new meat, so take my advice to heart, honey. Here we are, Dianne; follow me."

Margo stepped back for Dianne to enter the dancer's waiting area. Margo followed after her, closed the gate, and added:

"This is where we get a little rest between dances, usually not for long. The men buy tickets from Ruby, and pick one of us to dance. They change partners often. We turn in our tickets at the end of our shift to get paid. Behind that door," she said, waiving a hand to the closed one behind them like an afterthought "is where some of the women lay down."

"Oh, they get breaks to rest between dances?" asked Dianne. "That's good."

Margo's expression was a mixture of tried patience and disbelief at Dianne's naiveté as she responded: "That's where some of the women and men lay down.'

"But, I, uh... oh," said Dianne, and her face flushed pink. "Oh, my."

"They also turn in those tickets at the end of their shifts. No one is allowed to handle money except Ruby. The gamblers go in to the back room using that door." She pointed. "Now, if you'll excuse me, I see I've got a customer. I suggest you wait here to watch, for your own safety."

Margo opened the gate to enter the dance floor as the music ended, and Dianne followed her. Several men stood by Ruby; they were awkward, uncomely, and socially inept, swaying unconsciously to the *thump thump thump* of the music as they studied possible partners as they waited to dance, tickets clutched in sweaty, nervous hands, most of them still in work clothes.

"Dianne, I thought I said..." began Margo with naked petulance.

"I'll be fine, Margo. I'll stay out of your way, promise, but I need to move around to get what I need for my book. Go on. Go on. I'll be fine."

Savage wound her way through the dancing couples sharing only a sad parody of intimacy with cautionary glances at both Ebenezar, who shared his lust indiscriminately with everyone female at The Palace except Ruby, and at the off-duty cop who perfunctorily studied everyone in the dance hall for signs of disruption. When she reached the entry gate, Ruby was busy selling tickets to a new customer and ignored the reporter as she opened the gate, walked to a section of rail that would give Savage the best view of the entire dance floor, and leaned on it as the trickle of men and dancers entering The Palace grew to a steady stream.

As Dianne watched, the men, awkward, self-conscious, and out of step with the thumping music, and the women, indifferent behind feigned smiles and painted faces, some of the men's hands began to timidly stray to intimate places, in most cases to be met with firm resistance. But one of the flappers dancing close to Margo grabbed such a hand and guided her partner to and through the growing crowd on the dance floor to the waiting gate and then the door behind it. As other men entered to dance in their heavy work boots, stained plaid shirts, and mostly faded blue overalls, or cheap, coarse jeans, their hair matted and dirty or slicked back with hair cream, to pair with newly arrived flappers, one of the first customers of the night left the floor for the gambler's entrance.

As the newshound continued to watch, a man's hand successfully strayed to an intimate area and his partner placed both of her palms against his chest, and shoved him back. He staggered and fell *thud* hard on the unforgiving floor on his butt.

Ruby was though the entry gate, her hand on the butt of her pistol in its holster, and the off-duty cop was vaulting the railing as the humiliated patron, his face red and distorted with rage and shame, rose awkwardly to his feet, stepped up to the flapper, drew his right arm back with its clenched fist, and hit her a smashing blow in the face.

Her head exploded like a dandelion and she crumpled to the floor.

Time froze on extreme activity: Ruby and the bouncer stopped in mid-step; the music choked into silence; the couples on the dance floor turned as one to watch the man who had struck the dancer turn and flee, pushing Ruby to one side as the body on the floor flopped, its head lying in an oozing pool of yellowish ichor, then lay still. Savage vaulted the railing then stopped dead in her tracks.

Dianne covered her mouth and her eyes widened with horror as one of the men, from somewhere between reality and hallucination, wound his way through the frozen couples to the side of the fallen body, and knelt, and threw back his head. A deep uncanny sobbing rose from him, a moaning, a pressure rising in the air, and a gnashing of teeth, and something inhuman, but like a man, wailed in unabated fury like a siren.

The crowd blew apart and scattered and the musicians dropped their instruments and fled in terror, pushing others aside like chaff, as the thing put his arms under the corpse on the floor and rose with it, limp and seeping gore, and then began walking to the entry gate. As he passed Dianne, overwhelmed with the horror of the corpse's face, bile rose up searing in her throat, and she turned away, hunched over, and vomited.

For the pulsating, faintly iridescent face beneath the shattered human face was unutterably, irrationally, inhumanly alien.

Dianne's was a tortured dream that night. The teeth. The blood. The screaming, giggling, maniacal horror from which she fled was a monstrous obscenity of spider's legs writhing around the bloated head and gnashing razor teeth of a gigantic, pustulant maggot.

Savage woke in a cold sweat on Wednesday, October 17th, and lay in bed for hours, unnerved and questioning her own sanity. She had never believed even for a fleeting moment in centaurs, fairies, dragons, Abominable Snowmen, or gigantic maggots while at the same time believing in God, demons, and Heaven and Hell, all of which she had never thought of as separate from the natural or material universe but as the ultimate, or supernatural reality of which this world was an inferior mirror.

Yet she had unquestionably seen an uncanny horror at The Palace that she could not have possibly seen, and she was suddenly overwhelmed with an intense desire to return to Bangor and her little, simple apartment, the busy newspaper where she worked with her only friends outside of her church, her church and her Christian brothers and sisters, the stores where she shopped, and the town she knew with certainty like the back of her hand.

In her struggle to return her black thoughts to something approaching normalcy, she forced herself to set the impossible incident of last night in Bishop's Alley aside, and got out of bed, dressed, and wrote her third article on Bishop's Alley. When she had finished it, she laid her suitcase on the bed, removed, then unwrapped the oilcloth that protected her gun — a Browning "Grand Reudement" model 1928, 9mm, self-loading pistol — removed one of two magazines holding fifteen bullets each, and loaded the gun. She strapped the holster to her calf, then inserted the gun, shaking her pant leg back into place.

Savage walked to the Post Office to mail the article. The air was warm and smarmy for October, and she was nervous and alert for even the smallest aberration, but nothing out of the ordinary happened. At the Post Office, she checked with a clerk at a window for a letter by general delivery from Larry Allison. Inside was the cashier's check she would need to complete her undercover in Light's End and send Margo and Veyda home. She decided to wait until the following day when she felt more herself to walk to a bank and cash it.

As she returned down Dunlevy Avenue at the noon hour, she stopped at the Standard Grocery store and bought a copy of the Bangor newspaper.

Her initial story was on page one:

Lawlessness King In Light's End
Police Ignore Widespread Crime
Booze, Whiz-Bang Sold Like Water and Face Powder
This initial report begins a series by an undercover reporter on lawlessness in the red-light district called Bishop's Alley just north of downtown Light's End, Maine, on August Street.

In 'dance-halls,' saloons and whorehouses including Mother Murphy's and the Bucket o' Blood in Bishop's Alley— a three or four block section of Light's End — debauchery, booze and gambling are as commonplace as sliced bread. The polluted waters of the Abomination Bay east of Bishop's Alley are pure compared to the filth there.

The largest dance halls and saloons are The Palace, Blue Heaven, The '49er Dance Hall, the Bucket o' Blood and Mother Murphy's, The Big Sea and The Kentucky Rooms. There are also a few, shabby, 'legit' businesses including a barber shop and hamburger joint.

The situation is so nasty that unknown townsmen, or more likely townswomen, slop a line of whitewash across August Street at the mouth of The Alley early every morning before the sun rises. It symbolically separates Bishop's Alley from the downtown retail stores, a visual warning to proper folk to stay on the proper side of town.

What, there's more? A scandal is also brewing over the construction of a massive sewage and water maintenance system being built under Light's End. That's right. Under. Claims and counterclaims buzz like flies around garbage that a local man who owns the Ebaugh Construction Company lined many Selectmen's pockets to get the job and tons of money.

Your reporter in Light's End, reports the following:

Scum On Parade

Bishop's Alley's crooks and dopies outnumber saints in Light's End a hundred-to-one. They sell narcotics, hooch, loaded dice, and every perversion known to Pompeii as the good people of the town "turn their noses up" and close their eyes to what's going on during daytime hours. This "Alley" sits on land owned by V.T. Bishop, and bootleggers and hookers are seldom cuffed. If arrested, they post bond, forfeit, and trot away free. Shouldn't they be scared of the local cops? What a laugh!

"Law? What Law?"

"Have some hooch, pick a girl; ain't they peaches?" Alley folk can smell a cop a mile away. There's plenty of money to pay fines, and my guess is very little of it ends up in city coffers. Money talks, and those who have it can do whatever they like.

More to come.

Joe Seminole's expression, including a frozen smile in his bronze face, said that the baffling woman he was facing across a table and two Blue Plate specials was an idiot. However, his mouth said: "But you do know, Dianne. If what you saw was impossible, then you didn't see it. Maybe what you saw was just a bad cut where the guy hit her in the face."

"I wasn't the only one who saw it happen, Joe. Margo Willson was there,

"..what you saw was impossible..."

and a dozen other dancers and their customers, and Ruby and her bouncer all saw it before most of them ran away. I wasn't drunk or high on dope or overtired or hysterical. It was as real as you and I eating supper right now."

"Then I know even less than you," he responded, and picked up his cup of tea, and drank. He put the cup down. "Since this obviously still upsets you, Dianne, maybe we should just change the subject."

"All right, Joe. All right. Instead, you can tell me about the Church of Tenebrae, the giant maggot in the sealed cave under Elliott's Head cliff, and Jake Horne. Why they chew Asafoetida, and if you have a 666 branded under your hair on the back of your head. You know, the dirty little secrets in Light's End."

"Boy, you are feelin' cantankerous tonight! As my maw would say, you certainly got a red hot burr under your saddle. And I already told you I'm not a member of the church."

"Cantankerous? A burr under my what?"

"An Oklahoma saying. You're operating under a misconception, honey. I'm sorta new to Light's End myself. I stopped going to that church long ago when I was just a kid back in Oklahoma, and before we moved to Maine, so all I remember is the thing is run by a bunch of old men called 'the Sixes,' and I don't even know why they're called that. My mom and dad know how I feel about religion, all religion, so it isn't discussed. The maggot thing is just a local legend, a Maine 'boogie man' used to frighten kids and gullible people to get them to stay in line, and all I know about Horne is that I don't like him because he's got a bigger ego than even mine, and he runs most everything and everybody in Light's End... except me."

"Well, that isn't any help. And just how do you feel about 'religion, all religion,' Joe," Savage asked, grateful for the reality of the fork she held in her right hand.

"They make my head hurt," answered Seminole with the same frozen smile.

There was an extended, dead, thick silence that made the clink of silverware on plates in William's Cafe sound like exploding firecrackers.

"It's late," Dianne said. "I think it's time to take me home. Back to the apartment."

"But, honey..."

"No buts. Home, please. Now," the reporter said, and rose from her seat.

The sky and her heart were overcast with churning clouds that blocked out the stars as they drove back to the Van Sanford Apartments in Seminole's car without speaking.

The unsanitary stink of the ocean was palpable even in the stagnant, unmoving air, and Savage covered her nose and mouth with her right hand as she squinted at the short, railed pier before her. It was October and twilight, and the severe, short-sleeved, knee-length black dress that she usually wore to funerals nevertheless clung to her because of the hot sweat between it and her flesh.

Above her, the underlit grey clouds, like the bloated underbelly of a dead fish, moiled and threatened by its deep, rumbling anger to explode as she unpinned and removed the little folded, rectangular piece of paper with a Bible verse inside that she wore daily over her heart. She opened the paper.

It was blank.

To her left in the otherwise eerie silence squatted the mad throw of rock that was Elliott's Head cliff and the legendary mouth of Elliott's cave choked with a motionless, ragged flow of dirt and boulders and debris. To her right, the thin, yellow, dirty beach curved into oblivion. Dianne stepped onto the deserted pier.

Unaccountably, the slat of wood beneath her foot creaked and felt spongy. She stopped. She took a second step, and the new wood slat beneath her irrationally creaked, and a third, and then the fourth wood slat cracked and sunk down but did not break and fall into the muck beneath the pier as it tossed her sideways to her left so that she threw out her left hand to stop her fall and her hand broke the rail but saved her.

Dianne paused, regaining her composure and sure footing, glancing up as she did so to see a dirty swell of seagulls above her like vultures beneath the moiling clouds.

She gingerly took a fifth and then a sixth step, anticipating but without fear or trepidation and accepting the creak of each board as she did so until the reporter stopped at the end of the pier and looked ten feet down at the sluggish morass that was Abomination Bay. She looked down at the silver mirror of water that belched a sudden cluster of bubbles.

She looked down at the dirty water that belched a second time as a black mass rolled up just beneath the surface and belched a larger cluster of bubbles. She looked down as the mass rolled up and broke the mirrored surface and tender and tearful, in a dance of soundless, rising bubbles, the undine rose up and up and up, fey, voluptuous, beautiful, her thick red hair flowering in the water, the tip of her blue-green sequined tail breaking the mire behind her.

Dianne looked down and gasped and sat up in bed.

Chapter Six

On Thursday morning, Dianne watched as the rain spat outside of her apartment's single window and etched lines across its glass. Drowsy and sullen, she watched a handful of gulls swirl high in the muted light of morning. Above them, the charcoal clouds had thickened since last night, and she heard the pensive, October air outside heavy with a drowsy, deep-throated rumbling as the claustrophobic and threatening thunderheads rolled sluggishly in from the Atlantic Ocean. Then the storm exploded with profane, feminine power, and the unseen splatter of gulls burst apart and fled.

She tried to hum one of the songs she loved to lift her spirits, but it was a worthless effort. Her Spartan breakfast of eggs and toast had been tasteless. She hadn't even opened her Bible to copy a verse on a piece of paper to fold and pin to her blouse. Who would see it? A heavy rain shut down almost all movement in a town where the most prominent form of transportation was walking or riding a horse. One couldn't exactly call a cab in a backwater berg with few telephones, or cash a check or buy groceries in the rain.

Even though the bizarre images of the horror at Bishop's Alley were somewhat fading, Seminole's lame explanation had done nothing to dissuade her from what she knew she'd seen, or lessen the anxiety and confusion she still felt from having witnessed the impossible. So she resolved to choose a pulp or slick magazine from her thin stack sitting on the apartment's bureau and read until noon or so when she knew Margo and Veyda would be "up and about" and she could ask Margo to repeat what the dancer had seen.

At noon, she rose, set her magazine aside, strapped her gun to her calf under her blue dungarees, and left her apartment. It was the work of moments to walk down the hallway to the stairs that descended to the basement of the Van Sanford, descend, and rap her knuckles on Margo's door as she asked:

"Margo, it's me, Dianne. Margo, are you home?"

The door opened on Margo in jeans and a plaid shirt holding Veyda,

71

diapered and in a flowered night shirt, smiling, in her mother's arms.

"Well, if it isn't F. Scott Fitzgerald! Come in, honey," said Margo. "Have you had lunch yet? I'm making tomato soup and cheese sandwiches."

"Thank you," answered the reporter, and stepped through the door. As she did so, Veyda opened her arms to accept Dianne. "Oh, my gosh; isn't that so sweet! Hello to you, Baby Veyda! How is your mommy feeling today?"

"Her mommy is feelin' just great," answered Margo with just a touch of question in the tone of her voice as she handed her daughter to the reporter. "Why do you ask?"

"Well, I'm still a little shaken at what happened the other night at The Palace."

"You're kiddin'," said Margo, as she closed the door to her apartment. The thunder rumbled outside her apartment. "Fights in Bishop's Alley are just part of the job. Surely that couldn't have surprised you. Would you like a cup of hideous black coffee while I cook?"

"Yes, thanks," answered Dianne, as she sat Baby Veyda next to a scatter of illustrated, wooden, building blocks, and then sat on the floor next to her. She watched Margo with consternation and suspicion as the dancer poured coffee into a chipped cup from a gray tin pot on the stove in her kitchen. "Maybe we didn't see the same thing, Margo."

"I saw a jerk hit a woman in the face, and cut her pretty badly. That stuff happens all the time in The Alley; they don't even shut down the dives. The girls who ran, including me, got their pay docked, Ruby sent her bouncer out to round up the musicians, and they were back in business by midnight. Everything was business as usual the next night. Fist fights. Knifings. Shootings. Even gory murder. Happens all the time, honey. That's why I told you it wasn't safe for you to be there. But you wouldn't listen to me."

"But her face...?" Dianne protested and helped the toddler stack one *click click click* block on top of another one.

"What about her face?" Margo answered, as she handed the steaming cup of coffee to Dianne. Veyda placed a third block on top of the second, her face alive with concentration and smiles, as the reporter unsuccessfully tried to read Margo's guarded expression.

"Never mind, Margo," she responded with a reluctant resignation that she would not find confirmation of what she'd seen from the dancer who was again in the kitchen, pouring an opened can of Progresso tomato soup into a pan on her stove. Margo turned to the kitchen counter where a loaf of Hi-Lo bread, block of cheese, and stick of Seminole Maid butter were sitting. The dancer removed a small pan, placed it on the stove, and added two pats of yellow butter that instantly *sizzzzzled*. Something in the familiar sounds and smells of the mundane, everyday activity of cooking seemed to further anchor Savage in the reality of the moment instead of the bloody insanity on the dance floor.

Margo's unresponsiveness was forgotten amid gales of laughter as Veyda knocked down her tower of blocks and Dianne "the tickle spider" caught up the baby girl to tickle her stomach. Then she let Veyda escape so that the reporter could stalk her with baby steps and undulating fingers morphed into imaginary claws, and subtly and silently as falling snow, warm treasured memories of sitting on her own father's lap as he read to her or smoked his pipe, and snuggling, loved, in her mother's arms as her mother sang to her washed over Dianne, stirring deep maternal feelings, and the reporter's eyes welled with tears of joy, and she wished that Veyda was her child, and that she had the same love for one another that had enriched her parent's lives, and a brief image of Joe Seminole flickered in her mind.

She shook Seminole's face away as thunder pealed again and the low, impalpable sound of rain slowly filled the apartment.

"Come and get it!" announced Margo from the stove, interrupting Dianne's reverie.

The reporter handed a giggling Veyda to Margo who was already sitting at her small red-topped metal table set with a plate of three cheese sandwiches, and two place settings of spoons and plates and bowls filled with steaming, aromatic soup. Veyda was already reaching for a spoon when her mother said: "Dig in!"

Dianne added a sandwich next to her bowl, and without looking at Margo who was taking the spoon away from her disgruntled daughter, asked:

"Margo, do you believe in aliens."

"What? Put it down, Baby Veyda."

"Do you believe in, well, that there is life on other planets?"

Margo partially filled the spoon she'd taken from her daughter with soup, and offered it to Veyda as she shared her defeated and puzzled expression with the reporter.

"If you mean like 'The Man in the Moon,' no, of course not. Or those bugs like in that old flicker where they shoot a big bullet full of men to the moon? Nope."

"Yes, sorta like the ones on the covers of some of the pulp magazines, Margo."

Margo filled the spoon with tomato soup and offered it to an enthusiastic and very hungry Veyda, a halo of red tomato already ringing her mouth. "I don't read pulp magazines, Dianne. I can't read. It's one of the reasons I have trouble finding a decent job. Wasn't a problem when... when my husband was, well, you know." She waited for the reporter's condescension. She saw none, and the spoon dipped into the bowl and rose again to Veyda's pudgy face.

"Oh. Oh," the reporter stumbled. "Well, I continue to catch myself making assumptions that turn out to be stupid. I'm truly sorry that I've misjudged you several times, and I need to ask your forgiveness. In fact, I still haven't made it to the bank to get the money I promised to send you and Baby Veyda back home, Margo."

"Even Christians are human and continue to mess up, honey," said Margo, and the spoon fell and rose, most of it actually making it into Veyda's mouth. "We're never perfect, just forgiven. For sure, I forgive you, Dianne, and it turns out I owe Ruby some money that I'd forgotten about and will have to work awhile to pay her back and pay the rent I owe to the Sorenson's anyway, so don't worry about it."

As the susurration of the falling rain outside the Van Sanford Apartments diminished from a constant roar to a sigh and then to an intermittent whisper, and minutes blurred into hours, the two women continued to talk about the heartbreaks and joys of their young lives in Bangor, Maine and Nashville, Tennessee, respectively, of the colorful history of their families, of old friends and flirtations, of lost and found loves and lost or fulfilled hopes and dreams, and music and flickers and clothes and favorite foods, and Dianne Savage and Margo Willson became friends.

Veyda fell asleep in Margo's arms.

"Oh, dear," she whispered, gently rocking her body and her child lying against her chest and over her left shoulder, "I think the rain has stopped!" She patted Veyda's forever faintly stained cloth diaper. "That means I'll have to go to work. What time is it, Dianne?"

"A bit past four o'clock," said the reporter looking at her wrist watch.

"Dang it. Could you do me an immense favor?" she said as she rose slowly to her feet. "I don't have much time to get ready. Could you carry Veyda up to the Sorensonses' for me? They already have extra diapers and food and toys for her."

"Won't she wake up, Margo?" whispered the reporter.

"Not a chance," Margo answered, and transferred the sleeping baby who barely stirred to Dianne's arms. "She's used to it."

"See you tomorrow?" whispered Savage, as she moved gently to the front door that Margo had opened. "And be careful at that wicked, mephitic, place."

"Mephitic?" asked the dancer.

"Noxious," said the newshound. "Sorry. Sometimes, I get carried away."

"I'll be careful, Dianne," answered the dancer. "And since we're being completely honest with each other now, I'll confess a little lie before you go.

"I have seen men shining like silver in the dark," she whispered, and closed the door.

The apartment door opened on Gene Sorenson whose smile was immediate and broad when he saw Veyda in Dianne's arms.

"Oh, it's my little sweetie pie," whispered Sorenson. He placed a hand on the reporter's left forearm. "Please, come in. Where's her mommy, Ms. Savage?"

"Getting ready for work," whispered Dianne, as she stepped through the doorway and past the apartment manager who closed the door gently. "She's running a little late because of the depressing rain."

"We've got everything ready for the little angel," grinned Sorenson with a mouthful of off-white teeth, indicating a bedroom door located off of his living room with a hand gesture, "including her bed — our guest bed. Let's tippee-toe in and let her finish her nap. Mrs. Sorenson will be back in just a moment. She's down in the laundry room. How are you doing, Ms. Savage? Enjoying your apartment? Do you need anything?"

As she followed Sorenson through the doorway, Dianne formed a circle by touching the index finger of her right hand to its partner thumb and smiled, miming everything was all right in the world, and silently mouthed the word okay.

"Oh, I almost forgot," said the apartment manager as he opened the bedroom door with a surprisingly gnarled, free hand. "I was down at the library yesterday checking out 'Wild Horse Mesa' by Zane Gray, and I have a message for you."

Dianne gently laid the toddler on the bed in the space between two pillows placed parallel to one another. She spread a blue, fringed baby blanket that had been placed at the foot of the bed over the toddler. Sorenson leaned over the baby, lightly kissed her cheek, and drew an odd pattern on her forehead with a forefinger. As he straightened, he said:

"I'm afraid your request to use the Special Collections room has been denied."

On Friday, October 19th at 11:13 am, Dianne stepped out of the front door of the First State Bank on the corner of August and Lagle across the street from the train depot and under a stationary gray blanket of unclean, threatening clouds. She shoved an envelope containing the money from her money order into the right front pocket of her blue dungarees.

She wore her empty knapsack with the intent of filling it with groceries later in the day. Pinned above the left pocket of her blouse underneath her brown leather jacket was her traditional folded scrap of paper. Inside it read:

Be strong and courageous. Do not be afraid or terrified because of them, for the Lord your God goes with you; he will never leave you nor forsake you. Deuteronomy 31:6.

She did not wear her pistol on her calf.

It had been a busy morning that had included the mundane tasks of mailing the fourth of her series of articles that she'd written for her editor the night before, and dropping off her dirty clothes at the Seminole Laundry for cleaning. After a trip to one of the water and storm drain construction sites, Dianne's intention was to buy more food staples from the Standard Grocery as well as the day's edition of the *Bangor Daily* to see if they'd published another of her stories and the current copy of the disreputable *Citadel* newspaper.

Savage had used the bank's telephone to order the luxury of the Dixie Cab that was waiting for her at the curb. She took off her cloche hat and waved it at the taxi.

"Where to?" asked the cabbie as she plopped down on the cracked leather back seat of the cab and closed its shabby door behind her. As she began to wiggle out of her knapsack, she studied the cabbie's sallow, middle-aged, stubbled face under a soiled Porkpie hat in his interior rear view mirror; he was looking at her with weary indifference.

"I'd like to take a look at one of the construction sites where they're laying pipe for the new water system," said Dianne. The cabbie's expression changed to consternation.

"If you don't think it nosey, lady, what on earth for?" he asked as a cigarette appeared in his mouth and in the rear view mirror. He inhaled then blew out the smoke.

"Just curiosity," said Dianne as she glanced out of the cab's grimy window at a man on the sidewalk who had stopped and was looking at her. "And to kill some time."

She waved her right hand at the man on the sidewalk who fled like a deer.

"Well, that boondoggle is almost finished, Miss. The only active site left is down on the west end of Bishop's Alley."

"Then take me to the west end of Bishop's Alley, kind sir."

"If you don't mind my saying it, no can do, Miss. First, I don't take or pick up anyone into or out of that nasty place. Closest I get is the Chambers Hospital on the corner of August and Dunlevy. Second, that's no place for a lady to be walkin' around any time of any day for any reason. Every pervert, drunk, murderer and conman in the county end up there sooner or later."

"Then it's off to the corner of August and Dunlevy we go!" said Savage, feeling a little silly. "Make haste!"

"It's your dime, lady," grumbled the cabbie, and his worn face left the rear view mirror as the cab pulled away from the curb and into a "U" turn that would carry them west down August Street. The newshound heard him mutter "suffragette" under his breath.

"By the way," asked the reporter. "Why did you call it a boondoggle?"

"Who wants to know?" The cabbie's grim, sallow face was back in the rear view window again, the cigarette hanging out of the left corner of his down-turned mouth, and this time it was wearing a questioning mask of suspicion.

"No one special," said Dianne, looking out of a grimy cab window at the businesses on the north side of the street and the seemingly endless flow of people chatting in little eddies, window shopping, entering or exiting doorways, or walking up and down the sidewalk. "Just a brainless suffragette."

As they drove through the intersection of August and Ferry, Dianne turned her attention to the pernicious beehive of people and the businesses on the south side of the bricked street. Savage noted the small Liberty Theater and its sandwich signs on the sidewalk advertising a vaudeville show, the Jones Drug Store, and the William's Cafe where she had shared supper with Joe Seminole, then the larger Ritz Theater featuring both a flicker and vaudeville show, Collier Bro's Hardware and Furniture and Undertakers, and finally the Warecki Manufacturing Co. on the south corner of August and Wells.

As they drew nearer the second intersection, Savage saw more clearly an odd gathering of twenty or so agitated men in business suits and hats or caps standing around two waist-high meshed metal baskets. Two columns of gray smoke and burning embers rose from the gaping mouths of those baskets to merge into one and dissipate in the overcast sky above as something inside smoldered. Those Light's Enders on the sidewalks closest to this eddy of disgruntled men stopped to stare, or glanced back over their shoulders as they passed.

"Driver, could you slow down a bit?" Savage asked, grasping the back of the cabbie's seat for emphasis. He did so as Dianne searched the angry or outraged expressions on the faces of each man. "What on earth are those men burning?"

"Don't know and don't care," responded the indifferent cabbie as the scene slid behind the cab as it progressed down the street. He removed his cigarette and blew a smoke ring into the air for emphasis. "I try ta keep my nose outta other people's beeswax."

"Is this a common occurrence in Light's End?" asked Dianne as increasing distance blurred any chance of discerning with any certainty what burned in the baskets.

"Never seen it before." The cigarette stub went back into his mouth.

But her questions and statement were rhetorical because Savage knew instinctively that additional articles she'd written must have been published, and that Light's End officials and the town's movers and shakers were burning copies of the *Bangor Daily Register* in protest in those metal baskets, and that it was now only a matter of brief, indeterminate time before she and her mission in Light's End would be exposed.

An electric thrill of both fear and pride because of the consequences of her published words made her briefly shiver as the men, the baskets, and the intersection disappeared behind her from her field of vision, and she knew that the level of danger for her would rise as the window of opportunity to finish her work would rapidly slam shut.

Savage was greeted with the subtle but rancid odor in the still air of decaying food and refuse, stale beer, and urine as she stepped out of the cab on the corner of Dunlevy and August in front of the Chambers Hospital. The distant strings of unlit Christmas lights between the building before her in Bishop's Alley hung limp and motionless; there were only four or five dirty automobiles or buggies parked on the street. It was just before noon, and the aroma was subtle only because it was a block or so removed. The dirt road and throw of boards called a sidewalk in The Alley were swarming with random eddies of chattering and screaming seagulls feasting on last night's leftovers from the debauchery of Bishop's Alley. Dianne momentarily pinched her nose in defense of the noxious odor as she crossed the final intersection before entering the three squalid blocks that were a sorry testimony to the hedonism and weakness of man.

Her suspicion was that she would never pass that way again, so she paid close attention to the mostly silent businesses that she passed on the north side of the rutted and muddy road: the tiny, clapboard Epps Hamburgers, Conway's Used Furniture & Bail Bonds leaning drunkenly to its left on its makeshift foundation, the shanty that was Field's Barber Shop, The Palace and its next door hovels, The Big Sea and the Kentucky Rooms, and as she or one of the few patrons in sight approached, each eddy of seagulls would explode upwards into the gray, overcast sky with angry screams of protest, only to settle back to their horrid repast when no human was evident.

It was a depressing and slightly unnerving five minutes as the nauseous stink increased and she passed the huge, open-roofed Wintergarden dance hall, shabby Ada's Bar, an unsigned, unpainted, two-story house that Savage surmised was a brothel, unsavory and dirty Josephine's Boarding House, and a second single story Craftsman house without signage that was also likely a cat house.

On the third and final block there was only one retail business, the seedy Last Call Saloon, and four additional buildings of varying sizes and states of disrepair that were either private residences or brothels, or both, and here the reporter caught glimpses between the buildings of a huge mound of earth and the distant sounds of heavy equipment just to her west even as she approached the construction site.

The air was alive with the metallic, grinding, almost ear-shattering *clank clatter thud* of machines and the unpleasant smells of oil, concrete dust, and human sweat as Dianne stepped off of the rutted dirt road where a battered, muddy, Model A truck sat with its passenger side door open; the little wizened man who sat on its bench seat had both of his skinny legs propped up on its running board as he chewed something, a toothpick or that hideous witch's gum of the Azrealites, and watched her approach. He wore a baggy, gray, pin-stripped suit and Ripper hat pushed rakishly back above the hairline, and watched her with the eyes of a dead black lizard.

Thirty yards north of him lay a giant trench in the ground and the end of a huge, reinforced concrete conduit protruding from its gaping mouth. To its west and closer to August Street sat two additional concrete conduits, and next to them, a small wooden shed, and the entire muddy scene was, as the reporter thought to herself, swarming with men, tools, and lumbering earth-moving equipment.

"Hello!" Dianne shouted through cupped hands as she stopped at the Model A. The lizard said nothing as he stared at her, indifferent, unblinking, his sunken, stubbled cheeks lengthening then shortening with each chew of what turned out to be a bobbing toothpick.

"I'm looking for the foreman! *The foreman!*" she shouted. The lizard said nothing, his ball-bearing eyes never leaving her face, as he pointed an arm to a middle-aged man about twenty yards to his north standing at the mouth of the trench. The bullhorn resting in his left hand against his left thigh, dirty gray pants, his hard hat, and his general demeanor of authority was proof enough for the newshound that the lizard was pointing to the storm drain project's foreman.

"Thanks!" she shouted at the black-eyed stunted man who looked at her as if he'd heard nothing. "Thank you!" she shouted even louder, then waved a hand at him in dismissal as she walked way.

As Savage carefully picked her way through the muddy ruts left by the machinery, Dianne changed her mind about her earlier adjective describing the men at the site — swarming. While it was true there were probably more than one hundred uniformed workers — a number that, in itself, felt excessive — she observed that easily more than half were just milling about, leaning on shovels, chatting with one another, or sitting around the huge mound of earth just north of the trench doing no work as a dirty yellow Caterpillar excavator *clank clank clank* lifted one of the remaining conduits by a chain wrapped around its rough concrete surface.

"Hi!" Dianne shouted through cupped hands at the project manager who ignored her as he waved an arm and shouted an instruction to a worker whom the reporter could not find by the aid of his gesture. "Hi, I'm Dianne!" she shouted again, and this time the foreman turned to face her, his clean-shaven face wearing an expression of exasperation.

"Hank!" he shouted over the grinding racket of machinery and smiled to reveal uneven teeth. He tipped his hard hat in a gesture of respect. "Can I help you,?"

"Okay to watch for a bit?"

The expression on his angular and friendly face turned into mild consternation.

"Why?"

"Just curious!" yelled Dianne and gave him her best, innocent little girl smile.

"What?!" he yelled back, cupping an ear. "I can't.....?!"

"Can I watch!?"

In frustration, he gestured that the reporter follow him, which she did, as he turned and walked to and then past the mouth of the trench to the little shack. She noted the trim, healthy cut of his body and the easy, assured gait of his walk. He opened the door, smiled, and gestured an invitation for her to enter with the wave of his right arm.

The monstrous roar of the equipment was diminished by half when the door closed behind them.

"Sorry," he said, and grinned sheepishly as he laid the bullhorn down on a chair. "Didn't seem proper to be yellin' at a lady 'cause of the goddamned noise." He again gestured an invitation with his right arm that to sit in a shabby, armless chair in front of a small, scarred wooden desk by the wall opposite them. On the desk was a small, framed photograph of what Savage assumed was his wife with two small children, a son and daughter, both under ten years old. He walked around the desk and seated himself. He took off his hard hat and set it on the desk. "Now, what can I do for you, Miss?"

"Could you tell me a little about this project, Hank? May I call you Hank? I hope to write a book on little Maine towns, and I'm curious about the size of this thing for such a small berg. It looked like I could stand up in one of those conduits without coming close to bumping my head."

"I just follow my orders from the Ebaugh Company, Miss. I'm not an engineer or anything like that. But they told me they're buildin' for the future growth of the town."

"So these colossal tunnels run all over town?" she asked against the somewhat muffled cacophony of machinery outside the shed, as she carefully studied his body language and the tone of his rather pleasant voice.

"No, ma'am. Just mostly under the downtown area and the houses just around downtown for about four or five miles or so."

"But, I thought you said they were building for future growth?"

He shrugged his shoulders and smiled mechanically, indicating that he simply didn't know the answer. "That's true. And that's what they said."

"So the existing individual storm drain and water control lines and stuff from businesses and neighborhoods just tie in to these huge conduits, Hank?"

"I guess they've hired someone to come back in after me to do that." He shrugged his shoulders in ignorance, but the smile was gone. "Does seem kind of odd, though." He removed his hard hat, and, taking a soiled handkerchief from a breast pocket on his shirt, wiped his broad, sunburned forehead.

"Do you have a lot more of these questions, lady?" he asked as he picked his hard hat up off of his desk. "I don't mean to be rude, but I've got a project to run."

"Do you know where the water treatment plant is located where all of these conduits hook up?" asked Dianne with a growing conviction that she was talking to an honest man of average intelligence and nascent education except in the field in which he was employed who simply did not know the answers to her questions.

"Why, about six or seven miles west of downtown Light's End," said the foreman with sudden epiphany. "An old building out on the edge of Lost City. I never even thought of that until you asked. I guess the town Selectmen plan on someone else building a new one closer in after we're done here."

"Well, thank you for your time; I know you're busy," Savage said, disappointment obvious on her face, and stood up.

They left the shack side by side as the caterpillar swung one of the two remaining conduits in a slow arc high over the gaping trench.

As the massive concrete conduit swung, the chain *RUNK* slipped and the conduit teetered back and forth as it continued its arc.

"You might contact the Ebaugh..." Hank shouted, and looked up, startled.

The conduit swung past the trench, and the chain *RUNK* slipped again.

Dianne looked up.

The conduit swung over Hank and Dianne, and the chain *RUNK* slipped.

"LOOK OUT!!" Hank screamed, and shoved Dianne aside.

The chain *SNAP* broke.

The concrete conduit fell.

The shack exploded.

Hank exploded.

Everything and everyone stood still as the lazy broken chain swung back and forth.

And as their shock broke and workmen began to run towards the fallen conduit, the little wizened man sat in the truck with both of his skeletal legs propped up on its running board and smiled as he looked with the eyes of a dead black lizard at Dianne where she lay just beyond the rained chaos of crushed board and shattered glass and the growing red pool of Hank's blood.

CHAPTER SEVEN

Margo put her right arm around Dianne Savage's shoulder as the reporter wiped the remaining tears from her puffy eyes with the palms of her hands.

It was close to noon on Saturday, October 20, as they sat on a red and white checkerboard blanket spread on the ground next to a drained wading pool for a picnic at the Lincoln School Park six blocks south of the Van Sanford Apartments. The abysmal sun had struggled through the melancholy clouds to warm the air to a pleasant temperature for an October day in Maine, and a happy Baby Veyda played a few feet away, using a stick she'd found on the ground to beat at the withering blades of grass, dead fallen leaves like blotches of color on an artist's palette, and mysterious objects outside of her experience that had invaded her imagination. They were alone in the park, and the silence was a welcome salve for Dianne's jagged nerves.

"I'm sorry; I'm acting like a kid," said Savage. "It's just that I've never really seen a man die before yesterday."

"Honey, we're all school girls just pretending to be all grown up and in charge," said Margo, and brushed a wisp of Dianne's hair back from the reporter's lowered face. "But we're mostly only in charge of the choices we make in response to the things that happen around us that we can't control at all. I know you know that, just like me, but we all forget it most of the time."

"I was almost crushed into a bloody jelly."

Margo patted her back as Veyda threw fistfuls of blotted leaves into the still air.

"If I hadn't talked to him... if I hadn't gone out to the site..."

"Now don't go playin' the self-blame game. You're givin' yourself way more credit than anyone deserves, honey. Only God sees the big picture; only God is really in control. And you should take some comfort in that instead of pretending you can know more than is humanly possible."

"I know, I know, I know. On top of everything else, I've found out a lot of nasty little things about Light's End that I never expected to find that's put me on edge anyway. All completely out of my hands to stop, really. This is a corrupt, godless place, and you couldn't pay me to stay here one minute longer than I absolutely have to, Margo."

"Same here, and I thank you again for making it possible for me to leave and go back home. I've almost got the Palace paid off and I should be leaving sometime next week."

"If I can wrap up a few loose ends on my research, I may beat you out of here!"

"Over my dead body," chucked Margo as she began the slow process of standing. "I bet I know one something that may change your mind."

"It would have to be a gold mine or a field of diamonds or something," grinned Dianne, and, using her arms with her head to create a triangle, leaned back on the blanket. She noticed that Veyda had abandoned launching leaves into the torpid air and was now busy collecting blades of grass bleached by the Fall season for a purpose only known to her, and Savage felt the maternal warmth that had been awakened in her by Margo's baby begin to soften and distance her sorrow over Hank's hideous death.

"*Welllll*, that something begins with Joe and ends with Seminole."

"How did you know about that?" she coyly said as she bit the fingernail of the first digit on her right hand.

"A little birdie named Joe's mother told me. You aren't the only one who knows the few eligible, good-looking bachelors in this town, kiddo."

"Sorry, but you are dead wrong this time. I have no intention of permanently moving out of Bangor; I love the city. I admit Joe is easy on the eyes, and fun to be around, but he and I are just enjoying each other's company until I leave. Anyway, the trip to or from Light's End to Bangor is way too long to nurture any kind of long distance relationship.

"My dream has always been to be an ace reporter for a big newspaper in New York City or maybe Chicago, Margo. Or maybe even a best-selling author. And I've focused my entire life on nothing else but fulfilling that dream. But I admit your beautiful little daughter and Joe have made me pine a bit to add being a wife and mother to that somehow. Somehow. What is your dream for yourself and Baby Veyda?"

As Dianne asked, she turned her head to her left to see Veyda standing at her side and offering her a bouquet of dead grass.

"Oh, sweetie-pie, you are such a doll," she said, and accepted the gift. "You just made my whole day. Can I give you a hug?"

Dianne hugged and Veyda snuggled.

"Can I have a hug?"

"When I get home, Dianne, I hope to find a job to support us and maybe attend night school to get my High School degree. Then maybe a trade school; I think I'd like to be a social worker or a teacher or something. But my greatest dream is for Veyda to grow up to be a healthy young lady with a family of her own. And someday, maybe someday, I will find another man as kind and respectful and generous as my late husband who will love me. But, right now, the sandwiches have been eaten, the ants are full, and it's about time to head for home, I think."

"I'm not really looking forward to the trek, but I guess we ought to...." said Savage as she began to rise from her reclining position. As she did so, she saw an automobile rumble up to the curb of the road running next to the park and belch to a stop. "Well, look there! I may be wrong, but that looks like Chuck Walton's heap," Dianne said as she began to wave at the vehicle. "Do you know Mr. Walton, Margo?"

The driver's door of the automobile opened and a man exited and stood up by his car to return Dianne's welcome as Margo joined the reporter with her own wave of greeting.

"Want a ride somewhere?" Walton called out as he unconsciously touched the rim of his glasses and began to approach the women. "I promise I'm not an axe murderer."

Savage watched as Margo and Veyda turned briefly in front of the first step of the south porch of the Van Sanford Apartments and waved good-bye to Walton and her as the old professor pulled his shabby car away from the curb into the almost empty street.

"Thank you again for your willingness to drop me off at the Standard Grocery, Mr. Walton," Dianne said. "I sort of miss getting to telephone for a taxi like in Bangor."

"Call me Chuck. Are you sure you don't want me to wait," smiled Walton, "and give you a ride back to the Van Sanford? I don't have anything competing for my time."

"Goodness, no! I don't want to look a gift benefactor in the mouth, so to speak, and I'm only buying a couple of items. As you know, Chuck, it's only a few blocks back to my apartment; I'm a big, strapping, healthy female, and I'll be just fine."

"We're almost at the store," added Walton. I'll just drop you off in the parking lot by the entrance. How's the research going for your book?"

"Well. But I must tell you Light's End isn't exactly my favorite little town."

"Not town; blighted little jerkwater," Walton corrected. "It'll grow on you... like a malignant fungus. Here we are."

The old car spit and coughed to a stop and a high-pitched squeal of its brakes. Walton waited until Savage had entered the store, pulled his automobile to a distant spot in the parking lot where he would watch the front door, and turned off its motor.

It took only moments for Dianne to buy eggs, milk, bread, and a few canned items. At the checkout counter that had now been decorated for Halloween with paper witches, spiders, and orange pumpkins, she also picked up copies of *The Citadel* and *Bangor Daily Register* newspapers with the anticipation that one of her articles might have been published by her editor in the Bangor edition. But she rolled up and stuck both newspapers into her brown paper sack with her groceries before she left the store.

Outside, Savage sat her bag down on the ground, stepped to one side of the front door so she couldn't be seen by anyone inside, and removed the Bangor newspaper.

Walton watched her and, smiling in anticipation of her response to his surprise ride back to her apartments, placed his key in the ignition of his car.

Dianne's article was on the front page of the newspaper. She scanned it, noticing her byline and then the last line that announced a side-bar story on page three as well.

She raised her arms in exaltation, threw back her head, and silently mouthed the word "hurrah!" before rolling up and replacing the newspaper in her grocery sack.

Walton's smile faded into a puzzled expression. Then the memory of the anger felt by many in town over the recent articles on Bishop's Alley in the Bangor newspaper that had spilled over into the burning of copies of that newspaper on August Street replaced his puzzled expression with a frown. He removed his key from the car's ignition.

When Dianne picked up her sack and began to walk back to her apartment, Chuck Walton sat somber and disgusted and did not follow.

In her apartment five minutes later and before she put her groceries in the shelves of the kitchen, Savage read the first article she'd written that was printed above the fold on page one. It read:

ALLEY "CATS" PROWL

Cathouses are so prominent in Bishop's Alley, the red-light district of Light's End, that at midnight, Mother Murphy's patrons don't need to settle for exhausted girls. Because of an underhanded deal with corrupt leaders in the little, isolated town on our coast, flat-bed trucks back up behind the joint and unload fresh ladies of the evening. Worn-out dames then fill up the empty trucks and return to the smaller whorehouses in Lost City, just west of Light's End, where the population is mostly black. And the owners of Mother Murphy's and The Big Sea, and other whorehouses, and certain town fathers pocket a big chuck of the profits, big because of the huge influx of lonely men from out-of-town working on a very large water and storm drain project.

A Wink and a Nod

Prostitution is a cancer in Bishop's Alley, destroying the women who ply the trade, the men who buy, and their families. Police 'patrol' the rotten boardwalks and wink with bloodshot eyes and nod at the many half-naked hookers or, depending on their mood, guarantee protection from arrest for something other than money. Many of these women who are drug addicts and drunks stand behind the cathouses and deny no perversion to anyone with money. They know the worst punishment they'll get from County Judge White is a fine and a slap on the wrist. Bishop's Alley is so diseased that no one with a shred of morality would be caught dead in this seventh Hell of Maine.

Panties In Shanties

Why shouldn't they sell their wares? Prostitutes have no fear of Judge White, and gaggles of other "sisters," smoking cigarettes, snorting whiz-bang which is what they call cocaine, or swigging hooch, stand in doorways under cheap, flickering Christmas lights. My reliable source sniggers that, when confronted by a cop, a hooker may say something like "Where's the fire, honey? Sit down and take a load off!" And when a prostitute is brushed off by a potential customer, their cursing would make a sailor blush.

It is only a hop, skip and jump to The Alley which is how far it is outside the city limits of downtown Light's End, and that is a big part of the problem. Many are hard at work at the courthouse that supposedly delineates The Alley from decent citizens, but they aren't working hard to shut down V. T. Bishop's alley, the most debauched street in Maine.

Her second story, published on page three, read:

DRABS GUZZLE BOOZE LIKE LEMONADE
Thug Barkeepers Ignore Law
Disorderly Conduct Is Bootlegging?

Bootleggers, hookers, and gamblers are common in "The Alley" at the end of August Street just outside of the city limits of Light's End,

Maine. Competition is fierce and sometimes violent, prices and quality are cheap, and the barrels of booze seem bottomless. Many 'dance halls' and all of the saloons peddle whisky for $1 a pint; buy a gallon, it's even cheaper. Bootleggers are unafraid of anyone outside of federal prohibition officers who have no interest in disorderly conduct charges.

This reporter's source is solid: "Not a chance you'll go to jail. The cops arrest sots every day; they pay a $15 'fine' for disorderly conduct to the crooked county judge and walk out the front door. Half the fine goes in the judge's pocket, half back to The Alley."

As example, multiple disorderly conduct charges have been made in the past against Ava Hater who is one of the rare prostitutes that doesn't sell drugs or booze. Judge White argues her fines are the collection of a "fee" for operating in Light's End's "entertainment" district.

Hookers Hawk Whiz-Bang

Some prostitutes do sell whiz-bang by the pinch or the pound. Cocaine is legal, but a growing number of medical professionals believe it is crippling to a person's health in the long term. Spend a day or night in Bishop's Alley and that theory becomes fact.

Illegal business is conducted in the shadow of churches and schools built by the decent folks in Light's End who need justice and an end to corruption.

Savage tossed the newspaper on her bed, singing "I'm Looking Over a Four-Leaf Clover" to herself as she did so, and put her groceries in the proper kitchen shelves. Then the reporter spent the rest of her waking time alternately cleaning up her apartment and writing in great detail everything she could remember from the last several days — the facts she'd gathered, the events that had shaped her stay in Light's End, her impressions and even suspicions — in her journal.

She slept well, with no disturbing dreams.

"Thank you for the invitation for lunch, Pastor Miller," said Dianne as she sat in his little armless chair in the preacher's den after his Sunday worship service. Her cloche hat rested neatly on her lap. "I'm afraid I'm finding out what you said about ducks might be snakes in Light's End is true."

Miller chuckled. "Finally, someone remembered something I said! Just remember, Dianne, that anywhere is Hell without God, but anywhere is Heaven when He is with us."

"That's good; I'll have to remember that one as well. While we wait for your wife to change her clothes and get the kids ready, would you have time for a couple of hypothetical questions, just for fun?"

"Of course!" he answered. "I love to discuss hypothetical questions. Fire away."

"Do you believe that God still sends us messages through our dreams?"

"Why do you ask, Ms. Savage? Do you have such dreams?"

"Please call me Dianne. Maybe. But the dreams are almost always about little snatches of conversation that I hear days or months later, or little mundane events that don't add up to much," said Dianne with a cautious smile. "Just occasionally, it's about something big, even frightening. Some people would even call them nightmares."

"That couldn't be much *fun*, Dianne. But you surely know the Bible records many instances of men and women who had precognitive dreams, or receive messages while asleep; some of them even changed the course of history. But when you keep in mind that the Old and New Testament of the Bible record around six thousand years of history, these dreams are very, very rare.

"I do not doubt you dream, but I don't have that gift myself, and have never known anyone who did. And, more importantly, I don't have the gift of interpreting dreams either. I'm more than willing to listen to the ones that are bothering you, but they'll probably leave me just as befuddled as they leave you."

"When I was coming by bus to Light's End, Pastor Miller, I dreamed my left arm was being eaten by maggots," said Dianne, lowering her eyes.

"Oh, my."

"And, just recently," she continued without lifting her head, "I dreamed of that horrible, filthy, creature that is rumored to live under Elliott's Head cliff."

"Well, with the danger of sounding like I agree with that new heretic, Freud, that last one was probably due to hearing that silly little town legend while doing your research. Does that sound reasonable?"

"It does. It does," said Dianne, biting the fingernail of the first digit of her right hand and thinking *I believe help my unbelief this is not enough.* "And thank you."

"Now, what was your second hypothetical question?"

"Do you believe in non-human life-forms? Aliens?"

"Absolutely! The world is just teeming with non-human life, Ms. Savage; trillions on trillions of everything from squamous amoeba —yuck— to elephants, octopi to eagles, and mammals to reptiles to insects that don't look one jot like a human being. If fact, in the grand scheme of life, we are a tiny minority. On top of all of that, there are angels, fallen and unfallen, and Cherubim and Seraphim (and I don't even know what kind of creature those two are), some that have the uncanny ability to travel between the natural and the supernatural. And they existed even before we were created! It is undeniable that our amazing, Creator God is certainly interested in a cornucopia of life!

"But I'm guessing that really isn't what you are asking, is it? If you're asking me if I believe in green, tentacled things with fish bowls for helmets from Venus and Mars that are on the covers of some of those outlandish newsstand magazines that are popping up, it wouldn't surprise me one bit. Then again, I wouldn't be surprised if they didn't exist, either, I'm afraid."

"Ready, sweetheart!" interrupted a disembodied voice from the doorway of the den. Dianne turned to see the pastor's wife standing there as Miller said:

"Great! Let's go eat an alien life-form!"

"What?!" Dianne asked, startled, and jerked bolt upright at the waist in her bed. She wore only her white bra and panties, and she subconsciously crossed her forearms over her chest. Her apartment was gray with the palpable, ambient light of pre-dawn, and silent, and everything was forbidding, blurred shadow. The only sound in the room was the faint beating of her heart, the *susss suss susss suss* of her rapid breathing, and the rasp of:

"Hello, buttercup," from a disembodied, unknown voice diffused by the darkness and from everywhere and therefore nowhere. "It's party time."

She gasped, a thrill of electric terror running up her spine. She knew despite the black shadows that the blob leaning against the doorjamb of her apartment was one of the brutal thugs that had nearly beaten Vernon Thomas to death.

The thing that was shadow stepped from the shadows. It was the leering thug who had watched her at the Standard Grocery.

With the terrific energy of the fear of death, Savage leapt from her bed toward the chest of drawers where her pistol was hidden.

He lunged and was at the bureau first and thrust her back. She fell back and down hard *thud* on the floor by the bed. He seized a knob of the top drawer with his left ham of a hand, pulled the drawer out, and threw it behind him *thud* onto the floor behind him in one savage sweeping gesture.

He stepped to the fallen drawer and knelt.

"Someone... will... hear that," rasped Dianne.

"Let them," the thug said as he rummaged through her things. "There's plenty of room at the morgue. Well, lookee, lookee, lookee here!

"Steve found his ticket to Hell," he added and rose from his knees, holding her gun. Slowly, methodically, he shook loose the cartridge of bullets and let each clatter to the floor.

And Dianne knew his intention was not to kill her, and her resolve to not only live but to live unviolated hardened.

"Take off your undies, baby," the thug sneered. "You're in for the time of your life."

For a microsecond, Dianne thought of running to the kitchen and snatching a serrated knife from a drawer, but discarded the idea as useless.

"You m-murdered Vernon Thomas?" she said, thinking *fool; why did I say that, he needs nothing else to enrage him to rape me,* and struggled to rise to her knees.

Malevolent, he grinned and took a step toward her.

"Saw you at your apartment window seeing us. It was easy to follow when Vernon left your place the next day. Easy to board the train. Easy..."

"You killed him," Savage spat, her eyes never leaving the twisted face distorted by shadows and his lurid sneer, "because he knew too much about the storm drain project."

"I killed him because it was fun," he grinned, and took another menacing step towards the newshound as she straightened, steadying herself with the palm of her left hand on the top of the disheveled bed. "I'll be laughin' when I kill you."

"If you t-touch me, I'll scream."

"Sure hope so," he said, and "as above, so below," and lunged.

Savage kicked him in the groin.

As the hulk of a man groaned, doubled over, and clutched his groin with both of his beefy hands, Dianne grabbed the back of his head with both hands, feeling an anomaly beneath his oily, thin hair, and jerked her right knee up and smashed his face.

He fell like a sledge-hammered ox.

Limping towards the apartment door, Dianne stepped on the discarded gun cartridge. It shot out from beneath her foot, and the reporter fell hard and slid to a slapstick stop two feet from her goal.

In two great, limping strides, the thug was by her left side. He lifted his right leg, and straddled her, then buried the dirty fingers of his thick hand in her short, red hair and jerked her head up.

"OH!" she cried out. "OH! Stop! Stop!! Please," she gasped, her eyes welling up with tears. "Stop!! You... you... aren't thinking..."

"Sure am, baby," Steve snarled. "Be sure to name our baby Steve, Junior."

Dianne clenched her teeth, reached up behind herself with both hands, grabbed his wrists, and jerked down hard and forward.

"Wha... !?" The thug lost his clumsy footing, fell forward, and rammed his head against the door.

As he fell to his hands and knees on the floor, Savage frantically wiggled out from under him between his legs and leapt on his back, tearing at his face with her fingernails. Protecting his eyes from her slashing nails with his left hand, he bucked, arching his back until the reporter was thrown off. Then he fell heavily down onto his left hip, his back against the apartment door, still dazed and seeping blood from the lacerations on his face.

Dianne was on her feet and crabbing away from the thug when undeniable epiphany struck her; she was absolutely trapped, no one had responded to the tremendous noise of their struggle, she could not physically overcome her attacker, rape was certain, if not rape and death, and for the first time in her life, she was overwhelmed with fear and the stark realization of vulnerability. She put her right hand over her mouth to stifle her whimper.

And at that moment, her eyes narrowed, she removed her hand, and she resolved to fight and survive, and she screamed. And screamed. And screamed.

Breathing heavily, he was on her.

Steve punched her in the face, breaking her nose.

Dianne fell back on the floor.

The thug snatched up her legs. He tore at her panties.

Steve was on her.

Blood oozed at her nose and mouth. At that frenzied moment, frozen forever in time, Dianne knew that neither death, nor life, neither time nor distance, god nor demon, no law of man or nature, nor any other thing could stop the blood lust of his vicious, frenzied attack.

At the edge of unconsciousness, she felt his beefy right hand on her left thigh. She opened her swollen left eye and looked up.

Into the face of Joe Seminole.

She dry retched as a maggot crawled out of Joe's left nostril.

Then she woke up.

CHAPTER EIGHT

There was an illogical, exuberant bounce in her step as Dianne Savage walked east down the south side of August Street on the early afternoon of Monday, October 22. Looking most like a bunched up quilted blanket, the sky above her was a gray mess of stagnant clouds, and a cold, stiff, October breeze carrying the unpleasant smells of unseen Abomination Bay made her leather jacket almost useless. But Dianne pulled her cloche hat tight and down against the chill as she hummed "Baby Face" under her breath, and the little slip of folded paper above her heart and under her jacket read:

I can do all things through Christ who strengthens me. Philippians 4:13

That exuberance sprang partially from Dianne's belief that human beings were incapable of sustaining intense emotion, that she was certainly human, and that that was both a blessing and a curse. It was a blessing that deep emotions dredged up by death, or divorce, or terror, or shock, diminish with time; if not, they would surely lead to insanity. Therefore, the terrible, debilitating memories of the vicious murder of Vernon Thomas and of Hank's bloody, violent death at the construction site that would hover at the rim of her consciousness for years were already fading. However, it was also a curse that strong affection or the first, intense passion of love could not burn forever either. Today, she would reluctantly say good-bye to the first man who had shown a romantic interest in her for years, Joe Seminole.

But this belief wasn't the only reason for her light step and winsome smile in the face of a blustery, gloomy, October day in a dirty town full of nascent, dirty secrets. Her morning had gone extremely well: She had brushed off her rape nightmare from long experience with her odd dreams, most of which never came true, and after her hygiene routine, the preparation and eating of breakfast, and the cleaning of her apartment, she had written her fifth article for the *Bangor Daily Register*. It had almost written itself.

Her spirit had also been further raised by the sure knowledge that she would soon return to Bangor and the newspaper and its clatter of

94

typewriters, the pressure of deadlines, the thud of huge presses, the smells of ink and paper and sweat she loved. Nevertheless, she strapped her gun to her calf under her dungarees before leaving the apartment building.

Her first chore for the day had been uneventful. She had walked to the post office and mailed her article. It seemed like it had rained Halloween decorations everywhere overnight; orange pumpkins, pale yellow hay stacks, multi-colored fall leaves, full yellow moons, black witches, brooms, black cats, spiders, and bats hung from every light pole, lurked in every shop window, and were even strung on power lines at regular intervals across streets like Christmas lights. Several shop workers had waved at her, and the post office clerk had been particularly cheerful. That softened the crawling fact that the odd Azrealite symbol had also multiplied on the clothing of those she met.

She was filled with warm, childhood memories of Halloween and pumpkin pies, hot egg nog, and bags of candy apples and popcorn. It was a good day.

She stopped at a cluster of newspaper racks in front of The Boston Store, and bought a copy of *The Citadel* newspaper. A quick glance at its headlines lead her to read only one, a brief story about Hank's death. She was only mentioned as an "unidentified young woman"; everything seemed factual. She rolled up the newspaper and stuck in under her left arm, and then bought a copy of the *Bangor Daily Register.* The same quick perusal left her disappointed. None of her articles had been published in that edition. As she rolled up that newspaper, she glanced across the street, and startled.

Just at the corner of her eye, she thought she caught sight of the foul lizard of a man from the construction site as he entered the front door of a business. She shook the ugly impression out of her head, thinking: *not sure; not sure; will not give in to paranoia.* She stuffed the second rolled newspaper with the first under her left arm, and crossed the intersection of Ferry and August, no longer humming, headed for the Rex Theater.

The little marquee for Seminole's movie house above and ahead of her read:

Beggers of Life
Louise Brooks
Wallace Berry

She turned to the flyspecked, glass ticket booth in the middle of the recessed entrance to the theater and asked the teenaged boy there to see the assistant manager. He smiled mechanically and indicated she could enter by a nod of his head.

The lobby was full of the timeless smells of candy, salt, popcorn, soda pop and human sweat. The air was warm and smarmy. A teenaged girl stood behind the counter of the concession stand in the otherwise empty lobby.

"I'm sorry," the girl answered in response to the reporter's question. "I don't know where Mr. Seminole is right now. You might check inside the theater."

Dianne walked down the lush, clean, red carpet at her feet as she moved to the swinging door with the porthole in the center that separated the lobby and the theater, and pushed it open. It was a wasted effort.

"Dianne! You're early!" exclaimed the voice of Joe Seminole, and the reporter turned to see him behind her carrying a large, brown, cardboard box of candy to the concessions counter. "What a wonderful surprise!"

"I was in the neighborhood," Savage benignly lied. "I hope I'm not interrupting your work, Joe."

"No problem!" Seminole sat his box on the counter top and said to his employee: "Could you get these in the display cases, Susie?

"I think I can get away a few minutes early, Di. I've got a little surprise for my best girl, too. Come on. I'm parked behind the theater in the alley."

The surprise was a large, white, cardboard box, somewhat shallow, that sat on the passenger seat of Seminole's car. Its label read: Herrin's Ladies Ready-To-Wear. Dianne picked up the box, sat down, and lay it in her lap as Seminole positioned himself behind the white leather-encased wheel of his vehicle. He removed a package of Camel cigarettes and a matchbook from his shirt pocket, tapped out a cigarette, struck a match, and lit it.

"Should I shake it?" Dianne asked, biting a fingernail.

"No, you should open it," he commanded with enthusiasm, inhaled smoke deeply into his lungs, and then blew three smoke rings into the air. "Go on."

"I don't know, Joe, if I need to be accepting presents. We need to talk about something first."

"Talk last," he said, grinning broadly, "Open first."

Dianne opened the box. Inside was a modest, full length, beige winter coat.

"Got tired of getting the cold shoulder," Seminole said, and chuckled around the cigarette in his mouth as he turned his key in the ignition of the car.

"It's just lovely, Joe, but I can't accept this."

"What? You're kidding! Why not?" he asked, his smile fading as he began to maneuver his car down the alley. "It's getting colder. Your jacket isn't heavy enough. So I bought you another coat. Simple as that. I didn't exactly break the bank, honey."

Dianne held the coat up to examine it as Joe turned left out of the alley onto Ferry Street. "You didn't even break your piggy bank, dear."

"Hey! It's the thoughtlessness that counts," he quipped, and took the cigarette out of his mouth. "I got that from the best secondhand shop in town."

"I can't accept it because I'm almost finished with my research, Joe."

"Meaning...?" He rolled down his window, and flicked the cigarette out.

"Meaning I'm going home to Bangor, and Bangor is a long way from here, and because long distance romances never, ever, ever work, Joe. And because I don't like Light's End, and nothing, not even you, can convince me to stay here."

"I have a car. There's the trains. It isn't that far to Bangor!"

"Joe," she said, and there was an unemotional finality in her voice.

There was a long moment of silence except for the hum of the tires on Seminole's car as he turned left again onto August Street headed for the train depot.

"Does this mean I should turn this heap around," asked Joe, "and we aren't going to Elliott's Head like you wanted?"

"No. It doesn't mean we can't enjoy our remaining time today, Joe."

"Good. Does that mean I should cancel the interview I got for you with Jake Horne on Saturday, 7:00 pm, Crawford Hotel, second floor?"

"Joe....!?" she exclaimed a bit breathlessly.

"Surprise!"

Near dusk, Joe Seminole and Dianne drove from downtown Light's End in his 1928 Model-A Ford Four door Leatherback to the abysmal old ruins on top of Elliott's Head cliff, the barren, frozen crazy throw of slate gray stone that fell away below the ruins of the old lighthouse and continued to tumble motionless down its cliff to the yellow, dirty beach and the dead winter ocean that soughed into Abomination Bay.

Dianne left her own inadequate coat in the seat of the car and wore Joe's gift when they left the vehicle.

The sky was muffled by heavy, dirty sullen clouds. It was late evening on a cold October day and everything had sharp edges, but, as is true for the young, they did not care. The air tasted of salt and the ocean, flecked with foam, soughed against the unseen rotting pier far below them. Hand in hand, happy and quietly talking, sharing the intimate, delicate double laced innuendoes and mundane details of the lives of new lovers, they talked of the past and of their futures.

"You could have been killed," Seminole said, beginning to sit on one of the stones that lay half buried and moss-covered in an odd, chaotic circle.

"It's hard to imagine that people could actually believe," she said, ignoring his comment and looking down at the barren soil beneath her feet, "that somewhere beneath our feet lives a giant maggot that lives in a well and eats people, Joe."

"Well... "

"If you want to say something, say it."

"I think I'll do something uncharacteristically smart, and keep my mouth shut."

"Let me help," she said, and kissed him.

"Now, take me back to the Van Sanford before I start shopping around for an apartment for you in Bangor."

The bounce had returned to her step as she entered the Van Sanford by its east porch, and walked the short distance down the hallway to her apartment. The third surprise of her day was waiting there.

She pulled off the small, folded piece of paper taped to her apartment door and opened it. In simple block letters, it read:

Tuesday

7:00 P.M.

Lincoln School Park

Savage looked to her left down the hallway, and then to her right; the hallway was completely empty. The newshound put the piece of paper in the right side pocket of her new overcoat, opened the door to her apartment, and entered.

It was somewhat of a tedious, long walk from the post office where Dianne had mailed her sixth article to the *Bangor Daily Register* late on Tuesday, October 23, to the Lincoln School Park, and one filled with cloying anticipation.

A battered, muddy, Model A truck was parked next to the curb of the park with its passenger side door open, but no one was inside as Dianne approached, wrapped in her new, heavy coat against the deepening cold of advancing October. The sky above was blanketed with dead, gray clouds, and the park was empty except for an anomaly.

The little wizened man sat on a concrete bench in front of the wading pool with his skinny legs tucked one under the other as he chewed a toothpick and watched Dianne approach. Something was rolled up and tucked under his left arm held tightly against his chest. He wore the same baggy, gray, pin-stripped suit and matching hat pushed rakishly back above the hairline, and watched her with the eyes of a dead black lizard.

Her approach was cautious because she had no idea who had written and taped the odd note to her door, and it could have been one of the thugs that had beaten Vernon Thomas, or the thing at The Palace, as easily as a total stranger. Nor had she a clue about why this someone had wanted to meet with her, but she was no stranger to interviewing whistleblowers. It bolstered her confidence that her gun was strapped to her left leg under her dungarees.

The cold breeze of the day before had stiffened — her green cloche hat was pulled down tight on her head — but neither it nor the leaden sky above dampened her heightened senses. She had a premonition that this might be the break she had hoped for from the beginning of her investigation.

"Hello, Miss Savage," said the wizened man with his characteristic sick grin as she stopped about five feet in front of him. "I'm glad you could make it. I thought you might be too busy writing another one of these." He removed a newspaper from beneath his arm and extended it like a gift.

"I don't know what you're talking about," she said, ignoring the offered newspaper, and scanned the park for any other person or vehicle. "How do you know my name?"

"Light's End is a small town full of gossip; everyone knows everyone, but no one knows you." He laid the newspaper on the bench next to him under a rock he must have placed their earlier. "Everyone talks about everyone else, especially strangers in town. Ergo, you are the 'Undercover Reporter.' We accountants are analytical in that way. Or you can call it a lucky guess, if you want."

"Guess again, Mr....?" baited the newshound, pushing a red curl up beneath her hat.

His sick grin widened showing broken, yellowed teeth.

"Walter. But it won't do you any good knowing my name. I'll be gone from Light's End five minutes after I give you this. If I'm wrong, then I'll pay the price." He withdrew a manila envelope from beneath his suit coat. He stood up.

"What is this?"

"The works. Documentation of all of the under-the-table deals and kickbacks involved in the construction of the 'storm drain' project, Miss Savage. How the town Selectmen picked a DemiUrge in the Tenebrae Church who is also the owner of Ebaugh Construction to build the boondoggle; how Ebaugh laundries the money and funnels it back to the Selectmen who make sure it ends up in the Tenebrae Church. Interested?"

"I'm interested in how you got this information."

"I'm the accountant for Ebaugh Construction."

Dianne struggled to hide her surprise and growing excitement.

"After you read this, you should only have two questions left. Am I for real, or am I setting you up?" he said, handing her the envelope and then the newspaper. "Here's the answer for publication in this."

"There's one more question. Why would the accountant for Ebaugh Construction blow the whistle on something like this?"

His sick grin vanished.

"My last name is Thomas. My brother's name was Vernon."

Savage looked at the rolled up newspaper as Walter walked to his car, opened the *Bangor Daily Register*, and placed the envelope inside. Then she followed Walter's example, shoved the newspaper under her left arm, and walked away.

Back at her apartment, Savage opened the newspaper on her kitchen table only to discover it was two different publications, one stuck inside the other — the current *Bangor Daily Register* and *Citadel* newspapers. She put them aside, and opened the envelope.

It was the mother lode for which all journalists pray. She carefully returned the contents of the envelope, and then hid it under her mattress. It looked like she had uncovered another series of potential articles after her exposé of Bishop's Alley, and that she might be returning to Light's End and seeing Joe Seminole again after all that she'd said earlier. She might bring a Pulitzer with her for outstanding investigative reporting.

Smiling broadly, she opened *The Citadel* newspaper. On the editorial page, she read:

Editorial
by Publisher Mike Phillips
CITIZENS RENOUNCE ARTICLES

Many angry citizens gathered in cafes, our post office, library, and business offices as the word spread among our townspeople about the recent libelous article about Bishop's Alley written by an anonymous reporter for the *Bangor Daily Register*. Even the people of Lost City, afraid they will also be slurred by the state's largest circulation newspaper, met at a cafe drug store to write a heated letter that we have received at this newspaper with the request that we publish it (which we shall tomorrow) and forward a copy of their letter to the Bangor newspaper (which we have done). Meetings were also held by several protesting Light's End shopkeepers, and I must add that I am ashamed of the unprofessional nasty stink of a sister publication and the banana yellow cowardice of a reporter who won't identify himself with a byline.

If it turns out this anonymous reporter works for *The Citadel*, he will be fired.

I have been informed that newspapers across our fair state deluged the Light's End Chamber of Commerce wanting information about Bishop's Alley, which is not even in our city limits. Our Chamber of Commerce President said: "They [the *Bangor Daily*] are painting our whole town with the ugly broad brush of Bishop's Alley because the town of Bangor is jealous of our continuing growth and progress, and because the *Bangor Daily* just wants to sell newspapers."

At the request of its President and Board of Directors, we publish the following resolution from our Chamber:

"The *Bangor Daily Register* article about Bishop's Alley and our wonderful town is slanderous. It was published to promote the dishonest and salacious ambitions of certain elected state capital officials who are behind the newspaper, and degrades the wonderful men and women of Light's End. We pledge to tell the world that our morals were not represented by this article, and that we are an enlightened people. Thousands of dollars have been spent on our churches and schools, and parks and civic clubs thrive. Our library is unsurpassed for a town of our population. Our social life is the equal of any town in Maine. Since this malicious article is full of half-truths and foul out-and-out lies, we condemn the *Bangor Daily Register* for publishing it."

Dianne knew that her ability to hide her identity was now seriously compromised. Then she opened the copy of the *Bangor Daily Register*, and read:

GAMBLERS ESCAPE JUSTICE
by Your Undercover Reporter

There is real filth and a noxious odor behind the white picket fences that circle the polite houses of Light's End just southeast of Bangor, Maine.

Gamblers who flock to Bishop's Alley just west of August Street to let off some steam and win 'easy' money at cards, dice, and blackjack end up losing their steam, their money, their shirts, and, far too often, their lives. The majority of these men are working on the new water and storm drain construction in town and just outside of city limits (which hints at a greater corruption). But there is certainly a major sprinkle of 'proper' Light's End businessmen and workers who sneak across late at night. When they collect their wages, the scum that owns or manages Bishop's Alley scramble to take every dime from these men using hookers, bootleggers, dope peddlers, and loaded dice.

An employee in the Alley is one of your undercover reporter's most reliable sources, and reveals that gambling is wide open in Lost City as well. Lost City is the ghetto of Light's End, also west of the town, and is mostly populated by blacks living in poverty. The gambling joints there are not owned by Lost City citizens.

DIRTY LITTLE SECRETS

Gambling dens operate behind closed doors at the Last Call Saloon, Ada's Bar, the Kentucky Rooms, Salty Dog's Saloon, Blue Heaven, Bucket O' Blood, Gilette's Bar, and, last but far from least, The Palace. You'll need to know a "secret" password that changes daily to get inside, and will pay to even get the password.

The biggest dirty little secret may be a name that keeps popping up over and over again in my research as belonging to the man behind almost everything that goes on here. When I can confirm my suspicions, you'll read that name here.

HONEY GIRLS TOUT DENS

Smiling hookers hawk the gambling dens for a tiny commission if their names are mentioned by customers, but their smiles turn into indifference after the players are fleeced and there is no opportunity for them to ply their own wares. Guilty and penniless gamblers weep in the shadows behind these treacherous joints, blinded by the gambling fever to return and recoup their money, but are unable to do so, and many more are aware that the money they normally send or bring home to wives and children or mothers and fathers won't be sent this week.

TURNED UP NOSES

Games run nonstop, and some businesses own slot machines. Dice and poker are most profitable. Workers with calloused hands lose a month's salary in a single session. Self-righteous Light's End citizens and town officials continue to use the excuse that Bishop's Alley is outside of city limits and therefore is none of their business, and one after another, weak men are lead down the primrose path to self-destruction, and, ultimately, everyone suffers. If that sounds preachy, let it be so.

The Dixie Cab was waiting, so Dianne took off her cloche hat and waved at it.

"Again?" asked the dour cabbie as she sat down in the back seat and closed its shabby door. She recognized his middle-aged, stubbled face in his interior rear view mirror; he was looking at her with indifference.

"I'd like to see them laying pipe for the storm drain again," said Dianne.

"What for?" he asked as the cigarette in his mouth bobbed.

"Curiosity," said Dianne as she glanced out of the cab at Charles Walton and Joe Seminole on the sidewalk; they were staring at her. She waved her right hand at them; both turned away and fled like fawns. "Take me to the west end of Bishop's Alley, kind sir."

"No can do, lady. I don't go no further than August and Dunlevy."

"Then it's off to the corner of August and Dunlevy we go!" said Savage.

The cabbie's worn face left the rear view mirror as the cab pulled away and she heard him mutter "bitch" under his breath. "It's your dime," he said out loud. His rough face was back in the rear view window again, the cigarette hanging out of the corner of his down-turned mouth, and his expression a questioning mask of suspicion.

Dianne looked out of a grimy cab window at the businesses on the street and the endless flow of people chatting in little eddies, window shopping, entering or exiting doorways, or walking up and down the sidewalk, all of them moving in slow motion as if struggling against the immutable and irresistible tide of time and irrefutable fate.

As they drove, Dianne watched the small Liberty Theater and its sandwich signs on the sidewalk crawl by, then the Jones Drug Store, the William's Cafe, then the larger Ritz Theater, Collier Bro's Hardware and Furniture and Undertaking, and finally the Warecki Manufacturing Co.

As they drew near the second intersection, Savage watched a distant gathering of agitated men in business suits and hats or caps standing around two messed metal baskets. Two columns of gray smoke and burning flecks rose from the mouths of those baskets like fiery leaves to merge into one funnel and dissipate in the overcast sky above as something inside smoldered.

Something was wrong. The faces were wrong.

"Driver, could you slow down a bit?" she asked. He did so as Dianne studied the angry or somber expressions on the faces of each man began to come into focus. "What on earth are those men burning?"

Something was wrong. As they drew near, the men around the fire turned as one to look at the cab. Their grinning, dead faces were bleached

"Dianne looked out of the grimy...window..."

skulls crawling with maggots.

"You, you idiot," responded the indifferent cabbie, and turned to leer at her. The cab driver was Gene Sorenson.

Dianne jerked bolt upright in bed, covered with flop sweat.

She looked at her wrist watch.

It was 2:15 am, Wednesday the 24th.

CHAPTER NINE

"I'm the 'Undercover Reporter' that's been writing the stories in the *Bangor Daily Register* and outraging the whole town," said Dianne as she folded one of Veyda's tiny, yellow and blue and pale green flowered dresses. "I know I can trust you, Margo, and I felt you had the right to know before you leave."

"I can't say I'm surprised," answered Willson as both women stood at Margo's kitchen table. "I think Gene Sorenson suspects you, too."

"I promise you that the *Register* will break Bishop's Alley wide open and also expose the scam behind the storm drain project that took your husband's life before I leave this god-forsaken Hell hole. So, I'm coming with you to The Palace, and then I'll see you off at the bus station. I've got just a couple of things left to finish here, and then I'll be hitting the trail, to. I'm going to really miss you and Baby Veyda, my friend."

Veyda was terrorizing one of the cardboard boxes that Savage had helped Margo fill with the dancer's meager possessions. As the women began to pack the last of Margo's clothing in a box, the dancer stopped, turned to Dianne, and hugged her.

"You don't have to do that, honey, but I admit it's nice to have someone see us off." Margo held up an envelope and shook it. "This is the last of what I owe Ruby and Sorenson. I'll pay Gene when we drop off Veyda there for the last time, then it's ten minutes at The Palace, back here to pick up Veyda and to load this junk in a cab, and we're out of here!"

"May I carry the baby?" the reporter asked. "It's so hard to say good-bye."

Gene Sorenson stood with his left hand on the opened door to his apartment. In the crook of his right arm lay the horrible multicolored beak and black, empty eye sockets of an outré mask of a hideously ugly bird. He wore a white, long-sleeved shirt, but beginning at his waist and cascading down each leg was a chaos of huge red and yellow faux feathers ending in yellow, knotty faux claws tied by elastic straps over his shoes. From the safety of Margo's arms, Veyda recoiled against her chest.

"Oh, dear," Sorenson said, grinning sheepishly. "Is it that time already?

You caught me trying on my Halloween Feasting costume! Come in, come in!"

"Here's the last of my rent, Mr. Sorenson," said Margo, opening her envelope as she and Dianne followed him into the room. She removed several bills and handed them to the apartment manager. "I'll be out by late this afternoon."

"Judy! Margo and Veyda are here!" Gene yelled without turning his head.

From an unseen interior room, Judy stepped into its doorway wearing a heavy, dark, plum-colored dress with a lighter purple cape and light purple trim at the low neckline, a yellow studded, matching purple corset around her waist, and a dark plum mask covering half her face to the tip of her nose that then swept back over her head in a wild cornucopia of huge feathers. Strange black swirls tattooed her jaw and chin, and yellow discs with three dangling yellow beads hung from and hid each ear.

"Anyone for fried chicken?" Margo quipped.

Jazz thumped at The Alley as the naked, unlit, green and blue and white light bulbs that were strung between the buildings and across the street swung in a stiff, cold, salty breeze. The air was filled with low tittering, incontinent and slack singing, foul cursing and whooping as the Dixie Cab stopped in front of the worm-eaten planks of the boardwalk in front of The Palace. The underbelly of the gray clouds above were painted in subtle, impressionistic yellows, oranges, and reds.

As she stepped out of the cab, Dianne was met with the subtle smells of stale beer, human sweat, urine and feces. A drunken old man dressed in a dirty brown suit and hat staggered back on the boardwalk to lean against the wall of The Palace and leer at her with rotten yellow teeth in a stubbled jaw. He straightened, tried to tip his hat, but missed the rim with a disfigured hand, and stumbled away.

The door to The Palace swung open under Dianne's hand onto the dim hall and the same frowzy woman smoking a cigarette and sitting on a stool as during her first trip to Bishop's Alley. Beyond her was the same man in overalls wearing a holster and pistol on his hip and sitting to the side of the closed door to the dance hall.

"Evening, Judy," said Margo. "Is Ruby in?"

"Nope," the old woman rasped. "She's in the outhouse back of the hall. Go on in."

The man in the overalls rapped three times on the door with his knuckles. It was pulled open by someone unseen inside, and the disjointed, raucous music of a saxophone, piano, drums, and a guitar stumbling over a Ragtime tune swelled and joined the same nasty smell that was stronger inside the dance hall than on the street.

Ruby was not standing next to the gate in the wooden rail that partially enclosed the dance floor where a large number of men and women danced sluggishly on a worm-eaten, pine floor. The hulk of a man who had brutally beaten Thomas and tried to rape her in her nightmare was leaning on the rail about ten feet from the newshound. The reporter's blood turned to ice.

Margo spoke briefly with the Honey Girl who was selling dance tickets at the gate in Ruby's absence. The exhausted dancer shook her head in acceptance of a spoken word that the reporter could not hear over the noise of the crowd and the music.

"Let's wait over there," Margo said, leaning close to the reporter's ear, still a bit puzzled by Dianne's earlier reaction. "Ruby should be back in just a minute." Margo then turned to her left with Dianne following her, and both weaved through the expectant men behind the rail who were holding tickets and waiting for a partner.

Margo leaned forward with her forearms resting on the railing that mostly surrounded the dance floor as Dianne stood by her side, both watching the almost disembodied men and women on the floor sway to "Let's Misbehave."

"My husband loved to dance," Margo reflected, smiling whimsically but not looking at the reporter. "That's how we met, at a high school dance. It was my first time, and I was so shy and had two left feet, but he taught me how to move to the rhythm. And I grew to love to dance just as I grew to love him. He gave me so much. He taught me how to cook. To laugh. To compromise. To take chances. To give. To be a family with him. He gave me Baby Veyda. I don't think I'll ever find another man like him."

Someone touched Margo's shoulder, interrupting her reverie. Smiling, she straightened and turned around in one graceful, ineffably feminine movement.

"Yes?" she said.

Dianne turned to Margo, mistakenly thinking the dancer was speaking to her.

"Hello, Margo," rasped the thug who had beaten Vernon Thomas. "I'm Steve."

Her eyes dilated with fear, Dianne stifled her gasp with her right hand.

The stiletto appeared from beneath the thug's coat sleeve in his calloused left hand.

Its naked tip was on Margo's stomach just below her left rib cage.

"I'm your ticket to Hell," he sneered.

The serrated knife jerked in and up, lifting Margo off the floor.

Shock became terror became death on her white face.

Dianne screamed.

Someone else screamed, and then another. The music faltered and fell apart.

In a wave of senseless fear rippling through the crowd, dancing began to stop.

Margo collapsed on the floor.

The crowd exploded out like the head of a blown dandelion.

Trampling, shoving, screaming, biting, clawing.

A chaos of hands and feet.

Most fleeing not because they had seen or heard anything.

But by herd instinct.

The weaker fell and were trampled at the exit.

Shoving her shirt tail into the waist band of her trousers, Ruby stood in the back door, indifferent. She did not see Dianne, the courageous voice of the common people, the champion of the poverty stricken and downtrodden, and the lion of Bangor, Maine.

Dianne had fled in blind panic before Margo's corpse hit the floor.

Dianne Savage could not sleep that night, and spent the long, dissolute, silent, gray hours tossing, sweating, and turning in her twisted bed sheets, alternately praying and sobbing, overwhelmed with inexplicable grief, guilt, and shame. She cried out to God for understanding and forgiveness. Exhaustion finally brought her relief from her turbulent insomnia at 8:35 am on the morning of Thursday the 25th, and she slept the dreamless sleep of the dead.

No rap on her door by the police, or Gene Sorenson, or Chuck Walton, or even Joe Seminole woke her, and by the early afternoon of that day, the suffused half-light of the overcast October day finally crept in through her apartment window and onto her sleeping form to wake Savage at 1:37 P.M. in the afternoon. Red-eyed and unclean, she rose out of the mess of her bed sheets in a blue torpor; she could not eat —her stomach was a seething snot of bile — she could not read, she could not write, she could not pray or focus her thoughts on anything else as her restless soul mourned Margo's murder and beautiful, innocent, orphaned Veyda, and her cowardice ate at her like a ravenous rat. She teetered in a melancholy on the edge of a deep unrelenting depression that crippled her self-confidence and weakened her faith, her mind dredging up the old morose, painful memories of her parents' violent death, of Vernon crushed into a bloody pulp under the wheels of a train, and Henry ground into graveyard dust beneath a cement conduit, believing that death had dogged her every footstep in life.

But human emotions, no matter how intense, cannot long be sustained, and her impalpable grief was overcome with the growing, nagging belief that she should put her shame aside, go to the Sorenson's apartment, and hold Baby Veyda in her arms forever no matter what the emotional cost to herself. She sluggishly and indifferently dressed, and left her apartment.

No one answered her knock on Sorensonses' door. Savage rapped harder; there was no response, so she trudged back to her apartment, and her bleak ruminations.

At 7:45 that night, she sat at her kitchen table in front of a blank piece of paper torn from her journal, and wrote:

"Effective this Thursday, October 25, 1928, I resign my position as a reporter."

She signed the letter, fetched an envelope from her dresser, returned to the table, and addressed it. She laid the envelope next to her letter of resignation, returned to her bed, and, without undressing, fell into troubled, nightmarish sleep.

On Friday, October 26th, no longer thrown out of kilter by the intense grief of yesterday, Dianne's internal clock woke her at her usual time in the morning. Still frumpy, sluggish, and melancholy, she nevertheless performed her normal hygiene rituals out of long-established habit, then went to her kitchen in her pajamas to cook breakfast. The nearly empty refrigerator and bare shelves made it clear that her supply of groceries was almost depleted, but the idea of strapping on her knapsack and walking to the Standard Grocery to buy food was worse than distasteful, it was an outrage to Margo's memory. It took only a brief moment to cook the few eggs that were available and place her remaining two slices of bread on a plate. She neither hummed nor sang as she did so.

Savage pushed her resignation and its accompanying envelope to the furthest edge of her kitchen table without allowing them to register on her consciousness, placed her meager breakfast on the table, and ate without relish, tasting nothing. It did not satisfy her hunger. She fought down the self-doubt and misery that threatened to rise like bile out of her soul again, thinking instead of whether or not she should keep her interview with

Jake Horne on Saturday, and of buying a train ticket that day to get out of Light's End forever, and ashamed that she could even think of such mundane things in the face of Margo's bloody murder.

Almost her last words with Margo came to mind — the promise she would break Bishop's Alley wide open and expose the scam behind the storm drain project — and that fire in her belly that had made her a top reporter flickered and began to burn into anger, and she pushed the empty plate back, eyeing her letter with the conflicting emotions of its rightness and her hard-edged dedication to the truth, no matter how painful or what the cost to obtain it.

Savage stood up and began to nervously pace back and forth in her apartment.

She went to the kitchen table and picked up her dirty plate and utensils without allowing her letter of resignation to register on her vision, and carried them to the kitchen and deposited them in the sink.

Dianne left the kitchen, angry and energized, to pace back and forth.

She returned to the kitchen table and looked at the letter and envelope and moved them back to their original position. Then the reporter went to her chest of drawers, took out her journal and a pen, sat on the edge of her bed, and began to write.

Savage wrote slowly at first, updating her journal on everything, every crawling suspicion, aberration, and horror, that had transpired since her last entry, but her pace increased as she began writing passionately concerning everything she could remember about Margo's death. It was painful to do so, and her eyes welled up with tears, but she forced her hand to write despite false starts that she marked out before continuing, until she lay her pen down, emotionally spent, and closed the journal.

The newshound went to her chest of drawers and took out her money purse. She counted what money remained, shut the drawer, and placed the purse on top of the chest.

Dianne took off her pajamas and dressed, then strapped her gun on her left calf below her dungarees. She went back to the chest of drawers where her unopened Bible lay next to her cloche hat, opened it, tore a small piece of paper from her journal, and copied this verse from her Bible on the paper: *To everything there is a season, and a time to every purpose under heaven. Ecclesiastes 3:1*

She folded the paper and pinned it on her blouse above her pocket, closed her Bible, stuffed her money purse in the left front pocket of her blue dungarees, took her big coat off of the arm of a chair, and donned it.

It was 11:35 am. She put on her knapsack stuffed with soiled clothing over the coat —it was a clumsy effort— and left her apartment.

She carried Margo and Veyda in her heart.

The sullen, gray blanket of clouds above Savage was beginning to roll and turn dark and ugly, but the still, dry, cold of the day carried no salty breeze as she walked across the street to Harley's Drive In. Its gravel parking lot was empty, and no one sat at their picnic benches at the side of the eatery, so there was no delay in placing her order.

"Is this carry out?" asked the young girl behind the window.

"Oh, no; I'm on my way to get some groceries and get my clothes laundered, so I'll just eat it at one of your park benches," responded the reporter as she shrugged out of her bulky knapsack.

"Oh. Okay. But the weather will be getting dicey pretty soon; happens every year about this time. So we'll be throwing a tarp over the tables in the next couple of days and only doing carry out."

"I'll be throwing a tarp over myself pretty soon, too," Dianne responded, but not with a characteristic smile at her intentionally obscure simile. The young girl's puzzled expression was not unexpected, so Savage added: "I'm cutting my visit short, buying a train ticket tomorrow, and going back home Tuesday."

"Oh. Just thought you'd like to know since you've become sort of a regular. I'll call when your hot dogs are ready. As above, so below."

"Excuse me. That phrase. Are you a member of the Church of Tenebrae?"

"Yes," said the young girl with a wane smile painted on an expression of suspicion.

"Could you tell me what it means? I thought Azrealites didn't believe in God, so what do you mean when you say 'above'?"

"Well, I guess I never really thought about it. I always thought it meant something like things on Earth should be like things in Heaven. You know, good. But, you are right; we don't believe in God."

"Oh. Okay. I'll be sitting over there," she said, thinking *just like too many Christians and Buddhists and Muslims and Hindus (fill in the blank) she doesn't even really understand what her own religion means and just accepts what her parents teach her or her pastor says from the pulpit.*

As Savage sat waiting for her order, she studied the Van Sanford Apartments across the street with a growing sense of irrational uneasiness that replaced her initial indifference. She had already left and returned there so many times in the last couple of weeks that familiarity had relegated the building to her unconscious mind, but today, because of where she sat, or her state of mind, or the slant of shafts of diffused light through the clouds, something peculiar, something very large, looked different about the front of the building.

Epiphany struck her like a lightening bolt that sent a hard, racing chill over her entire body. A pattern of bricks of a slightly lighter shade than the rest formed the simplified but outré Azrealite diamond-shaped symbol of the Church of Tenebrae on its face. She reflexively placed her right hand over her mouth.

"Miss!" she heard someone call from somewhere a million miles from her. "Miss! Are you all right? Your hot dogs are ready!"

"What?" Dianne asked, turning from the apartment building to look unfocused at the young girl behind the window. "Oh, I'm sorry. I'll be right there."

She ate her two hot dogs and french fries in their paper diaper in silence. Her eyes never left the Van Sanford until she had finished her lunch. Then she rolled up the remaining papers into a ball, rose and threw them in a wire trash receptacle next to the Drive In, and walked to the Seminole Laundry.

Joe Seminole's mother was not there. She emptied her knapsack of dirty laundry.

As she approached the Standard Grocery, Dianne saw that the two parking spaces next to the grocery store were occupied with small bales of yellow hay, witches brooms, orange pumpkins of varying sizes, and large multi-colored, queerly shaped squash that had obviously been picked over by Light's Enders making last minute preparations for the Feasting. Next to this display sat a Dixie Cab; the cabbie inside was eating a sandwich as Dianne approached.

"Excuse me..." she said to the driver whom she did not recognize.

"What...?!" said the startled cabbie inside, one cheek still fat with sandwich. "Oh. How can I help you, Miss?"

"I need to buy a few things in the grocery store," she said; she did not recognize the driver. "Could you wait and taxi me back to the Van Sanford Apartments when I'm done?"

"Certainly, ma'am. Don't mind waiting." He pointed to his half-eaten sandwich with his free hand and grinned. "Dynamite sandwich. I'm on break myself."

Since she only needed enough food to last through Monday morning, it took only a few minutes for Savage to buy a half dozen eggs, a small block of cheese, a quart of milk, a small loaf of bread, and some sliced ham. As her items were being tallied at the checkout counter, she glanced to her right to the end of the counter to add a copy of the current issue of the *Bangor Daily Register* and *The Citadel* only to see the stacks of newspapers had been joined by a herd of hideous, small, stuffed maggot dolls reared up on their back quarters like snakes threatening to strike.

"Excuse me, sir," she asked the clerk, biting the fingernail of the first digit of her right hand. "Could you tell me what those terrible little dolls are all about?"

"Oh, that's Percy," answered the clerk, who did not stop ringing up items as he spoke. She noticed he was wearing a little Azrealite pin on the collar of his shirt.

"Percy?" she asked, as she put her eggs in her knapsack spread out on the counter. "That foul, eldritch thing is named Percy?"

"Yeah, sure. He's sort of a local bogeyman, so to speak, for the kids during Halloween. You know. Based on the legend of our town's founder, Caleb Elliott. 'The issue of god and man.' Just for fun. On Halloween, they break them open for a surprise inside."

"No offense, but your town is more than a little weird," she observed, and zipped up her knapsack and began to shrug into it.

"As am I," the clerk answered, and grinned like a death mask. "That's $1.80, total. And Happy Feasting."

Outside, Dianne sat down on a bale of hay, removed her knapsack and laid it on the ground, opened it and pulled *The Citadel* newspaper out of it.

The article on page two said that Margo had died at The Palace in Bishop's Alley in a tragic accident, that her body had been shipped by train to a distant cousin in New York City, and that a memorial service would be held at the First Baptist Church of Light's End on Monday. There was no mention of Dianne.

She folded the newspaper and put it back in her knapsack. Then she took out the *Bangor Daily Register*, and read on the front page:

GOVERNOR DEMANDS REFORM
Tough Jury Pending
by Jim Copeland, Managing Editor
Governor Orders Crime and Corruption Stopped
Through the efforts of this newspaper, and your managing editor, and due to the excellent reporting of our fearless, crusading "Undercover Reporter" in Light's End, Governor William Tudor Gardiner announced yesterday through an official letter that a special prosecutor will soon

convene a grand jury investigation into the town of Light's End. Gardiner also sent this directive to Raymond Fellows, Attorney General of our state, in which Fellows is instructed to "send our best into Bishop's Alley and sweep it clean."

The letter states: "A grand jury will investigate the alleged illegal bootlegging, drugs, prostitution, and gambling reported in a recent series of articles in the *Bangor Daily Register*, and any violator of our laws in Light's End. No one is beyond the law or this probe into the crime and the terrible, destructive debauchery that is openly celebrated in Bishop's Alley. This grand jury will bring justice and relief to the people of Maine."

Judge White of Light's End was also notified of a state Supreme Court decision to remove him from overseeing this jury or being involved in any way with the state's investigation of this shameful situation.

In addition, the *Bangor Daily Register* plans its own investigation into the Ebaugh Construction Company, several Selectmen and other town officials, the Church of Tenebrae and its leadership, and the tangled web of suspected kickbacks and under-the-table deals that were possibly made concerning the huge storm drain system near completion in this shameful town.

Savage rose from the bale, her spirits somewhat uplifted, and carrying her knapsack and the rolled up newspaper dangling from her right hand, walked to the taxi.

"Ready, ma'am?" the cabbie asked, tipping his cap.

"Ready," she answered and opened the right, back door to the cab, sat down and threw her knapsack and the newspaper on the seat next to her, and closed the door. "By the way, tomorrow, can you pick me up around..." she paused to estimate the time needed. "Around 1:30 in the afternoon? I need a ride to the train station to buy a ticket, and I've got an appointment at 7:00 pm. to interview Jake Horne."

"Jake who?" asked the cabbie, turning partially around in his seat to face her with a puzzled and concerned expression.

"Jake Horne, at the Crawford Hotel."

"Excuse me for saying so, but you couldn't pay me to get within half-a-mile of that monster for no reason no-how. Why do you need to talk to him? He'll eat you alive."

CHAPTER TEN

On Saturday, October 27th, Dianne stood on the street corner by a black, cast-iron lamp post and squinted up at the angry, gray, churning blanket of clouds above the hotel before her that, corpulent and feminine, rose like a huge, three-layered cherry cake, and reminded the reporter of the gumdrop houses, naughty German children, and cannibalistic witches she'd enjoyed in Grimm's Fairy Tales. Above the roof, a dirty splatter of gulls hung and then swirled and hung again in restless search of a roost.

In her left hand was a rolled up copy of the *Bangor Daily Register* for that day. Her article on its cover read:

SICKNESS IN ALLEY
by Your Undercover Reporter

If the tragic consequences of gambling and addiction aren't enough of a reason to shut down the red-light district called Bishop's Alley, here's another nasty problem confirmed by my preliminary research before traveling to Light's End, by two admittedly second-hand but reliable sources, general observation, and even by the town's own newspaper.

Black diseases from dance halls and "cat" houses in Light's End are infecting the "johns" that frequent Bishop's Alley, and when those who aren't citizens of the town return to their homes in other towns and states, they infect the unsuspecting, decent citizens of our state including their own wives. This terrible hypocrisy exists side by side with the scam of the huge storm drain system meant to improve the health of the city that is now under construction here.

HONEY GIRLS DISEASED

Most "johns" who don't live in Light's End patronize dance halls to escape the grinding work building the storm drain system and to escape loneliness. But every day, men and women are waiting for help from the understaffed and overworked doctors of the medical clinic in Light's End for treatment for the diseases transmitted in this way. Almost all are from Bishop's Alley according to the reported observations of Dr. Bay, the clinic's director. In many cases, multiple treatments are necessary for each client, and at least 200 or 300 such treatments have been administered to patients coming from the Alley. Obviously, this medical treatment will also be needed for those in other parts of Maine who caught it from Bishop's Alley prostitutes before returning home.

Treatment at the clinic is for indigents, and patients pay 25 cents for bismuth. Unrepentant, heartless women from The Alley get the few doses sufficient to stop their pain before returning to their illegal trade and spreading their affliction.

MANY REMAIN SICK

Hookers and their "johns" seldom receive enough medical attention for a sufficient time to be cured. The hookers sometimes go to personal physicians while continuing to seduce men. Those physicians only slow the progress of the disease.

Of course, disease is not the only consequence of prostitution. The town, our state, our nation, and the world are filled with broken homes, abandoned children, and broken hearts because of uncontrolled lust.

You say, it isn't my problem; I live in Bangor. If nothing is done by the decent people of Maine, then everyone will own a part of this horrible travesty called The Alley.

The massive hotel rose in sedate, ethereal, Victorian beauty. The Crawford was the most famous building in Light's End, rectangular, symmetrical, and alive with static movement. A round turret capped with an inverted, sky-blue cone faced the street and Savage. On the ground floor, a door with a burgundy cloth awning opened onto the restaurant where Seminole had met Horne on numerous occasions.

The reporter walked across August Street to the servant's entrance, a set of weather-beaten double doors in the hotel's west face, raised her right hand, and knocked. The door swung partially open onto a small vestibule, a door to her right, and almost vertical stairs in front of her bathed by somber light. Dianne wrinkled her nose at a subtle but foul smell.

A smear of black with white paws and luminous yellow eyes crouched at the foot of the stairs. The cat looked at Savage with the utter disdain of complete ownership of the material universe and unequivocal, occult power.

"That's Oreo," said a disembodied voice at the top of the stairs. "She actually owns the Crawford. Please, come up."

In one silent, graceful movement, Oreo swept fearlessly, a whisper of cool air, up the narrow stairs, pausing once to glance suspiciously over her midnight black shoulder at Savage before she finished her ascent and was gone.

Horne was old with a face like a crumpled paper bag full of wet flour. "Come up," the fat old man said with a mouth full of yellow teeth.

The patron of The Feasting, goat-headed Baphomet, leered from his t-shirt as the newshound began to climb the steps. Above the demon's twisted horns was hand-painted THE FEASTING. Beneath its cloven hooves was hand-painted RAM IT. Before Savage could answer, he smiled from an acerbic cut of a mouth, turned, and disappeared to the left of the stairwell.

Horne sloshed ahead, his shifting internal organs seemingly disconnected from his skin, until he reached the end of the hall and lumbered through an open doorway. Behind him, Dianne entered a cramped, dark room puckered by shadows that, except for a flimsy card table and two chairs set in its middle, was otherwise empty. Dust motes hung, somber and timeless in the muffled air.

"Take a load off," said Horne as he waved a flabby invitation with his left ham of a hand at the reporter to sit and did so himself behind the table. She watched as Oreo meticulously curled herself into a ball at his feet beneath the card table.

"I hope you'll excuse Oreo." Horne picked up a smoldering, cheap cigar from the card table that was sitting next to a plate filled with what looked like fried ground hamburger and stuck the cigar in the cut of his mouth in his flabby, stubbled face. "She's my favorite demon familiar; I implicitly trust her to repeat nothing that is said between us today."

"Of course, Mr. Horne. I actually like cats. And thank you so much for taking some time out of your busy day to talk to me."

"Please accept my apology for the afternoon snack," Horne added, picking up a fork by the plate. "It takes a substantial effort to maintain my... metabolism." He speared and ate a forkful of the meat on the plate. "Bite?"

"No, thank you," Savage said as she runked her metal folding chair back and from beneath the table, and sat down. She took her cloche hat off and laid it on the table.

"I have a few questions that I hope you'll answer about the Church of Tenebrae, some of the local legends about Light's End, and even about you, Mr. Horne," said Dianne, trying but failing to smile because there was something outré, something unsettling, even frightening about the great, greasy, hulk of a man.

"Please, call me Jake. May I call you Dianne? I always tell the truth when it serves my purposes." The fat man removed the smoldering cigar from the cut of his mouth and laid it on the edge of the table. "So, you may ask

"Take a load off."

me anything you'd just die to know, and I'll spill my guts. Where's your little pad and pencil?"

"I have a photographic memory, Mr. Horne... Jake, and I promise that I won't miss a word. My first question is about a phrase that pops up when I talk to members of your Church. 'As above, so below.' I've been led to believe that the first tenant of the Church of Tenebrae is that 'there is no god but man.' Doesn't 'above' imply a heaven and God?"

"Not to the non-thinking rabble that makes up most of my members, dear. If I told them the sky was red, they'd accept it without question. The little people need their bread and circuses, their empty symbols and rituals, ergo the meaningless 'as above, so below,' the stupid little diamond-shaped emblem, the maggot in the cave crap. But the inner circle of the Church knows the dirty truth, as I do, that there is a creative power in the material universe that most people call 'god.'" Horne picked up the cigar, placed it in his mouth, and inhaled and exhaled slowly and deeply, the muscles in his jaw relaxing. "Indeed, it is against that tyrannical egomaniac that I and the Azrealites and others on Earth and countless other beings scattered across realities beyond number wage a war for freedom."

Do you think I'm an idiot you big lurking toad Dianne thought to herself as a spark of anger at this affront to her intelligence flushed her cheeks pink. But she said nothing, trying to hide her emotional response on her face with a blank expression.

"What's wrong, Dianne? Cat got your tongue?" grinned Horne. He looked down at his feet. "Oh, there's Oreo. No tongue that I can see."

"Are you telling me that you lie to the majority of your congregation, Mr. Horne, about the beliefs of your own Church?"

"Oh, dear me, Dianne, I lie to the majority of everyone I meet, including you, about anything and everything if it serves my purpose. Didn't I just say that? It is by far the most important, powerful tool in my very old tool belt of manipulations. I am proud to claim that if Satan is the father of lies, I am at least the Son."

"All right. Who are these 'others' you mentioned that are warring against God, and why was Light's End chosen as the headquarters for your church?"

"My 'church,' as you continue to mislabel it, is older than dirt, Dianne, and there are branches of it all over this world, all of them relatively small but potent, and under dozens of different names. Some don't even know I exist.

"Light's End sits on a metaphysical 'crack' between realities. It's through this crack in space and time that those beings that Caleb Elliott mistakenly called naiads came to build their first city underneath the dirty waves of Abomination Reef eons ago. It's those alien beings and their submerged city that foul the bay. And it's through the unique coupling of one of those aliens with Caleb Elliott that a cosmic aberration, a seed of chaos, an abomination to your god, and a symbol of our cosmic war against that blubbering sycophant you call god, was born.

"But the 'naiads' were not the first to crawl through the breach between your reality and their own, honey. Indeed, some of the others traveled from planets other than Earth, and not from a parallel universe.

"It is here in Light's End that we lay up arms, each in our own way, for the final cosmic battle that will destroy your god and liberate all of creation." Horne inhaled and exhaled slowly and deeply, the muscles in his stubbled jaw relaxing. His smile was antiseptic. "What? You don't believe me, again, sugar?"

"No, Mr. Horne, I don't. But I will play your game for a little longer. Giving you the benefit of my huge doubt, is this abomination the Azrealites worship still alive?"

"We worship nothing, sweetie. He is called The Other, and lives in the well in the cave sunk by Caleb Elliott beneath Elliott's Head cliff. Yes, yes, I know I just said the maggot doesn't exist. For some inexplicable reason — perhaps because he is neither here nor there; slightly out of sync with either of two realities — that The Other is stark raving mad and ravenous for human flesh. It is not an easy or pleasant task to keep him fed." Horne took a forkful of meat, put it in his mouth, and began to chew. "He's not a him, actually. But what can one do?

"Are you sure...?" Horne asked again, extending his fork towards the reporter.

"Why are you doing this?" Savage sighed. "Why do you keep lying to me?"

"I'm telling you the absolute truth," said Horne, as Oreo jumped up onto the table and began to eat from his plate. Horne laid a beefy hand on the cat's back, and Oreo arched her ebony body as he pet her.

"And how do you Azrealites feed this horrible, ravenous thing, Mr. Horne?"

"The dead in Light's End are not buried here because of a high water table beneath the city that prevents it. The Light's End Crematorium actually just burns trash. The dead are not buried here because The Other eats human trash."

"And I suppose you'll tell me the town legends are all true. The old lighthouse was really an inverted well into Hell," said the reporter, barely able to repress a sneer. "And Isaac Azreal shot an angel, and the Special Collections room in the library is full of arcane, occult volumes that contain the Azrealite's secrets, which is why I'm not allowed in."

"The old lighthouse was a supernatural beacon guiding some in this universe to Light's End, Isaac Azreal did shoot an alien, and yes and yes and yes about the library."

The fat man speared a morsel with his fork as, purring, Oreo circled around herself and then curled up in a ball by Horne's almost empty plate to stare at Savage.

"And the storm drain project?" asked Savage, biting the fingernail of the first digit of her right hand. "Why is it so large that a person can walk through it?"

"There is a crevice that runs down from where the old lighthouse stood inside Elliott's Head cliff to the cave of the well, a natural fault in the earth," continued Horne as he scratched behind the cat's ears. "It took forever to widen it and carve out some rather primitive stairs, but we did it to feed The Worm and hold our nascent rituals in their season. The storm drains all lead to the cave. Much more convenient for my disciples and I, and it will make it so much easier to transfer corpses from the crematorium to The Other."

"That's it. We're done. This whole conversation has been a disgusting waste of my time, Mr. Horne. And, frankly, you are a pathological liar."

"Yeessss. Some things in life are rather disgusting," Jake continued, ignoring most of her statement, "but real and necessary as well. As example, at about 7:00 P.M.this Wednesday, as the crowds above celebrate Halloween on August Street by getting drunk and feeling each other up in dark alleys, the chosen of Tenebrae will sacrifice a human baby — a 'goat with no horns' — in the well in the cave beneath Elliott's Head cliff. It's quite a to-do. If you want to see bloody disgusting, you should come."

"I don't believe you, Mr. Horne; you are mentally ill. I don't believe anything you say," said Dianne, her voice rising in pitch with her anger, and her revulsion naked on her face. "I have heard you called Satan, Cain, Caligula, and Judas, and a cannibal. But I think you're a pathetic, nasty, lonely, filthy rich, power-mad old man who is hated and feared by everyone around him, and I believe you belong in a mental institution."

"I am The One," said Horne with an acerbic smile.

There followed an angry, pregnant silence except for Oreo's purr for what seemed like eons.

"Does this mean that none of my comments," added Horne, "will end up in one of those articles you've been writing for the *Bangor Daily Register*, honey bun?

The blood drained from Dianne's face. Horne forked a morsel of meat from his almost empty plate, placed it in his mouth, and chewed. The cat continuing purring.

"I admit I'm disappointed in you as well. I've had my eye on you since you got off the bus, cupcake. We are a close-knit community, so it's easy to keep track of out-of-towners. I've done nothing up to this point to stop you because your little stories served my purpose. Bishop's Alley has been a son-of-a-bitch money-making machine and it's played its roll and fattened the pockets of the Church, but has become more trouble than it is worth. You and your newspaper closing it down means you'll be the fall guy to certain 'investors' and concerned parties instead of me."

Savage runked her chair back from the table and began to rise.

"Sit down, Miss Savage." said Horne with the cold of black death in his tone.

Dianne reluctantly sat down, defiance and fear burning in her eyes.

"I'll tell you when we are done." Horne stroked Oreo. "I had hoped your native intelligence and tenacity would make you an asset for the Church if you could be... *turned*. But our talk has convinced me that isn't going to happen. You've had your chance and blown it. Now, you must soon share the fate of anyone who doesn't fit my needs, indeed like another wrong-headed lady who was about your age. In fact, I think she was your friend... what was her name? Harlow? Fargo? A tasty piece of feminine pulchritude."

Savage covered her mouth with her hand.

His burning eyes locked on Dianne, Horne speared a morsel from his plate, raised his fork to his mouth, and said: "She was so yummy then..." He ate the morsel.

"...and is so very, very yummy now."

Dianne cried out from behind her hand, and cringed back,
and flailed out, and runked her chair back,
 and toppled back and out, and fell hard,
woman and chair, to the floor,
kicking her right foot up under the table,
and the table jerked up
and Oreo jumped up and off
and the almost empty plate hopped and spilled onto Jake's t-shirt

Savage lay still on the floor, embarrassed, hamstrung with fear, her chest heaving, her face hot with shame, her eyes dilated and pooled with tears. She rasped "oh god oh god," to the rhythm of the erratic pounding of her heart. Her tongue found the thick taste of blood in her mouth and she put a trembling finger to her lips and it came away with blood.

"Now look what you've done," said Horne, smiling as he straightened the table, and replaced the plate. He began to brush meat from his t-shirt.

"You've upset Margo!

"Now, get out." Jake's eyes were red slits, and his teeth showed. He began to laugh, a painful laughter, a laughter that twisted his face and convulsed his gelatinous stomach.

If anything, the rolling blanket of gray clouds above her seemed even more oppressive and threatening as Dianne sat hunched on a cement bench in Lincoln School Park on Sunday afternoon, October 28. Nevertheless, her black and chaotic mood left the threat of rain or even storm impotent. There wasn't the slightest of breezes, and yet the subtle stink of dead fish and rotting seaweed hung in the chill air.

Earlier in the day, Savage had gone to the Sorenson apartment once again only to find a note on their door: they had taken baby Veyda to live with the distant relative mentioned in the newspaper article about her mother's death, and wouldn't return until Dianne had already left Light's End. A name and phone number for renters needing assistance of any kind ended the letter. Dianne cried inside.

Oppressive also described the emotional turmoil churning in the reporter. Her feelings of debilitating paranoia — of being constantly watched and reported on to Horne, of being driven from Light's End, physically harmed, or even killed — and of her helplessness to control any of these external situations, had become overwhelming; she could not bring herself to go to church that morning, or to stay in her apartment. After packing her few possessions for her departure from Light's End on Monday afternoon, Dianne dressed herself, strapping her gun to her left calf under her dungarees, donned her long coat, and took a circuitous route that skirted the church to the park.

The change in locale had done nothing to relieve her depression however, so, with the hope of raising her spirits, the reporter began to examine her relatively young life and, in particular, the personality traits that had lead to her rise through the ranks of reporters at the *Bangor Daily Register*. She had grown up with her nose constantly in a book, which self-taught her to write and inspired her to apply at a newspaper. It was her self-confidence that had given her the incentive, the drive, even while initially writing obituaries, to begin to write some society features without any assignment to do so. That led to a major break in her career when she uncovered a malicious scandal involving a highly-placed and powerful socialite and a powerful man who wasn't her husband. The article had given Savage her first byline and brought her to the attention of the managing editor who promoted her to cover city hall. But it was her tenacity and courage in the face of threatening letters and the occasional red face-to-red face confrontation with the subject of one of her scathing exposés that had elevated her to the position of the first female, full-time reporter of hard news at the Bangor newspaper. Self-assured. Talented writer. Self-motivated. Bold. Unflinching. Courageous. The Champion of the Little Guy. The relentless pursuer of Truth and Justice.

Yes, she was the fearless reporter who ran away when Margo had been murdered, the dauntless reporter who had slunk away from Jake Horne like a whimpering, beaten dog.

The yellow coward.

She was overcome with guilt and sorrow and her eyes welled with bitter tears. Then an incongruous question leapt into her mind about Margo's packed boxes. What had become of her friend's possessions? Dianne stood up. Was there a possibility they still sat untouched in her apartment? It was certainly a long shot, but...

Savage left the park using the most direct route back to the Van Sanford carrying with her the hope of some form of closure, of a chance to say good-bye to Margo and Baby Veyda even if it were really only to the memories and smells of their apartment.

In five minutes and with a growing, uneasy anticipation, she was ascending the steps to the main entrance of the apartment building, then walking through the front door and down the stairwell that lead to Margo's former apartment. The empty laundry room with its weird door sunk in the floor earned only a passing glance before Savage stopped and knocked on the apartment door. She thought how stupid that was even as her hand fell to her side.

There was no answer. The reporter tried turning the doorknob. It turned easily, and a gentle shove sent the door in a long arc open onto another surprise.

The room was utterly empty; no packaging boxes, not one piece of scarred furniture, not even a dust bunny remained. It was as if the room had never been occupied and as if Margo and Veyda Willson had never existed.

Dianne sat down, cross-legged, in the middle of the apartment on the floor, and buried her face in her hands, her elbows resting on her knees, but she did not cry. She prayed for Margo's soul and for protection for Veyda throughout the baby's life.

As she prayed in the almost eerie silence, she heard a queer click clack like the claws of some huge animal on the stairs outside the apartment. Dianne looked up. The apartment door was open. She sprang to her feet. Tiptoed to it, and closed the door quickly, quietly and partially, leaving only a crack open. Then Savage watched as Gene Sorenson descended the stairs wearing his grotesque, outré, bird mask, a white, long-sleeved shirt, and, from his waist down, a cascading chaos of huge red and yellow faux feathers ending in yellow, knotty faux claws that *click clack click clack* fired with each step. Without pause, he entered the laundry room.

Savage waited ten breaths, then tiptoed to the open door to the laundry room and pressed herself against the wall to the right of the entrance.

She watched as the door held by his left hand and Sorenson sunk slowly and noiselessly into the floor of the laundry room. Then, waiting another twenty breaths, and looking behind her to her right and up the stairs to make sure no one else approached, Dianne entered the room herself, padded forward, her canvas shoes whispering on the floor. The door lay on the basement floor and the furnace soughed. Her heart rose and thudded. She licked her lips and tasted the salt of sweat; her flesh was clammy in the muggy heat. Dianne bit her lower lip and fought down her fear. Trembling, she knelt and reached for the glass onion doorknob and began to open the aberrant door, rising as she did so.

Beneath that door, she saw a sheet of what logically could only be faux concrete, flush with the floor. Sorenson must have pushed it closed from below as he descended. The reporter searched for the stud or device that would open it, found it with her right hand, raised her head and looked around the laundry room and outside to the stairs — all were empty except for the weirdly flickering shadows thrown by the red-toothed grate of the furnace. She pressed the stud, and the false concrete fell, noiseless, down and back.

Savage rocked back onto her haunches and looked at the eldritch, yawning hole before her, and the impalpable doubt and shame and the gnawing fear of the last several days momentarily fell away from her, and her infamous curiosity and a tenacious determination for revenge for the death of Margo and Vernon and Hank were sparked, and an epiphany sprang to her mind that the answer to the foul mysteries and endless enigmas that surrounded Light's End, Bishop's Alley, the Church of Tenebrae, and the shining alien face on the floor of The Palace, lay at the end of that tunnel. On Wednesday night. Halloween. And Savage knew that, even if she were to end up beaten or raped or crippled or cremated or in Horne's stomach, she would crawl down that Stygian tunnel and uncover the truth of the horror or the folly that was the odious, filthy ritual of the dreadful, insane Azrealites.

The Goat With No Horns.

The newshound pushed the stud on the floor by the door a second time, and the faux cement rose silently back into place. She rose, and closed the door in the floor, then the reporter left the laundry room, ascended the stairs to her floor, and walked to her apartment.

Savage stood in the open doorway and looked at a package wrapped in brown butcher's paper and tied with twine on her bed. On top of it sat one of the disgusting maggot dolls, and in its fanged mouth was a piece of paper.

She looked around the empty apartment, and then entered, moving to the bed. She took the piece of paper from Percy's mouth and unfolded it even as she read the label stuck on the brown butcher's paper which read: "Seminole Laundry."

The note read: "Let's see you worm your way out of this one! Joe Seminole."

She threw the note and the doll in the trash.

Dianne stepped onto the deserted pier.

The slat of wood beneath her foot creaked, feeling spongy. She stopped. She took a second step, and the rotten wood beneath her creaked, and a third, and then the fourth worm-eaten wood slat cracked and sunk down without breaking and falling into the bay as it tossed her sideways so that she threw out her left hand to stop her fall and her hand broke the railing.

Dianne regained her composure and sure footing, glancing up as she did so to see a dirty swell of seagulls hanging above her like vultures beneath the moiling clouds.

She gingerly took a fifth and then a sixth step, anticipating and accepting the creak of each board until the reporter stopped at the end of the pier and looked down at sluggish Abomination Bay. She looked down at the dirty silver mirror of water that belched a cluster of foul bubbles.

She looked down at the dirty water that belched a second time as a black mass rolled up beneath the surface and belched bubbles. She looked down as the mass broke the mirrored surface and, tender and tearful, in a dance of soundless, rising bubbles, the undine rose up and up and up, fey, voluptuous, beautiful, its thick red hair flowering in the water, the tip of its blue-green sequined tail breaking the mire behind it.

She looked down as the undine leapt.

Savage looked as the undine leapt and arched up out of the muck, shedding an arc of watery sludge around and beneath it. And Savage followed the arc up with her eyes as the undine rose over her, and as it rose, its jaw unhinged and its rapacious smile split into a gaping wound of gnashing, razor-sharp, jagged teeth, her wealth of thick red hair flowered into writhing snakes around her thick, scaled neck and the flaring sucking gills there. Below her waist, her blue-green tail stretched and twisted and morphed into the hideous coils of the gigantic, hairy, legless aberration that had borne a monster with Caleb Elliott.

The teeth. The blood. The horror. The undine rose up and up.

And plunged down on Dianne, and jammed its mouth over Dianne's head.

And blew exquisite pain and death into her.

And Savage and the undine were one.

And Dianne looked down at the bloody almost unrecognizable empty sack that was her body on the pier as the undine slid from the pier back into the ooze below.

And Dianne rose off of the pier as the bloody mass that was her body beneath her feet became to dissolve like mist, and she rose up beneath the swirl of seagulls hanging above her who rose up beneath the under lit, roiling clouds.

And Dianne rose up, spreading her arms crucified on a cross of ether beneath the rising gulls and rose up and up and up.

Dianne rose up in bed.

Chapter Eleven

It was Monday, Oct 29, the day of Margo's memorial service at the First Baptist Church, when Dianne went through her morning hygiene ritual, dressed in one of her newly cleaned and pressed blue denim blouses, her blue dungarees, canvas shoes, and her green cloche hat. The reporter pinned her daily reminder to herself on her blouse above her heart. It read: *For God so loved the world that he gave his one and only Son, that whoever believes in him shall not perish but have eternal life. John 3:16*

Because she knew it would be chilly outside, Dianne put on her long coat, grabbed her clutch purse, and left her apartment. It was a chilly morning under the same angry blanket of gray, rolling clouds that seemed locked to the sky. The denuded trees stretched brittle skeletal fingers like spider webs in shattered glass. She stopped on the landing of the Van Sanford before descending the stairs, stopped at its foot, pulled her coat around her, shivered, glanced at the small used car lot in front of her, and then to her left at the Standard Grocery Store and the ice company beyond it. There was little traffic on the road.

Dianne's brisk walk to downtown Light's End and the Majestic Cafe on August Street took about ten minutes; the few people she passed did not greet her in any way; most of the retail businesses were opening, and their windows were decorated with Halloween displays of orange pumpkins, bales of yellow straw, black bats, scattered colored leaves, and the hideous stuffed doll like a worm with blood-tipped teeth. No one she recognized was among the customers inside the Majestic, and she didn't recognize the waitress who methodically took her order.

After her breakfast was eaten and her bill was paid with no one staring at her and no threatening incident, the reporter left the cafe and walked east on August Street to the train station to exchange her ticket for a new departure date on Thursday.

It was a brief but unpleasant walk. As earlier in the day, her growing paranoia caused her to question if someone was watching her from a doorway, or from a clutch of people, or behind her, and Dianne turned quickly again and then again only to find indifference in the growing number

"Savage stopped on the landing…pulled her coat around her…"

of Light's Enders near her. Nevertheless, reaching the architecturally incongruous Mexican style train depot was a relief.

"Certainly, I am happy to do that," said the middle-aged clerk to Savage with a overly toothy smile like the Cheshire cat from "Alice in Wonderland" as he slouched behind his barred ticket window. "May I have your boarding ticket, Miss?"

Because of her journalistic training, Dianne noted the clerk's pub cap, tilted slightly and rakishly up and back from a pimpled forehead, his Ben Franklin frameless eye glasses, and his worn, black suit and tie, and the queer Azrealite diamond-shaped pin on the suit's lapel, as he took her ticket and began to check it against a list on a clipboard he'd taken from the wall at his left side. His unnatural, antiseptic smile froze. He hung the clipboard back on the wall.

"I'm sorry Miss Savage," he said as his smile faded to guarded indifference. "I can't exchange this ticket."

"I don't understand..." the reporter objected as her blue-green eyes narrowed and she wrinkled her nose at the fetid smell of Asafoetida.

Raising the ticket to the level of his chest, his eyes never leaving her face, the clerk tore it into two pieces that fell to the little shelf behind the window.

"Company policy." The acerbic smile was back on his dour face.

"Then I'll just buy a new ticket for Thursday when you refund my money for the one you just tore up," she said firmly.

"No refund." His face was a blank mask.

Dianne felt her face flush hot with blood from her growing anger, but for the sake of her witness as a Christian, she forced it down.

"Then I'll just buy a new ticket for a Thursday afternoon departure for Bangor," she said, her voice even but cold. "Surely, there can't be that many people traveling to Bangor."

"There are no tickets available," said the clerk, and he leered with bared teeth like yellowed ivory dominoes.

"Then I'll buy a ticket for Friday."

"There are no tickets available for Friday," repeated the clerk. "Next," he said although there was no one behind the newshound.

"I want to speak to your supervisor. Now." The tension was palpable.

"Certainly, but my supervisor has nothing to do with this situation."

"Then I'd like to speak to the person," said Dianne adding a strained pause after each word for emphasis, "who *did* have 'something to do with this situation.'"

"Certainly, Miss," grinned the clerk and leaned forward. "He lives at the Crawford Hotel. His name is Jake Horne."

Her blood ran cold, and she fought to keep the sudden fear from her face as she clenched her fists at her sides. The moment seemed an eternity until she finally said:

"Then I'll buy a ticket at the bus station."

"I wouldn't bet on that," said the middle-aged clerk with his Cheshire cat smile, and contemptuously swept the two halves of her ticket off of his shelf onto the unseen floor.

There were only nine modestly dressed men, women, and children, including Dianne Savage, who were sitting quietly on a worn couch or one of several common house chairs or metal, folding chairs facing Pastor Darren Miller at Margo's memorial service in the little Craftsman house on Angell Street that was also the Light's End Baptist Church.

Dressed in his typical blue shirt and gray trousers, the pastor stood in front of his brown, overstuffed chair, his arms outspread during his closing benediction praising the Creator God of the natural and supernatural universes. The first couple to originally greet her, and the only members she now knew by name, Rebecca and Joshua Nantier, with their sons Schlomo and Kenneth, were praying together with bowed heads.

"Amen," said Miller, ending the service as Dianne wiped tears from her eyes. "Good-bye, and God be with each of you until I see you here on Sunday."

Dianne was intentionally the last person in the short line of people to shake the pastor's hand and wish him well. When she reached Miller, she said:

"Thank you for the wonderful, memorial, Reverend." She extended her hand. The preacher took it. "Although I'd only known her a brief time, I'd really grown to love Margo and her Baby Veyda. Could I talk to you for a moment?" she added, dropping her hand from his, and her eyes as well. "In private."

"Certainly, Miss Savage. Is my 'office' okay?"

"Of course," said Savage, and they turned and walked to the open door at the back of the living room where Darren moved to and then behind the same small desk where he'd sat during their first conversation. With a gesture of his hand and a friendly smile, Miller sat down as he indicated a chair for Dianne.

"How may I help you, Miss Savage?"

"I need a ride to the next nearest town early Thursday morning, Pastor Miller. Do you think there is someone in the congregation who could help me?"

"Why, of course. I can borrow a car and take you, if you like. But if this is a matter of having enough money for a train or bus ticket..."

"No. No, Reverend," she said, lowering her head as she spoke. "I have plenty of money, and am more than willing to pay someone for the ride."

Miller arched his eyebrows in question, encouraging more detail.

"I need to tell you something in strictest confidence, Reverend. Do you know Jake Horne? He has made it impossible for me to buy a ticket out of Light's End."

"May I ask why on earth he'd do something like that?"

"Have you been following the series of articles in the *Bangor Daily Register* on Bishop's Alley and Light's End, Pastor Miller?" Savage removed her hat.

"Of course! I am thrilled that someone has had the courage to stand up and expose the graft, corruption, and debauchery of Bishop's Alley, in particular."

"I wouldn't be so quick to equate courage to that person, Reverend. I am 'Your Undercover Reporter.'" Dianne covered her eyes with the palm of her right hand as she spoke. " And a coward."

"Oh, my stars. You?" For extended moments, the only sound in the room was the hum of an unseen heat vent.

"Yes, me, Reverend. At first, it seemed like the things happening to me or around me here in Light's End were random or coincidental." The reporter lay her hat on her lap. "But then it felt like someone wanted to scare me out of town. But, after an interview with Jake Horne yesterday, I suspect he wants to shut me up permanently."

Then Dianne told Miller with exacting detail about the savage beating and death of Vernon, her recurring nightmares filled with maggots and monsters and rape, how Hank was crushed in what she now believed was a violent 'accident' possibly meant for her, and about the hideous, alien face of the slain dancer at The Palace. Then, fighting to control her emotions, Dianne told the preacher about Margo's death.

"I was standing right next to her when... when an off-duty policeman who works as a bouncer at The P-Palace knifed her, Darren." Despite her efforts, her eyes began to well with tears. "Not twelve inches from me. One second she was alive, and the next she was dead on the floor, and not only did I d-do nothing to protect here, to stop it, I... I..." She buried her face in her hands, and began to cry. "I ran away."

Miller stood up, moved around the desk, and gently placed his hand on her shoulder.

"There is no shame in tears," he said, patting her shoulder, "but if these tears come from guilt on your part because of Margo's death, could you tell me a little more about what happened, my friend?"

"I'm all right, now," said Savage as she removed her wet hands from her face and began to wipe the tears from beneath her eyes with her fingers. "I'm okay."

"Good. Good. Did I hear you say that our dear friend Margo was 'alive one second and the next she was dead'?"

Savage nodded her head in the affirmative as she bit the fingernail of the first digit of her right hand.

"That's certainly not what *The Citadel* reported, I'm afraid, but I haven't put much store in their honesty for some time now. Hard to put much faith in a newspaper owned by Jake Horne and the dirty little Azrealite's cult, you know."

"Horne owns the newspaper?"

"Yes, he does, as well as two-thirds of every business, and every Selectman in Light's End. I suspect he owns Bishop's Alley somehow, under-the-table, so to speak. This little church exists only so he and his lot can claim they are tolerant. Now, Miss Savage, please tell me exactly what happened."

"We had gone to The Palace so that Margo could pay off a debt before she left Light's End. We had only been there moments, both of us leaning on the rail that separates the dance floor from the outer wall, when a thug that works as a bouncer there must have come up behind Margo and tapped her on the shoulder. As she turned, I turned to face them both and saw a serrated knife in his hand. In the blink of an eye, he'd buried it in her heart, Pastor."

"And, 'in the blink of an eye,' you could have stopped him?" asked the young pastor. "That's why you feel guilty, Miss Savage?"

"No," said the reporter. "No, I couldn't have stopped him. But I could have held him until the police arrived, or even killed him on the spot."

Miller arched his left eyebrow as he placed palm against palm, intertwined his fingers, placed his thumbs against his lips, and planted his elbows on his desk. Dianne pulled up her left pant leg, revealing the holstered pistol on her calf.

Miller said nothing and showed no emotion on his face as she lowered the pant leg back over her calf.

"I've been wearing it for some time, ever since I began to suspect my life was in danger, Pastor Miller. And I can shoot the eye out of a weasel at a hundred yards."

The preacher nodded his head, thinking *and there it is again.*

"Certainly, you could have held him for the police," he said," but I think you know that most of the police in Light's End are inept or corrupt. It probably wouldn't have changed much, and you likely would have ended up in a jail cell, badly beaten or dead, Ms. Savage.

"And you certainly have the right to protect your life or the lives of others around you. There is no question of that. As for killing Margo's murderer in cold blood, that's not an option for Christians.

"But I suspect your crippling guilt concerning Margo's murder is unfounded. It happened so quickly that you couldn't have prevented it, and you didn't murder her yourself. I'm sure you know, when your mind is quiet, that you aren't responsible for the actions of others, even though we sometimes suffer not only from our own bad choices and their consequences, but also from the consequences of the actions of others in this beautiful but befouled, fallen world of ours."

"I know that's true, Pastor Miller. But it doesn't change the fact that I ran away like a yellow, spineless coward. I still feel like I should have done something."

"Is it possible that you believe you have an ability and responsibility that actually belong only to our creator God? Even though I haven't had the time to get to know you well, I have noticed a very, very strong streak of self-reliance in you, my friend. That can be a blessing or it can be a curse if it crosses over into self-deception and self-absorption for us weak-willed humans.

"As for our abilities as human beings, I'm sure you know here," he said, untangling his fingers and then pointing with the index finger of his right hand at his right temple, "that neither Christians nor nonbelievers created themselves. Nor did we create the air we breathe or the lungs with which we breathe it. And yet, without air, we'd each be dead in less than three minutes. Neither do we create from nothing the food we eat without which we'd starve to death in the matter of days. We are also not the authors of any of the laws of nature like the law of gravity that holds us to this planet. We did not create the tumultuous planet where we stand. In fact, no human being has ever created anything from nothing.

"But do you know it here," he continued, pointing with the same finger at his heart, "in your soul?" He then webbed his fingers again and placed his thumbs on his chin. "I think it's important to keep our role in life in the correct perspective.

"I have also learned that there is an arrogant self-confidence that borders on insanity," he continued, "by which I mean a disconnect from reality, and that we humans can act like we control almost everything in life when we really control nothing but the choices we make from the choices presented to us. And we influence even less — people don't change inside unless they want to, not because we can make them change. Yet, even with our limitations in mind and body, look at what a dirty, selfish mess we've made of the tiny little awesome thing we are in charge of... choice."

Miller webbed his fingers again, tapped his thumbs against his lips, and grinned thinly.

"On top of that, there are some who believe human beings can know everything. I always get a little chuckle when a scientist tells me that he knows, with certainty, what happened two hundred million years ago, but he can't tell me, with certainty, whether it will rain tomorrow or not.

"Sorry, I think I'm getting a little preachy.

"So, from what you have told me, you had no advance knowledge of and nothing to do with the murder of Margo. By your own eyewitness account, she was killed by an off-duty cop. He and only he is responsible for her death. Nor could you have prevented it. That is simply a fact. If you are feeing guilt over her death, it is unfounded.

"Second: holding him at bay for the police would not have accomplished justice, would not have stopped the maniac from killing again, and would have most likely endangered your own life. Not a fact, but almost a certainty.

"And, my final point, even if you had had advance knowledge of his intent, you had no right to kill him in cold blood before he stabbed Margo, nor after the murder.

"If I'm correct, is it possible that you aren't feeling guilt at all, my friend, but a genuine sorrow at Margo's death, and, at the same time, a bitter remorse at playing God and doing it so very, very poorly? Has the Empress realized that she has no clothes, Dianne?"

Savage did not raise her lowered head.

"As for the 'no clothes' part — your running away —I can't know why you ran, Dianne. I can't see into your heart and know your motive. I can't see into any man's or woman's heart, and that is why God makes it very clear that we are not to pass judgment on other people. That's His job. Our job is to simply try to have the wisdom to discern between right action and thought and wrong action and thought.

"But I will give you an irrefutable truth that you can mull over. When faced with the possibility of their own deaths, all of the apostles ran away from Jesus when he was crucified. Every one. So you are not alone. And yet, they went on to revolutionize the entire world after they met the same risen Christ that you have met. If you need forgiveness for this, *thing*, Dianne, ask for it. It will be given, and then you, if only in a small way, must go out and revolutionize the world as well.

"And remember, we of all peoples should have no fear of death. To leave this temporary body is to be eternally with the One we love.

"And that leaves us with only two remaining questions, Dianne," he said as he separated palm against palm, untwined his fingers, removed his elbows on his desk and leaned back in his chair. "If there is a Creator God who died for you and I and for every fallen man or woman so that we might live forgiven..."

What seemed like an eternity of silence tempered only by the hum of an unseen heat vent was really the stuff of moments before Dianne raised her head and looked clear-eyed at Miller thinking *okay, let the other shoe fall.*

"...can we do any less?" Miller asked.

Dianne picked up her cloche hat, placed it on her head, runked her metal chair back, and slowly stood up.

"And the second question?" asked Dianne.

"Can you be here at 4:00A.M.on Thursday?" asked Miller, and grinned.

"I hate traffic."

On Tuesday, October 30, the angry blanket of gray, moiling clouds that seemed locked to the sky had become a clenched fist threatening to strike. The trees stretched brittle fingers like spider webs in shattered glass as Savage stopped on the landing of the Van Sanford before descending the stairs, pulled her coat around her, shivered, and glanced at the small used car lot in front of her, then to her left at the Standard Grocery Store.

Early that morning, she had written her will and now she would mail it and her diary to James Copeland at the *Bangor Daily Register*. She had left all of her earthly possessions and her modest savings to the orphanage where she had lived as a child.

On her blouse above her heart was pinned a small, folded piece of paper. Inside was a verse from the Old Testament. It read:

Even though I walk through the valley of the shadow of death, I will fear no evil, for you are with me; your rod and your staff, they comfort me. Psalm 23:4

She had chosen the verse carefully.

Chapter Twelve

It was Wednesday, Oct 31st, the day of the insane, cabalistic night of The Feasting on All Hallows Eve, when Dianne awoke in the Van Sanford Apartments at 9:13 am. She whistled "I Can't Give You Anything But Love" out of mundane habit instead of joy as she went through her morning hygiene ritual, dressed in a blue denim blouse, worn blue dungarees, canvas shoes, and her green cloche hat. She put her latest article for the *Bangor Daily Register* in the left pocket of her dungarees, then pinned her daily reminder to herself from the day before on her blouse above her still uneasy heart.

Because she knew the weather would be ugly outside, Dianne put on her long coat, grabbed her clutch purse, and left her apartment. It was a cloudy and chilly morning outside. She stopped on the landing before descending the stairs and looked at Quality Motors — the small used car lot hadn't opened yet — and then to her left at the Standard Grocery Store. A teenage boy was loading groceries into the back seat of a 1926 Buick 4 door Master Six Sedan. The cacophony of light traffic, both by foot and vehicle, met her, but nothing else to daunt the newshound, and nothing seemed out of place or threatening.

Dianne's brisk walk to downtown Light's End and the Majestic Cafe took about ten minutes; the few people she passed did not greet her or even recognize her in any way, most of the retail businesses were closed, but their windows were fey with brittle fall colors and Halloween displays of pumpkins now too ripe, bales of straw, paper bats, scattered colored leaves, and "Percy," the eldritch stuffed doll like a worm with teeth that left a foul taste on her soul. No one she recognized was among the few customers that were in the Majestic as she sat down at a table, and she didn't know the waitress that took her order of two eggs, over easy, ham, hash brown potatoes, wheat toast, and coffee.

Dianne added an order of two peanut butter and strawberry jam sandwiches wrapped in wax paper to carry with her when she was finished eating. They arrived with her bill.

At Maritime Supplies on August Street, Savage bought a flashlight, a first aid kit, and a small compass, then the newshound continued east to the Light's End Post Office on Dunlevy Street wearing a false expression of casual indifference on her face to hide her gnawing anxiety and mailed her brief article to the blind address of the *Bangor Daily Register*. Then she strolled to the Western Union office next door and sent a telegram to "Larry Allison." It read: "I'm going in. d"

It was 11:00A.M.when Savage reached the Van Sanford Apartments, the picture of assurance and calm determination. Inside, she was a nervous wreck.

Back in her apartment, Dianne took her suitcase out of the room's closet, placed it on the bed, and opened it, tossing her little packages from the Majestic Cafe and Maritime Supplies next to it. She removed her knapsack, unfolded and opened it. She took out the flashlight, small first aid kit, and the compass from one package and put it on the bed. She turned to the top of the bureau next to her stack of magazines and pulps that she had purchased earlier at Park's Drug Store. She looked through the magazines, rejecting "Amazing Stories" because its editor had rejected her submissions, "College Humor" and "Goblin" because they didn't appeal to her at the moment, and chose a pulp horror magazine, "Weird Tales," to carry with her.

On its cover, a woman clad in a diaphanous gown was chained and ready to be burned as a cowled man with an axe crouched at her feet. The cover story within was "The Werewolf's Daughter" by H. Warner Munn. She thought *maybe they'll publish one of my short stories if it's about this weird, filthy place.*

She walked back to her suitcase and lay all those things next to it, then unwrapped the oilcloth that protected her Browning "Grand Reudement" model 1928, 9mm, self-loading pistol, removed the gun, her calf holster, and two magazines holding fifteen bullets each, and strapped the holster to her leg, inserting the pistol. Then Dianne removed her new Eastman Kodak No. 2 Hawk-Eye camera from her suitcase and added it to the knapsack, as well as the flashlight, first aid kit, compass, "Weird Tales," and her two sandwiches. She closed the bulging bag with some effort.

"Don't weaken, don't weaken, don't weaken," she said to herself, "it's a great life if you don't weaken," she added, quoting her editor, then knelt by the bed, and prayed.

"This is it," she said to the fear that haunted her, and rose and closed her suitcase, returned it to the closet, and, wearing her knapsack, left her apartment.

Directly across the street, Dianne ordered a jumbo cheeseburger with lettuce, tomato, and mayonnaise, fries, and tea. It was an act of will that her voice did not tremble. She ate everything on the little red metal table in front on Harley's Drive In as she fought back the paranoid feeling that a man at the now open Quality Motors was watching her for an inordinate length of time. She ate every morsel because she knew that, besides this meal, her peanut butter and jelly sandwiches might be the only thing available for a long time. She looked at her wristwatch; it was 12:15pm. Then she walked back across the street to the Van Sanford, trying to control the shivering in her stomach that was not due to the cold weather. Dianne entered the main entrance facing the street; she did not go to her apartment.

She went to the stairwell that lead to the basement, put her hand, clammy but firm, on the doorknob of the closed basement door and turned the knob easily; the door swung in, creaking. The instantly familiar, low, red glow from a furnace huddled against the far wall, hot and dangerous and reassuring, rose as she entered, throwing wild, undulating shadows and a red half-light everywhere. The furnace soughed through its red teeth. With a growing confidence and a curiosity too fierce to be smothered, she stepped into the laundry room.

The newshound padded forward, her canvas shoes whispering on the floor. The aberrant door lay on the basement floor, and the furnace soughed. Her heart rose and thudded. She licked her lips and tasted the salt of sweat; her flesh was clammy in the muggy heat. Dianne bit her lower lip and fought down her fear, reminding herself that descending into the tunnel that she believed led to the Azrealite's secret underground temple six hours before their outré "Goat With No Horns" ceremony almost guaranteed she would meet no one. But she was equally aware that she might find herself standing like a fool in the mouth of a conduit emptying into the foul, odorous Abomination Bay. Trembling, Dianne knelt and reached for the glass onion doorknob and opened the door.

The sheet of faux concrete still lay beneath the door, and the reporter touched the secret stud that would open it with her right hand. She looked around the basement, but it was empty except for the damnable flickering shadows thrown by the red maw of the furnace. She pressed the stud, and the false door fell down and back to her left, and she laughed nervously at the shameful fear inside her because, whatever the reasons for Walton's or Horne's lies, she knew she stood on the threshold of finally uncovering the truth.

Dianne removed her knapsack, opened it, and took out her flashlight. She closed her knapsack, and, carrying it hanging from her left hand and with the flashlight in her right, she pulled the door above her closed as she slowly began to descend into what only God and Jake Horne and Chuck Walton and apparently everyone else in Light's End knew but her. She looked along the stairs that fell down and pushed her fear, the violation of logic, down hard into its animal place.

Even as she stepped down, the reporter saw a uniform row of light bulbs to her right hanging from the roof of the concrete tunnel throwing enough dim light to make her flashlight unnecessary, and her camera useless. At the bottom of the stars, she lay her knapsack down, replaced the flashlight in it, and took out the compass and two extra clips of bullets for her gun. Lifting the back of her jacket, she pushed one clip into each of the front pockets of her pants. Then she palmed the compass in her right hand, and paused to push the faux concrete floor above her closed against its outer door above her.

"Don't weaken, don't weaken, don't weaken," she whispered. A pressure of warm, smarmy, moist air registered beneath the trepidation and very real fear clouding her senses. Savage stepped off the last stair into the tunnel, and put the trembling fingertips of her right hand at the end of her outstretched arm on the wall for balance.

Dianne jerked back. She brought her fingers to her nose and sniffed, smelling nothing beyond damp earth and clammy flesh. She illogically wiped her fingers on her coat.

Possibly fifteen or twenty feet to her left, she could see the mouths of at least three tunnels intersecting with her conduit and fading into obscurity because of distance and diminishing light to the West of downtown Light's End, to the North under part of the town's retail district and possibly under part of Bishop's Alley, and to the South and West of her position under several neighborhoods. She could discern no sound or movement from these tunnels.

The tunnel to her right that stretched east towards the unseen sea looked to be about eight feet high and wide to the reporter; it was warm and the silence was oppressive, compromised only by a faint chittering no louder than her own intake and expulsion of breathe that, she thought, must surely be the electricity in the light bulbs. The air was still, antiseptic, and claustrophobic. Dianne guessed that if she headed east and slightly north to the temple beneath Elliott's Head, and if she did not stumble onto a dead end, or run into intersecting tunnels that would confuse her direction, or if she did not collide with an Azrealite acolyte or the gnashing maw of Horne's monster, she faced about a two mile trek that would take her at least an hour to complete. She looked at the compass in her right hand.

Her heart thundering painfully in the silence, she took another step into the tunnel.

Savage squinted at her wristwatch in the dim light. It was 1:30pm. The reporter had been walking east northeast cautiously for almost fifty minutes, her hearing acute for the slightest sound of human footsteps, which meant that by her calculations she must be very near the subterranean Tenebrae temple, when she had arrived at the fourth anomaly in the tunnel. The first three had been additional, unoccupied, intersecting tunnels that had, nevertheless, made her heart leap as she approached and then passed each one. To her left was a slightly recessed, unmarked, steel door in the wall. She placed her right hand on the grey door; it vibrated almost imperceptibly with a muffled, rhythmic *thud thud thud.*

Dianne knew that every decision she now made, no matter how seemingly trivial, might lead to discovery, or failure, or even a horrible death for her. She thrust that crippling thought aside and slowly and quietly turned the knob, opening the door.

The suddenly thunderous *thud thud* that first startled her and then obliterated her sigh of relief came from a huge furnace in the center of the room. It was flanked by an equally monstrous unit that Dianne could not identify with certainty. Large metal vents ran from both mechanisms to the walls of the room, those from the furnace explaining the warmth in the tunnel. She guessed the vents from the second unit ran up and outside of Elliott's Head, drawing down and circulating fresh air from above.

Savage turned, stepped from the room, and closed the door behind her, pausing outside to lean against a wall with one equally unnerving and exhilarating certainty: She would not end up standing in the open maw of a conduit overlooking noxious Abomination Bay.

The electric chittering was an erratic, damnable, perceptible gibbering in the otherwise preternatural silence. Anxious and raw, Dianne stood in the mouth of the conduit opening onto the cavern that was the nightmarish Azrealite temple. No one stirred inside. Nevertheless, she quickly unslung her knapsack and held it in her left hand as she pressed her back against the rough concrete wall of the tunnel.

Despite the dim lighting, Savage memorized every aspect of the unsettling Azrealite temple; it was unimpressive, primitive, and shabby with crude chisel marks on its gray stone walls. The ancient cavern had obviously been enlarged by human hands. She counted a crescent line of eighteen high-backed, wooden thrones with ichthyoidal carvings, red padded seats, and armrests that lined the rough-cut walls and ended at the edge of a stone well far opposite her. Four other tunnels opened onto the temple, breaking the line of thrones, as did three large, ornate iron grills probably covering air or heating vents.

The well rose about four feet above the floor, by her estimation was twelve feet in circumference, and was of mortared, raw, gray stone probably quarried from Elliott's Head cliff. But it was not the gray of granite; it was the gray of dead, human flesh. The temple was lit by smoking torches in sconces embedded in its walls that threw squirming shadows everywhere. The implacable charnel smell of dead, rotting flesh permeated the warm air.

Dianne realized she faced an immediate, possibly insurmountable, dilemma. She could see no space between the outré thrones and the walls or at the well where she could hide, and she certainly could not do so in any tunnel emptying onto the temple. But the thought struck her that the iron grates were large enough to hide a small, reclining person.

Suddenly, a monstrosity of green spider's legs haloed around an expressionless blue human mask above a neck wrapped in white bandages emerged from one of the dark tunnels close to the stone well. Its eye sockets white and pupilless, a green robe hung open from its shoulders exposing a torso of what insanely could only be human internal organs. The chilling rush of the fear of discovery ran through Dianne, and she quickly slunk further back into the tunnel as the heavily robed man carried three small, bronze lamps shaped as dragon heads in each of its hands to the well and set them down on its lip, one after the other.

Savage turned on her heels and began to tip-toe into the tunnel, her clothing drenched in flop sweat, her bloodless face white with tension.

And as she fled down the tunnel, the undine leapt and arched up out of the well, shedding an arc of watery sludge around and beneath it. And Savage followed the arc up with her eyes as the undine rose over her, and as it rose, its jaw unhinged and its rapacious jaws split into a gaping wound of gnashing, razor sharp, jagged teeth, and she shook the absurd terror-induced image from her mind.

Savage finally reached the recessed steel door that she had breached earlier, quietly opened and then closed it behind her. She covered her ears from the demonic *thud thud* of the machines as she went to a large metal vent attached to the second unit; its path along the floor seemed to lay in the direction of the temple. Bending at the waist, the newshound ran her right hand over and along it, searching for access through a maintenance panel or some other opening and, finding a panel, slid it back.

"Don't weaken, don't weaken, don't weaken, girl," she inaudibly whispered to herself beneath the hideous pounding as she sat on the floor next to the vent. Savage removed her knapsack, and, holding it in her left hand, slid into the opening. Dianne pulled the knapsack in after her and felt her heart slowing and her breathing returning to normal as she grasped and slid the maintenance panel back into place, somewhat diminishing the hellish *thud thud* of the machines. She sat still in the dark vent for several moments, composing her emotions and reviewing her options. Then the reporter opened the knapsack by feel, removed the flashlight, and shone it around the interior of the vent. It was even larger than she had remembered and easily would allow her to crawl on her hands and knees along its length. The reporter began to crawl, dragging the knapsack along at her left side.

Her first trip from the furnace room to the temple had taken scant moments. Now, the same distance on her aching hands and knees seemed to drag on forever. But dozens of irregular pinpoints of light thrown through the holes formed by the pattern in a temple grate slowly grew in size in front of her until her flashlight was no longer necessary. She stopped and opened her knapsack, took out her copy of "Weird Tales," closed the knapsack, and painstakingly crawled the four or five feet remaining to the iron grate.

Her arrival was bittersweet. Although someone outside of it would literally have to press an eye against an opening in the outré pattern of the grate to discover her, therefore making her hiding place secure, the same small openings made her camera useless. Holding her wristwatch close to an opening, she saw it was 2:15 pm. Resigned to a long wait of what she guessed might be as much as five hours, she placed her knapsack against the grill, sprawled out in the vent with her head against it, and, using her flashlight as a makeshift lamp, began to read about blood lusting werewolves and eldritch horrors and death. And as Savage read, the electric chittering swelled in the otherwise oppressive silence and again impressed itself on her raw nerves.

When she was almost finished reading the last queer story in "Weird Tales," the reporter heard the scraping of feet in the temple underscored by the now constant, infernal chittering. She lay her magazine down as she twisted around and placed an eye to the grate as the same spider-haloed priest of indeterminate gender that had carried in the bronze lamps emerged again from the tunnel behind the stone well. High above the bizarre acolyte hung an almost imperceptible agitated heat shimmer. Using a burning taper, the Azrealite lit the six small, dragon headed lamps on the lip of the well as he chanted in a dead, lifeless monotone:

"Y'ai'ng, H'ee-l'ged, F'ai Throdog Uaaah, Ogthrod Ai'f," over and over again.

With some effort, Dianne took out the small notebook and pencil she always carried in the front pocket of her dungarees and wrote down the priest's gibberish.

Savage held up her wristwatch to her face; it was 4:10 pm. As she pressed her eye against the grid again, a second acolyte wearing a pale purple robe over an outrageous human skeleton beneath, and an abhorrent, elongated, beaked mask with a row of hooked spines ascending up its center, emerged from the dim entrance. He or she carried a small, ornately carved ebon box. She watched as he or she placed what looked like a small shot glass on the arm of each of the eighteen thrones. A third worshipper entered dressed in a peaked witch's hat with a yellow flame burning at its tip, a purple robe draped diagonally across its chest from the left shoulder to the right hip, and a faintly purple sash with arcane symbols cascading down from its left shoulder to its waist. Moving behind the well, this acolyte used a velvet pull cord to release a rolled up, high mounted tapestry that unfurled with a muffled *whoosh* to reveal a blood red, diamond-shaped mesh of crosses, the weird symbol of the Tenebrae church. Then, as unceremoniously as the three priests had entered, they all shuffled out of the temple.

Savage abandoned her watch at the grate, twisted back to her original position, and took her gun out of its holster.

The newshound again pressed her eye to the grate as what she knew must be some kind of manufactured, recorded trick—a scratching and a faint, unnerving, deep sobbing like a woman—rose from the well and joined the festering, maniacal chittering that in turn was underscored by the faint *thud thud* of the heating and air circulation machines far behind her. The sobbing sent a shudder down her spine as the soft, eerie music of Pan flutes, the sambuke, sistrum and tympanum also swelled from nowhere and everywhere in the shadows and joined the cacophony of delirious sounds.

From the black maw of each conduit, more acolytes began to shamble into the Tomb of the One, a hideous procession of six deformed blasphemies of unnaturally amalgamated carnivores and spiders and scorpions and slimy octopods that, led by a yellow-robed priest carrying a white book and a long, curved serrated knife beneath it in his upturned hands, bleated, "*Y'ai'ng, H'ee-l'ged, F'ai Throdog Uaaah, Ogthrod Ai'f Y'ai'ng, H'ee-l'ged, F'ai Throdog Uaaah, Ogthrod Ai'f*" as they limped and crawled and stumbled on the cavern floor. Each but the yellow-robed priest carried a musical instrument or a black torch whose yellow aura of flickering light added more fantastic squirming shadows on the cavern walls and the Azrealite priests.

Because of her research and queer old Charles Walton's bitter exposé of the "dirty little secrets" of Light's End, Savage knew she was witness to the Presentation of the Black Book, the most treasured arcane fetish of the inner circle of the Azrealites.

The bizarre procession of costumed Azrealites continued to fill the murky chamber and laboriously seat themselves, leaving one empty throne, until seventeen monstrosities chanted in a broken, low, guttural, gibberish unknown to Dianne as the sobbing from the well and the tempo and volume of the music intensified and the bearer of the Black Book drew near the well's mouth. The yellow priest stopped and laid the book on the stone lip of the well, and opened the tome as the chanting surged and reverberated in the cavern, and the priests on their feet and seated acolytes rocked back and forth where they stood or in their chairs.

Like the sudden intake of breath, every sound stopped except the chittering of the agitated impalpable swarm hanging above the heads of the congregation of blasphemies and the melancholy sobbing from the well.

"*Ogthrod!*" shouted the yellow-robed priest facing the obscene mockery of human flesh, and threw his arms and hands in the air above his head. "We gather the seeds of chaos. And we plant. *Y'ai'ng, H'ee-l'ged, F'ai Throdog Uaaah, Ogthrod Ai'f!* Hail The One! Hail the Conquering Worm!"

Suddenly, Jake Horne stood unhooded in the black mouth of the cavern behind The Well of the Worm in a blood red robe, a dagger at his left hip holstered on a black rope around his enormous girth. He smiled with the slit of his mouth full of yellow teeth in his yellow, stubbled face and smirked at a dirty joke that only he knew and loved.

"*Y'ai'ng!* We plant!" he shouted with jubilation and a great flourish of his arms and each of the seated worshippers stood, removed a small serrated knife from the left sleeve of their robe, and, drawing back a sleeve, nicked the flesh of their left forearm.

"We sow!" Horne shouted. "*H'ee-l'ged!* We sow!" And each of the eighteen acolytes laid down a blood-tipped serrated knife on the arm of a throne and picked up the glass from the opposite arm and began the profane chant as their blood dripped into the cup.

The sobbing in the well became an obscene angry gurgle as the few turned to pick up flutes, the sambuke, sistrum and tympanum from the thrones where they had been placed, and the eerie, dissonant music again swelled to join the cacophony of sounds..

"This is the real covenant in blood; do this, as often as you drink it, in honor of Man," Horne said in a gleeful frenzy, and each worshipper except the first who had filled two cups handed his glass to the acolyte on his left who drank; the first drained his cup as the last at the end of the crescent drank their neighbor's and their own warm blood.

"*Y'ai'ng!*" Horne spat, he voice now pregnant with threat. "By the ashes of unholy wafer, and the blood of tainted flesh, He burns His on my name; He adds His to my power. And when the earth shall hang where heaven be, and the Goat with man shall lie, then the damned will draw down blasphemy, from a well sunk in the sky!

"*Khoda! Khoda! Khoda! Y'ai'ng, H'ee-l'ged, F'ai Throdog Uaaah, Ogthrod Ai'f!* Hail Man! Hail the One!" Horne barked, and threw his own hands and arms up and out in jubilation. "Bring me the sacrifice of the goat with no horns!"

The raucous music and chanting stopped, only intensifying the unholy otherness of the angry wet gurgle in the well and the chittering from the now maelstrom shimmer above, and, one by one, the Azrealites began to remove their grotesque masks. There was no surprise for the newshound as Judy and Gene Sorenson shed their disgusting masks, but she suppressed a gasp with her right hand when the yellow priest of the Black Book removed his hood.

It was Chuck Walton.

"*Y'ai'ng!*" Walton barked. "Bring forth the goat with no horns."

Dianne watched as Azrealites continued to unmask; a face of tattered, yellowed pages like the fanned sheets of an opened hardback book sitting on its spine fell away, then another the slobbering mandibles of a spider, yet another a face stripped bare of all flesh, then the next acolyte who took nothing from or off a face that shone like the sun.

The reporter saw two diabolic masked Azrealites suddenly appear in the ebon maw of the tunnel behind the well, one a squirming head of worms atop the same purple and red robes of most of the Azrealites, and a female in a blood red caftan wearing an expressionless, off-white porcelain, Kabuki mask in front of a cascading wealth of auburn hair carrying a tightly wrapped bundle. They began to skirt the well.

"*Khoda!* Hail the Feasting! Hail The One! Hail the Urge!" both chanted with dead, monotone voices as they first reached the well and then knelt before the Black Book, individually kissed its open pages, rose, and approached Horne.

"I am the Urge," hissed Horne as both knelt before him. "What do you bring?"

"The mother of the goat with no horns," said the writhing ball of worms, "and the initiate DemiUrge of the Three Sixes," and removed his mask.

It was Joe Seminole.

"And who is the initiate?" asked Horne with a queer gesture of dismissal as the female acolyte removed her mask, raised her face in supplication, and said:

"Body and mind, I belong to the One and his image on Earth, the Urge."

"Oh my god!" hissed Savage between clenched teeth.

It was Margo Willson.

Dianne stifled a sob with her left hand, her face distorted by overwhelming shock and fear as an epiphany like a sledgehammer struck her: that 'the best damn, investigative reporter' at the *Bangor Daily* had been lied to, manipulated, betrayed, and conspired against by everyone she had stupidly trusted from almost the moment she'd gotten off the bus, that she'd been a fool, a patsy, a pawn in a hideous game, and that she was undeniably trapped. Savage fell back from her squatting position against the stone wall of the air vent thinking *I am dead I am dead I am surely dead.*

Then she bit her lower lip, drawing blood, and steeled herself and pressed her eye against the iron grate to see Margo removing layers of cloth from the bundle cradled in her left arm as Horne snatched his serrated knife from the black cord around his obscenely fat belly, and the macabre music fell apart, and the sibilant chittering of the swarming shimmering alien cloud above them all and a gnashing from the well merged and rose to a roar, and the Azrealites fell prostrate as one on the cavern floor with cries of ecstasy.

"What blood offering does the mother give," asked Horne with the slit of his mouth.

Margo held up Baby Veyda in her arms.

Horne raised his serrated knife above Veyda as, horrified, Savage twisted around until her legs were drawn tight against her stomach, her feet were on the grate, and her gun balanced in her right hand.

"This is the body," chanted Horne, "which is for you. Praise The One! *Y'ai'ng, H'ee-l'ged, F'ai Throdog Uaaah, Ogthrod Ai'f.!* Take and eat. Do this in honor of Man.

"There is no God but man," he droned, and placed the serrated knife in his left hand against Veyda's throat as the scratching and slobbering in the well became frenzied.

Dianne kicked the grate clattering to the floor, and swung out into the temple.

"STOP!" she screamed, and the horrid sound of frenzied slobbering from the well and the chittering from the alien cloud above filled the cavern, and Horne, the priests, and the mendicants turned as one to see the reporter standing in front of the fallen grate, holding her pistol with both hands pointed at Jake Horne's chest.

"Well, hello, Dianne," cooed Horne. "What took you so long. You know, you look good enough for Percy to eat." And Horne raised the knife above Veyda again as, abhorrent and reeking, in an unseen dance of soundless, rising bubbles, a monstrous obscenity of spider's legs writhing around the bloated head and gnashing razor teeth of a gigantic pustulant maggot rose up to the lip of the well, out of the well's silent womb, spit its slobber out onto the floor and leered at Dianne.

"OH MY GOD!" Savage screamed and fired, and the shot struck Jake Horne in the left shoulder. Horne's legs buckled, and Margo dropped the baby as he staggered back against the lip of the well below the writhing horror there. Walton threw up his hands, his face twisted by fear, and took two steps to the left and away from Horne as Margo, in one movement, rose and fled toward the black maw of a conduit.

Dianne fired, and the second shot struck Horne in the face at the corner of his left eye. Gushing blood, he collapsed to the floor against the well as the swarm of alien light above broke apart and fled up into the ebon blackness above the light of the torches and the aberrant maggot horror rose howling in the well.

Savage fired, and the third shot struck Horne in the heart.

She turned to flee down the tunnel by which she had come only to face an unmoving wall of acolytes mad with rage that had closed in behind her.

She raised the pistol thinking *God in Heaven, it is finished, accept my soul* and swept it down the line of Azrealites.

"Yes, you'll take me in the end," she hissed, "but I've got twelve more bullets in this pistol. Who wants to die first."

No one moved. Two giggled.

Savage turned on her heels to find another escape route only to see Joe Seminole standing by the well under the swaying, slobbering, unspeakable abomination of blood and gnashing teeth and horror, place his right hand under Horne's left armpit. As he lifted, Jake Horne impossibly staggered to his feet with an acerbic smile like a cut in his face. He placed a finger to the seeping hole by his left eye, and brought away a smear of blood. He placed the bloody finger in his mouth and sucked, then opened his mouth full of yellow teeth in a face full of stubble and distaste, and said:

"My dear, you have become a bore."

Low and filled with black fury, the Azrealites began chanting: "*Y'ai'ng, H'ee-l'ged, F'ai Throdog Uaaah, Ogthrod Ai'f.! Y'ai'ng, H'ee-l'ged, F'ai Throdog Uaaah, Ogthrod Ai'f.! Y'ai'ng, H'ee-l'ged, F'ai Throdog Uaaah, Ogthrod Ai'f!*"

"I think," said Horne, "I'll send a letter to your editor."

Jim Copeland stood in a heavy coat and gloves on the south landing at the top of the short flight of painted concrete stairs that led to the ground floor of the Van Sanford Apartments just as the sun had sunk below the horizon. It was bitterly cold and the light from the bulb over the landing was a wane halo of yellow. The editor stomped the snow that had delayed his arrival off his boots, and opened the door onto the hall that ran the length of the building. It was empty and silent.

His first impression of the Van Sanford was of cleanliness and the subtle but sharp smell of antiseptic. It was unusually warm. He glanced to his left, noticing that the tarnished brass number on the wooden door of the first apartment was 1A, then to his right, ran his right hand nervously through his black hair, and stepped inside.

Copeland stopped at the next apartment to his left, 3A, raised his clenched, gloved fist to knock, but hesitated. He knew that, at best, his earlier telegram ordering his fiercely independent reporter not to enter the storm drain until he arrived would have been interpreted by Dianne as a lack of confidence on his part in her abilities as an investigative reporter, or, even worse, as a woman. He knew he would face real anger, but Copeland steeled his resolve, and knocked. There was no answer.

He rapped again, louder, and said: "Dianne?" There was no response.
He knocked again, even louder, and raised his voice. "Dianne!"
Silence.

Frustrated, Copeland tried the doorknob with his right hand, and found it turned without resistance. If she were not in the apartment, he knew that this 'intrusion' would be met with irritation as well, but, considering the possibility of real danger to her, the editor pushed the door open a crack, and, moderating his voice, said: "Dianne."

The door slowly swung open on well-oiled hinges onto a room of dense shadows. A blacker blot in the dark room, Dianne sat on a straight backed chair facing the door.

"Dianne!" said Copeland, and stepped into the room.

Copeland took another step and then another closer. Dianne sat upright in her chair by the apartment's only window. He could see she wore her trademark gray suit with its outrageous, bell-bottomed pants, and her cloche hat was pulled over her bobbed, red hair, but the suit looked uncharacteristically awkward, as if someone who didn't know how to dress a woman had dressed her. He knew her silence meant she was as mad as Hell.

"Hey! Dianne!" said Copeland and wrinkled his nose at an unpleasant smell as he approached her. "How's the best damn investigative reporter in Maine doing this...?"

He stopped. The subtle thin line at the middle of her neck that was the first sign of advancing maturity seemed more pronounced. She was tied to the chair. Her dungarees hung limp as if they were empty beneath her waist. Dianne's daily note to herself was pinned to the lapel of her suit.

On the cover of her note was scrawled, "Dear Editor" in red ink. The blood drained out of Copeland's face as he gingerly reached out with his trembling right hand and touched her unnaturally pale cheek. Dianne's head lolled back slightly to her left side, and the dungarees collapsed inward on themselves like a fallen cake, and the thin line in her neck became a gaping mouth rimmed with dried blood.

Copeland clapped his left hand over his mouth to stop the bile rising there as a maggot crawled out of her left nostril.

EPIL⊙G

T*he Citadel* newspaper reported that Dianne Savage, the *"Bangor Daily Register* undercover reporter whose articles on Light's End and Bishop's Alley have outraged our fair city," was found dead on November 5. According to the Light's End newspaper, details were lacking, but authorities claim she died in a bizarre accident involving earth-moving equipment while investigating a line of the massive new storm drain system being built by the city. The body was mangled almost beyond recognition, and would be released to relatives pending an autopsy.

The next day, November 6, 1928, *The Citadel* newspaper published the news of Dianne Savage's accidental death on page three, above the fold, in its afternoon edition. In that same edition, the "All Around Town" gossip column reported an unrelated story that Ebenezar Azreal had mulled over his opportunities and decided that twenty-one was a good age to leave town and attend college in Calcutta.

On November 8, Jim Copeland's scathing article on the cover-up of her murder by *The Citadel* newspaper, the police, and the authorities in Light's End was published in the *Bangor Daily Register.*

The upstanding citizens of Light's End who read the report of Dianne's death in *The Citadel* and bothered to comment on it because gossip was thin that day threw up their hands and said: This proves there isn't a God or He would have stopped it. Some Light's Enders believed it was Dianne's fault for being in the wrong place at the wrong time, or the fault of the *Bangor Daily* editor for sending her to stick her nose into business that didn't concern anyone but Light's Enders. Some said it was no one's fault, or the fault of ignorance and poverty, or nonexistent governmental safety regulations, or that it was her insatiable curiosity that killed her.

The pastor at the Baptist Church in Light's End told his tiny congregation that Dianne's parents had eaten sour grapes and Dianne's teeth had been set on edge, meaning that we live in a fallen world created by fallen people, and we therefore suffer the consequences of not only our only sins but of everyone's sins. He also said that this world created by God had been recreated by Man in Man's dirty image.

Those Light's End citizens who read the *Bangor Daily Register* were outraged by Copeland's article, and the city fathers sent a telegram to the publisher of the newspaper demanding an immediate retraction. In his response published the following week, Copeland publicly called for an FBI investigation of the leaders of Light's End, Jake Horne specifically, and its corrupt newspaper, charging all with conspiracy and an attempt to cover-up Dianne's brutal and tragic murder.

Righteous indignation began to burn white hot in Light's End for the next three weeks. Almost every subscription to the Bangor newspaper was cancelled, day-to-day petty squabbles, conflicts and misdemeanors were ignored by the town gossips, and the injustice and hypocrisy of Bangor, Maine was the first topic of every conversation in the homes, at the cafes, restaurants, drug store lunch counters, and on the sidewalks of Light's End.

The Citadel began its own series of articles on government corruption, brothels, gambling dens, and drug dealers in Bangor, some of which were true. Jake Horne seemed to disappear, swallowed up by the earth. But he and the high officials of the town and the First Church of Tenebrae were putting intense pressure on state officials and others in positions of power and influence who were also members of the Tenebrae Church, or had other connections with Light's End, to silence Copeland and the *Bangor Daily Register*.

No one really believed that Copeland would stop, but any mention of Light's End became conspicuously absent from the *Bangor Daily Register* for one week, then two, then an incredible three consecutive weeks. Behind closed doors and in clandestine meetings, there were sighs of relief and even gloating among Light's End's elite, and the mundane grind of living with its little triumphs and sorrows resumed in the stunted, isolated town on the coast of Maine.

Like an unexpected slap in the face, the first new article by Copeland in the Bangor newspaper appeared the first week of January in 1929. It was a general re-indictment of Light's End, a statement that the FBI was considering an investigation, and that the wheels of government had been set in motion to convene a Grand Jury.

An intense and obscene fury was reignited in Light's End, and Copeland began to receive death threats, but the second article that was published without a byline in the next week threw a sudden chill in the souls of her citizens. It mentioned recent events in the town, and that meant only one thing: There was another undercover reporter among them.

Ebenezar Azreal left for Calcutta.

In the third week of January, heavy equipment seemed to disappear overnight as construction on the massive storm drain project ceased abruptly and without explanation, leaving little mountains of excavated earth in multiple locations around Light's End. No one ever noticed that there wasn't a single manhole cover leading to the storm drain anywhere in the town or its neighborhoods.

In the final week of January, Jake Horne shambled up to the pulpit at the First Church of Tenebrae and laboriously reasserted the accidental death of Dianne Savage, and denounced Jim Copeland and the *Bangor Daily Register* with uncharacteristic heat.

In February and March of 1929, paranoia spread like a cancer throughout the community. With each passing day, a growing number of citizens would not talk to anyone in fear that it might be an FBI agent or a reporter, and no one would be caught dead straying into Bishop's Alley. Hour after hour tensions and fear rose, business fell off at The Alley, and petty squabbles, conflicts and misdemeanors between those who would still talk multiplied and intensified. Several men suspected of being undercover reporters were found by the Light's End police beaten almost to death, but no charges were filed and no stories about the assaults were published in *The Citadel*. Articles condemning Light's End continued to be published in the *Bangor Daily Register*.

In the first week of April, Charles Walton's body was discovered in the dumpster behind the Mermaid Cafe, riddled with bullets. Dianne Savage's ashes arrived in an urn at the *Bangor Daily Register* with a note of apology from Light's End officials for the mistaken cremation of the reporter. The photographs she had taken were published by a Light's End printer as a series of postcards, each signed "Savage."

Then several anonymous letters to the editor of *The Citadel* newspaper called for the impeachment of a number of city officials as anger and violence in Light's End escalated. Isolated fist fights became common, even on school playgrounds, and by the end of the month the town fathers reached the only conclusion that could have been reached.

Enough was enough.

It was whispered that in an outpouring of self-righteousness, a furious mob of citizens stormed the red light district and burned Bishop's Alley to the ground around midnight on May 13, 1929. Some believed, however, that the federal government had sent special agents to torch it. One person claimed to have seen the silhouette of a very fat man, his head thrown back in maniacal laughter, dancing in the flames.

"...a very fat man...dancing in the flames..."

Deemed as acceptable punishment for failing to shut down The Alley, the town put the whole matter behind it and incorporated the land where The Alley had plied its drugs, booze, and prostitution into the city, therefore putting it under the jurisdiction of Light's End's police. Almost at the same time, the FBI investigation was terminated, the Grand Jury was squelched, and the publisher of the *Bangor Daily Register* fired Jim Copeland for his 'one man crusade,' therefore putting an end to the articles against Light's End.

The narcotics, booze, perverted sex and violence that had been celebrated openly in Bishop's Alley was moved indoors.

Margo Willson emerged as a DemiUrge in the Church of Tenebrae.

And Veyda Willson grew and grew and thrived as unspeakable horrors opened one after the other of countless doors scattered like stars between the worlds and traveled across a vast, unfathomable abyss to Light's End.

Where the seeds of chaos gather.

The End

CIRCUS SONG

LYRICS BY SCHLOMO NANTIER

While gently out tripping in moonlight, stewed—I—
stumbled, seen a stone carriage pulled by four outré dragonfly.
Knuckled dew from my eye amongst multi burning dandeli — I —
my pickled scream in a brain dream — watched circus wheeling by.

Ass on my in the grass, four hundred sang birds sung,
Four thousand church chimes belled, once upon a rung.

In shattered eye-glasses, the ant clowns mimed — I,
humbled, seen a bone carriage phat with six squeamous piggie eye.
Spiders chute from the sky as countless maggots multiply — pi —
a tiny daft in their love craft — as circus shambling by.

As churning and clabbered, the buttered bugs — fly,
chromed, comes a lone carriage armed with eight eldritch octopi.
Blind rats strut, tailless, by, amongst two thumping tympani — high —
I, fevered brain in a pickled scream — watched circus flopping by.

Ass on my in the grass, four hundred sang birds sung
Four thousand church chimes belled, once upon a rung

While heaving down circus in vestments, bloody — magi
juggled; as this blind maggot, flanked by ten gnashing cockeye,
tossed balls in foul air among water spraying elifly — aaiii! —
its putrid tail leaves a slimy trail — as circus crawling nigh

Of crystaled balls juggling, the magi tossed, matt'ring,
inside, eyed my soul mirrored and my dead carcass, tatt'ring.
Stumbled, my globe amongst the magi worm's magicry, fumbling,
its toothless mouth in a silent scream, stupidly dropped mine, shatt'ring.

Ass on my in the grass, four hundred sang birds sung,
Four thousand church chimes belled, once upon a rung.

Cannibal

"Looks a cannibal sort of chap, don't he?" said the constable confidentially to Cutler. The Man in the Passage/G. K. Chesterton

"Dr. Sangor?" enquired Schlomo Nantier who was sitting on the cool, cracked but smooth, red vinyl bench of one of more than two dozen booths and freestanding tables in Pat's Cafe. "Dr. B. S. Sangor?"

"That's me," answered the old man of average height and weight whose words were almost lost in the sounds of silverware clinking on Blue Plate Specials, the hum of ceiling fans stirring the too warm air exhaled from an overtaxed air conditioner, and the undulating murmur of the sparse group eating lunch at the small cafe. Sixty-seven years old himself, Sangor stood looking down at the old, hawkish face of Schlomo Nantier with mild and somewhat hidden surprise at the modest clothing of Light's End's only internationally known scholar and part-time resident. "Mr. Nantier?"

"Please, Dr. Sangor" answered Schlomo, signaling his visitor to sit down on the bench opposite him with the wave of his gnarled, open-palmed hand. "Have a sit. I've been looking forward to meeting you since you first called a few days ago. It's a rare pleasure to meet someone who is not only interested in the history of this little whitewashed town, but who also played a very interesting part in that history. You and I are rare old birds, doctor."

"Please, call me Bruce," said the doctor as he impatiently kneaded the pale temple of his bald head with two fingers. He hugged a sheaf of typewritten papers under his left arm that was held tightly against his body. "I understand you wish to learn something about Russell Anderson for an article or some such that you are writing?"

"As I mentioned on the phone," Schlomo said as his guest sat down. "I am actually writing a short story, Bruce, about that most colorful and unnerving bit of double death. I believe you wrote something about Russell Anderson yourself?"

"I think he may have been my very first patient when I was a young man and working as the contract psychologist for the police department here." The doctor sat down. "I've lived in Light's End all of my life, Schlomo, and old age has made me somewhat nostalgic about the place and the people.

"His story ends in 1942, as I suspect you know, Schlomo, when he was only twenty-four years old. May I call you Schlomo? I love a good story, myself, and this one comes from second or third-hand sources except for my investigation into his past, and is clouded by the distance of quite a few years. If you don't mind, I think I'll order lunch while I collect my thoughts.

"Of course, the 'facts' about Russell Anderson were almost forgotten after the initial, yellow journalism in *The Citadel* newspaper, which was intentionally or mistakenly half-wrong. The officer who arrived on the scene couldn't explain much about Russell or what happened.

"The 'discovery' of his diary by his mother sometime later burned red hot in the press and then turned into ashes in Light's End, so to speak. I reviewed the diary. I believe Russell did what he did so that, unlike his unfaithful father and his tragic mother, the mermaid in the side show couldn't betray him and run away. Although the image of a mermaid running away is kind of funny, eh? The horror of his mother's tragic decision and his father's physical abuse, to him in particular and to his mother as well, struck a black and primitive chord in the hearts of everyone who read my evaluation in the newspaper about four months later."

"Yes, he had a tough life as a boy, but I don't see him as a victim of his environment and/or his nurture." Schlomo cut a piece from the ham slice on his plate. The ham spiked on the fork in his right hand began a brief journey to his mouth. "No one can control much of his circumstances, but everyone can choose how to respond to them."

"Of course, yes," continued Sangor, "Russell's story begins when the circus came to Light's End. It ends with a question, Schlomo. One I've never been able to answer."

Schlomo's piece of ham stopped in midair on its trip to his mouth. With his left, Dr. Sangor pushed the sheaf of yellowed, typewritten paper over to him.

"Here's what I've written," said Dr. Sangor. "It should answer most of your questions. Most, I regret to say, except the most important one:

"What ate Russell's hands up to his slit wrists?"

In the drowsy quiet before dawn on Sunday, a silence disturbed only by the subtle buzz of an occasional street light, the clink of milk bottles being left on doorsteps, the slap of a newspaper in the bushes next to a front door, the chirrups, clicks, and rustling of hidden insects and small animals, and the broken snores of jaded and indifferent adults, the children of isolated

Light's End, Maine began to wake up, their heads exploding from sheets and comforters like superheated popcorn, to the distant trumpeting of an elephant.

Thirteen cars of the Bangor and Aroostook Railroad had rumbled to a slow, creaking stop at the train depot, and a moveable smorgasbord of the flotsam of society called circus people was crawling out like ants, hauling the bones and guts and skins of illusions and dreams to a large, pre-selected cow field behind a once white, two-story frame house on the outskirts of Strother Street. Eighty-four sweating, cursing gaffs, acrobats, clowns, geeks, and creeps of the Carson Circus would once again drive battered tent spikes, raise shabby canvas tents, and breathe a smarmy and foul life into their third-rate carnival in the dog days of summer in 1942.

The headline above the fold of yesterday's Citadel newspaper had shouted "The Circus is Coming" and all over Light's End on the sides of buildings and telephone poles posters with drawings of outré, threatening, broken things, nature's train wrecks, tempted: the Unicycle Riding Dog, Brunhilda the Dancing Bear, Dardenalla The Fat Girl, The African Ape-man, Psmathe the Undine, and Geraldo and his Amazing Dancing Horse, "White Fire." Circus Day was a rare, exhilarating feast for the mind, body, and soul, and retail business and city offices had ground to a halt, and schools stood empty in the little town that lay at the mouth of a dead bay, a town that had been bypassed by any state highway or air field, and ignored the aberrant and occasional traveler who passed through the bus station. There were movies at the State or Seminole Theater, of course, and Jack Benny on the radio, but Vaudeville was dead, school plays were agony, and live entertainment was as rare as the hen's teeth on display in one of the circus sideshows.

Flushed with awe, giggles, and pounding hearts, children in young and old bodies pushed and elbowed their way into the low roar of the Carson Circus that Monday morning: a congested mass of milling human flesh, hungry to eat up illusions at dozens of worn canvas stands stocked with rows of cheap Kewpie dolls and gaudy trinkets, to gulp exotic iced drinks as they stood under gently swaying, naked light bulbs strung on wire over their heads and between the tents, and smell strange animal stink and taste strange tangs, and to gawk at puerile exotic dancers or creepy freaks. Electric with anticipation and eager to escape life, teachers and clerks and delivery boys and shop keepers would soon throw nickels at fishbowls, and wade through discarded popcorn bags, candy wrappers, and cotton candy cardboard cones as a calliope mourned and a brown monkey spun about in a wire cage strumming a banjo.

That Monday, awkward and stunted, his oily face pitted with acne, his black hair unclean and uncombed, Russell Anderson stood in front of a kiosk of toy cranes and rubbed his pudgy hands nervously as if he were washing them. In his left hand had been a half-eaten Dynamite sandwich that he'd laid gingerly on the top edge of a dirty toy crane. With his right, he reached into the frayed, front pocket of his jeans, removed a dime, and gingerly stepped up to a crane.

Anderson dropped his nickel *clink* into a slot on the front of the machine with a pudgy hand that belonged to a prepubescent boy, not a twenty-five year old, and cranked the knob of a round disk next to it in a slow careful circle. The jagged, tin teeth of the crane rose and then fell, but missed a cloth Popeye doll that was tangled in a jumble of yellow, red, blue and gold gewgaws and gaudy junk covering the bottom of the game.

"That's it, that's it, ya almost got it," cajoled a barker squinting behind and between two rectangular glass boxes housing toy cranes that were part of the square of games surrounding him. He pushed a scuffed, black derby that was noticeably too small up and back against small, pink ears. "Jest a little more to yer left."

Anderson stood at the crane, cranking, his forehead beaded with sweat. He did not glance up or raise an eyebrow to acknowledge the gaff. The cacophony of a distant calliope mingled with the crowd and was fading into a low, distant hum for him, leaving only the dull thud of his heart and the click of the crane as it turned. He cranked the knob as he squinted through the thin patina of grime that covered the glass box and felt like grit under his handful of dirty fingernails.

"That's it, that's it," said the shill as he studied his mark, Russell's dull black eyes set just a bit too far apart, the slack mouth set between fat cheekbones. The crane ground slowly over the mound of trinkets, the jagged mouth opened, and fell, and rose with nothing.

The toy crane rose and ground over the mound of worthless treasures; the jagged mouth opened and fell, and rose tenaciously over the opening that released a prize, clutching a small, silver-plated cigarette lighter.

"Got it," Russell hissed without emotion.

"Nah, nah, look fella," grinned the shill. He turned and spit on the ground, and turned back. "It's hanging on the lip, there, see. Bad break. Tough luck. Tough to be a loser."

Russell stood for a moment, not unexpectedly cheated, picked up his now unsanitary Dynamite sandwich from the top of the toy crane, and stuck the chewed end in his mouth.

Lori sat at a tiny vanity in her bedroom, an attractive woman and something more, quietly beautiful, using a cheap turtle shell comb to brush her wealth of red hair flowing around her pink neck, her delicate shoulders, and the front of her blouse. On her vanity lay a slightly cracked, matching mirror. Her deep green eyes were dull with resignation, and glancing at her son sitting at their little, scarred, wooden table reading a tattered *Startling Comics* comic book that had been handed down (like the table) because with her husband, M.R. it could not be anything new and booze, she said in her head: *it's late; M.R. could be here any second.* She wouldn't say out loud any ugly thing that would disrupt Russell's fantasy world and bring him back even for a moment to the sordid dirty real world of their lives because she loved him.

Next to her son's elbow lay a half-eaten Zero candy bar.

There had never been money because, even though her son's father, M.R., once had a good job with the Bangor and Aroostook Railroad, he'd selfishly spent almost every penny since on booze. So it was money for food, but not too much, so that M. R. could pay his bar bill or there would be Hell, filthy profanity, and purple bruises to pay.

"It's time for bed, Russell," she said in a guarded voice with no hint of fear or anticipation or anything except resignation, and rubbed her beautiful, tired, green eyes. "You know daddy doesn't like it when you're up." But her little fourteen-year-old son picked up the Zero bar, took a bite, and lay it down again without any acknowledgment.

Implacable, Lori sat in a faded, muslin dress she'd sewn from discarded cloth, without buttons or lace or adornment because it could not be a new dress and booze, and placed her comb on her vanity in the shack they'd lived in in Stonebreaker Heights for more than ten desperate, hopeless years. She rose and moved to the side of her son, and gently laid her right hand on his left forearm.

"The taxi could be here any minute," she said and thought of M. R. coming home again in a taxi because he couldn't drive since the car wreck that had almost killed several people. Russell looked up into the eyes of the only person on Earth who loved him.

Lori thought about Russell who (emotionally, physically, and spiritually too immature, and lacking the life experience to be a real husband so that two can truly become one) had been her actual husband for at least five years.

"Did you hear me, Sweetheart?" she asked out of habit and duty.

She thought about M.R. at the Belleview Bar downtown on August Street, where the smell of stale beer that had been spilled and not mopped up and the odor of Lucky and Camel cigarettes, whose stink was as much a part of the walls as the paint, mixed with the pungent odor of grease, hard boiled eggs, fried cod and dirty men. In the back in its darkest corner sat a ragged shuffleboard table. She thought of M.R.'s rage building.

That night, Lori did not hear M.R. say in a barely audible slur to the owner and barkeep of the Belleview (who ladled potato soup for him because by then it was all that M. R. could stomach) not to worry about him (M. R.) because he was going to be gone for awhile.

Lori and Russell did hear the front door open and saw M.R. framed there, reeking of booze, just as his left hand swung the axe (that had been partly hidden behind his left leg) up into the open palm of his right hand just below the blade. His eyes burned red with a maniacal fire as he giggled.

"So what's eating you this time," Lori said without inflection and in hopeless resignation, instantly knowing it was the last thing that she should have said out loud and might very well be the last thing she said in her life. Lori began screaming, "Russell, run! Run!," but they both knew it was Lori that the axe wanted to eat.

M.R. swayed slowly in the doorway on the unpainted, untreated porch, a string of salvia hanging from the corner of his ragged mouth, the axe in his left hand, when he stumbled an unexpected and unwanted step back, and then another.

And he fell.

The axe lay on the porch.

Befuddled and surprised, M. R. struggled to rise, then swayed slowly on the porch, his mouth open, and he fell again.

The axe lay on the porch.

Russell turned his back on the arcade crane and, lured by the distant, low, whooping cough of an unseen calliope, weaved through the meandering crowd of Light's Enders, touching no one, shunning eye contact, and imagining himself invisible. As he entered Freak Row, he ignored the huge, garishly colored canvas banners that hid smarmy little trailers behind them, and mutely hawked The Worlds Smallest Horse, The Nine Foot Giant, The World's Largest Boa Snake, The Fat and The Thin Man, and The Lizard Lady. Russell stopped on the fringe of an eddy of twenty-seven other people by the moaning, decrepit calliope at the exhibit for Psmathe.

Above a scarred, wooden platform, a scroll at the top of a tattered canvas banner claimed in red English lettering on a yellow background that she was THE ONLY LIVING MERMAID in Captivity. Smoldering in the center of the canvas, Psmathe reclined on a rock in a cerulean blue ocean, her right hand combing a wealth of red hair that tumbled down her pink neck, her delicate naked shoulders, and her pink breasts. On her lap lay a mirror with a clamshell back. Below her waist, her blue-green sequined tail ended in delicate blue-veined fins. In the distance behind the undine lay a hazy reef sparsely necklaced with stunted palm trees.

As Russell stared at her, an unexpected door opened in the mermaid's canvas tail to frame a neatly dressed man carrying a bamboo cane in his left hand, wearing a yellow straw hat, a red vest and carefully pressed white shirt, and canvas shoes. He smiled with a mouth full of teeth in a pleasant face and waved his cane as a visual exclamation point.

"Yowza, yowza, yowza!" he barked as the cane flourished. "My name is Washington Tubbs, your guide into a world of horrors! Step right up to see the EIGHTH WONDER of the WORLD for one thin dime!

"The Babylonians worshipped the fish-tailed god Oannes, and the Semites the mer-goddess Atargatis—the Greeks and Romans called her Aphrodite and Venus—and even Pliny the Elder wrote of sighting their daughters, the sirens of the seas, the horrors of the deep, riding hippocamps and singing irresistible celestial harmonies to ensnare lonely men.

"They are the unnatural children of gods and men, a forbidden, salacious pleasure, passionate, temperamental, harlots of the unfathomable ocean— the watery womb of creation, the cradle of monsters. At the sweet taste of human blood in the water, they rise up and up through the turbulent sea to entangle drowning sailors and eat their eyes, their noses, the tips of fingers and toes, and their... private parts!"

Someone in the audience giggled nervously; a woman.

"Sideshows fooled you during the Renaissance and the Baroque days, calling a shaved monkey stitched to the tail of an ocean trout a mermaid! P. T. Barnum made a monkey out of y-o-u when he claimed Dr. J. Griffin caught the Feejee Mermaid in a net in 1842! But you will be fooled NO MORE! Ten feet away, just behind this canvas painting, waits the seductive..." he cooed as he formed the outline of a woman in the air with his hands and cane, "beautiful, ALL-woman, half-fish that is Poseidon's daughter, the amorphous PSMATHE!

"Step this way for your admission into the weird, the wonderful, the wild!"

Like a drop of oil on water, the eddy of humans scattered and little cliques of people moved around the right side of the platform to the sideshow entrance to drop their dimes in the outstretched hand of the barker.

Waiting nervously until the last person had entered, and clutching a half-eaten hot dog in his left hand, Russell paid his dime and went inside.

The dim interior of the claustrophobic, windowless trailer had been gutted and replaced with a narrow passage running its length, now filled two or three deep with Light's Enders, and ending in a door and exit sign. The wall to Russell's left had been painted with the same faded, exotic, and isolated reef necklaced with stunted palms that was depicted on Psmathe's banner, and a thin layer of sand and mostly broken sea shells carpeted the floor. To his right, a moth-eaten, sea-green curtain hung in heavy folds from ceiling to floor, and a blue, velvet cord threaded through a number of freestanding brass poles cordoned the audience back four feet from the curtain. The subtle, unpleasant smell of dead fish and rotting sea weeds hung in the close air.

The barker in his straw hat hobbled in, unhooked a velvet cord, stepped inside the cordoned area, and rehooked the cord behind him.

"Ladies and gentlemen," he bellowed and flourished his bamboo cane at his audience. "You all know of Caleb Elliott, the founder of Light's End, and how he swam out to the forbidden reef in your Abomination Bay, and down and down until he found a rift between realities, a tear between the invisible wall that separates our world from the world of the half-people, the mer- and wer-people, until he found the nest of undine there, and fathered on Psmathe his unholy offspring, the horrible blasphemy whose unnatural bones are still buried in the black well beneath 'Elliott's Head' cliff.

"But only I know how Hiram Percy would later rediscover that same nest, and through deceit and guile, captured Caleb's weird whore, and sold the mermaid to my family where she has remained on display to this very day.

"Do you snicker and doubt still?" he questioned as he moved to the right hand side of the heavy curtain and laid his hand on the pull hanging there.

"Behold!" he said, and yanked the pull down. "PSMATHE, THE ONLY LIVING MERMAID IN CAPTIVITY!"

There was a whispered gasp from someone, and a young boy pointed and giggled nervously at the rectangular glass tank twenty feet in length and twelve feet in height filled almost to the brim with blue-green water and a wriggling of odd, silver, saltwater fish. Russell stood mesmerized, unconsciously clutching the velvet restraining cord with both hands. She had beautiful, sensual, green eyes.

On Tuesday, the Light's End Home for Troubled Boys would not give Russell the day off from his janitorial duties. When Russell arrived at the Carson Circus, a gibbous moon hung broken and yellow above the slightly swaying, naked light bulbs strung on wire over their heads and between the tents. The eddy of fifteen men, women and teenagers at Psmathe's exhibit scattered, and cliques of most of the people moved around the platform to the freak show entrance. Waiting impatiently until the last person had entered, Russell took the final bite of a turkey drumstick, tossed the bone aside, paid, and went inside.

The trailer's passageway was partially filled with Light's Enders standing in front of the wall painted with the exotic reef and on a thin layer of sand and sea shells. The barker stood in front of the sea-green curtain hung from the ceiling, and behind the velvet cord threaded through freestanding brass poles. The subtle smell of fish hung in the close air.

"Ladies and gentlemen," he bellowed, flourishing his yellow bamboo cane. But Russell ignored the rest of the talk he had heard fifteen times since Monday as he stood mesmerized. The barker laid his hand on the curtain pull.

"Behold!" he said, and yanked the pull down. "PSAMATHE, THE ONLY LIVING MERMAID IN CAPTIVITY!!"

Oblivious to time and place, Russell stood alone, mesmerized, his face flushed, his breathing shallow and too rapid, both hands clutching the velvet restraining cord.

Psmathe reclined at the bottom of her cerulean blue pool, wholly woman and something more, beautiful, using a clamshell comb to brush her wealth of red hair flowering in the water around her pink neck and the flaring gills there, her delicate naked shoulders, and her pink breasts. In her corpulent lap lay a mirror with a clamshell back. Her attractive, deep green eyes were dull with indifference to the weird, silent dance of water plants in her tank, to the wriggling little silver fish, and to Russell. Below her waist, her blue-green sequined tail swayed gently as she adjusted her position.

A hand fell on Russell's shoulder, and Russell jerked away and forward, staggering into one of the freestanding brass poles.

"Easy, son, easy," said the barker. "Something eating you?"

She had beautiful, sensual, green eyes.

Russell did not answer.

"They call me Washington Tubbs," continued the Barker, cocking his head towards his left shoulder as he studied Russell. "After the comic strip.

"You're one of the rare ones, ain't ya. You believe. I get one of you every coon's age."

Russell did not respond.

"Listen. They all come to the circus to find something, kid" said the barker. "Most, it's to find a smile, to see the clowns, to laugh. We have sort of an unspoken agreement; they come to be fooled, and I fool 'em. So they don't get mad when they pay to see The Worlds Smallest Horse only to find a dead, stuffed, baby pony. Same for The Lizard Lady who is really a sweet, quiet woman with some kind of skin disease.

"So, don't think I don't know what's goin' on. Thanks for all the dimes, but you're startin' to give me the heebie-jeebies. So, go home, kid..."

"My name is Russell Anderson."

"Aaaahhhhhhh. You can talk. So go home, Russell Anderson," Tubbs said with a quiet smile, "to your little room under the stairs or over a greasy spoon. Find something else to do. Get a life, kid; none of them last very long, and you're wasting the life you don't have. So go on now. Go on. Get out."

Reluctantly and looking neither to his left or right, Russell walked down the brackish narrow passage to the exit door. He went outside. He walked around the front of Psmathe's freak show, and stood at the back of the eddy of five people waiting on the barker to reappear.

When they finally went inside the freak show, Russell went inside.

"His mother left Russell," continued Dr. Sangor, "at the Light's End Home for Troubled Boys when she couldn't even feed herself. In his diary, Russell wrote in crabbed handwriting that she promised he wouldn't be there long.

"She never returned.

"He also wrote he loved her and hated her and wished that he could do just one thing in his whole life that would have pleased her."

Nantier looked at the sheaf of papers that the psychologist had pushed over to him as the hum of ceiling fans stirred the too warm air in Pat's Cafe. Nantier put at bit of ham in his mouth and chewed.

"He also wrote about 'feeling empty,' watching his mother's brother's Ford pull out of the orphanage driveway, of bleakness, of a dirty, brick building, and off-white walls that left him feeling hopeless and abandoned.

Russell would learn of her suicide two months later.

"That and another particularly harsh memory would haunt him the rest of his short life was this: Russell was in the backyard where boys were playing on one of those little merry-go-rounds. He needed to go to the restroom badly and was leaving to do so when the other boys stopped him, laughing as he tried to move around them, circling and taunting him. Mad and afraid, Russell screamed at them to let him go. They didn't.

"He wrote of then standing in a large shower area with dingy white walls and high windows. Everything was dirty: the stools, stall doors, urinals, and showers. A disgusted matron in her starched white uniform was glaring at him. Russell was ashamed because he was naked, his clothes on the floor, and his underwear and pants were soiled. She crouched over him and said: 'you should be ashamed, messing your pants at your age.' She shoved him in a shower stall, turned on the water, and called out to another other matron: 'OK, bring them in!'

"Them" was the other orphans. Russell never felt so alone, humiliated and frightened as when the kids pointed and laughed, his wet hair in his eyes, hands covering his 'private parts,' sobbing, sobbing, his tears and the water running down his pudgy little body. Russell wrote: 'If only I could have gone down the drain into blackness, into nothing.'

"He eventually could no longer stay there because of his age, but they knew he wouldn't survive outside 'The Home,' and hired him to live on-site as a janitor. So, over the long, dreary, festering years at the orphanage," said Sangor, "and because he was not accepted in the world outside the orphanage, Russell made his own 'compartment,' his own inside world, and he went inside himself."

On Wednesday, Russell knew the Light's End Home would not give him the day off, so he didn't even ask, skipped breakfast, and snuck out of the orphanage before dawn. When he arrived at the circus, hungry, anxious, and excited, the naked light bulbs strung on wire over his head and between the tents were noticeably swaying in a stiff, salty wind blowing in from Abomination Bay. The sky wore a grey blanket of threatening clouds sotted with rain, a deep throated although occasional rumbling promised lightening, and the Carson Circus was empty of Light's Enders, waiting in their homes to see if their anticipation of a storm was fulfilled. It was too early for the food kiosks to open, so Russell fidgeted, thinking of dynamite sandwiches, cotton candy, corn dogs, and soda pop, as he sandwiched himself in the space between two closely anchored tents.

He waited as, one by one, a head poked out of a tent, eyes focused on the sky, or a hand was extended from a trailer, palm up, to test for rain. Eventually and cautiously, the people of the bizarre came out of their canvas or aluminum caves to prepare for the few stragglers who would brave a storm to see an elephant stand on its hind legs. Eventually, Russell came out of hiding as well.

No eddy of men, women and teenagers waited at Psmathe's or any other exhibit.

Russell moved around the platform to the freak show entrance, laid his hand on its doorknob, and turned the knob. The door creaked open.

Inside, the passageway in front of the wall with the rocky reef, swaying palm trees, leaves beaded with raindrops, fell into a beach of sand and multicolored sea shells. Washington Tubbs stood in front of the thick sea-green foliage behind him; the salty smell of the ocean tainted a brisk, cool breeze.

Psmathe reclined, a fey, voluptuous woman and something tantalizingly more, radiantly beautiful, combing her wealth of attractive, thick red hair flowering in the water around her delicate, pink neck and the flaring, transparent gills there, around her rounded naked shoulders, and her alluring pink breasts. A mirror lay on the sand next to her. Her deep green eyes danced as did the weird, silent dance of water plants and little silver fish. Below her waist, her blue-green sequined tail swayed gently as she raised her hand to her face.

"I can't say I'm surprised," said Tubbs. "So here you are again, my friend. Don't think I haven't seen you gawking around here all day yesterday and the day before. Son, you've got a problem; a big, serious problem."

Russell did not answer.

"I told you yesterday you're one of the rare ones, the ones who believe," said Tubbs, his eyes sparkling. "I didn't mean that as a good thing, son. In fact, you're a little morbidly sick; you have an unwholesome obsession with a dream or maybe a memory. You need to get out of here, son; go home."

Russell did not answer. Tubbs extended both of his hands to touch his shoulders and Russell recoiled, his face twisted by suspicion, fear and anger.

"The circus starts packing up Saturday night to get away from this sad little backwater, and I don't want to see your dirty face in my freak show again. And since I don't think you talk to anyone regularly, and that if you did they wouldn't believe you anyway, here's the truth, the whole truth, and nothing but the truth about Psmathe.

"You have nothing to offer her, and she has nothing to give you. She's a fraud. Do you understand, son? The whole thing is fake. Caleb Elliott did not find an inhuman mermaid and father a monster that is buried under Elliott's Cliff, and Hiram Percy didn't catch her and sell her to my family. There are no gods and no mermaids. There are only men; you and I. There isn't even a glass tank," he said, taking several steps backwards and rapping the knuckles of his left hand with a solid thup on Psmathe's prison behind him. "Behind two thin sheets of glass filled with water is a special movie screen, my friend, and a ladder on the side of the screen so I can keep it clean. Behind that is a rear-screen projector. What you think is a preternatural mermaid is a cheap actress on a film loop that repeats every twenty minutes or so."

"She is real," hissed Russell, shaking.

"Go home, son! Go home now, and don't come back!" barked Tubbs who saw Russell jerk involuntarily back as if he were struck, and did not see the seething anger in Russell's eyes or the little slits already bleeding red beneath his fingernails digging into the palms of his clenched fists, rigid at his sides. "Go help someone else; get your mind off of yourself. I know that always helps me out of a dark place. Go. Go.

"NOW! RIGHT NOW!" shouted the barker, brandishing his cane like a sword.

Reluctantly and looking neither to his left or right, Russell walked down the narrow passage to the exit door, his rage hidden, coiled to strike with the deadly venom of his pain.

As he stepped from the trailer, the sky began to spit fat drops of rain. But Russell did not return to the Home for Troubled Boys. He walked in the steadily increasing rain, shoulders slumped and head bowed, to a clutch of trees behind and out of view of anyone in the circus.

He stopped in the trees, already drenched, and his rage broke, savage and raw and naked, and Russell began to violently tear at his shirt as he growled and cursed until it hung in tatters.

He stood in the shower, ashamed because he was partially naked, and his underwear and pants were soiled. With his arms spread wide at shoulder height, his palms with their little bloody slits opened and turned up, he threw back his head and screamed.

No one heard him.

That night after the rain was spent and as the town and circus people slept and when the hot doorknob to the entrance opened without resistance under his clammy hand, Russell went to Psmathe. The hot, jagged reef and its necklace of palm trees still wet with rain fell into the unclean beach of yellow sand and multicolored sea shells under his feet. The sound of the cerulean blue sea susshed against it as the ocean breathed in and out and the distant chirp of unseen sea-gulls above and tropical birds below on the reef whispered in his ears.

Washington Tubbs was waiting in his pressed, white shirt, without his cane.

"I've been expecting you, my son; some people just have to see the truth to believe," he said, shaking his head in regret, and turned his back to Russell, and reached up to pull the velvet curtain cord hanging from a tree limb. "Look!"

Gritting his teeth, and his eyes burning with a maniacal fire, Russell reached back and pulled his shirt out of the waist band of his pants and removed his father's hand axe that he'd hidden in the bottom of his chest-of-drawers for years. He swung the axe back over his shoulder, and swung forward and down with terrific, savage force, cleaving Tubbs' straw hat and embedding its blade in the back of the barker's head with a sickening, bone-cracking thud.

Tubbs threw his hands and arms up and out as if he were worshiping, and fell forward, dead, on his face.

"I'm not your goddamn son," Russell snarled, and dropped the axe in the spreading pool of blood under Tubb's head.

He stepped further up onto the unholy reef and inhaled the subtle but salty smells of the ocean carried on the hot breeze. To his left rose the worn ladder of ancient, natural, lichen-covered stone steps that led to Psmathe's pool. He carefully ascended.

Russell laid himself at the lip of the pool, mesmerized, his face deeply flushed, his breathing very shallow and very rapid, both hands opened and palms down on the ferns that grew there as he looked down into the eyes of the only person on Earth who loved him.

Psmathe reclined at the bottom of the pool, fey, voluptuous, beautiful, combing her wealth of thick red hair flowering in the water. Below her waist, her blue-green sequined tail swayed gently as she raised her hand to her face.

And Psmathe, the blinding light that would kill the horrors in Russell's black soul so that two could truly and forever become inseparably one, looked at him. He began to cry as he removed the folded straight razor from his left pants pocket. Sobbing and trembling in complete surrender, he opened the razor.

Hanging himself over the lip of the pool by his arms, Russell slit his left wrist with the straight razor. He threw back his head and screamed without sound, his eyes ballooning from the unutterable pain. Then punching through the excruciating pain and the fierce tears that blurred his vision, he slashed his trembling right wrist.

He lay his hands in the pool and screamed as his open wounds filled with unclean salt water and a red stain spread in a watery halo of blood, and Russell faced death and judgment and Hell as, tender and tearful, in a dance of soundless, rising bubbles, the undine rose up and up and up.

She dropped her comb, and the mirror fell from her lap, and as she rose, her jaw unhinged and her rapacious smile split into a gaping wound of gnashing razor sharp, jagged teeth, her wealth of thick red hair flowered into writhing snakes around her thick, scaled neck and the flaring, sucking gills there. Below her waist, her blue-green sequined tail stretched and twisted and squirmed into the hideous coils of the gigantic, hairy, legless aberration that was Psmathe.

The teeth. The blood. The horror. The undine rose up and up.

And placed her mouth over Russell's nose.

And blew exquisite pain and death into him.

And Russell and Psmathe were one.

Schlomo Nantier laid his fork on his empty plate. Dr. Sangor watched the old poet's expression with the detachment most associated with his profession as he repeated: "I have no knowledge of what ate Russell's hands up to his slit wrists. Like you, I can't bring myself to accept any supernatural mumbo-jumbo either. All I know is what I know.

"I can tell you that the police were never able to answer it either. I know because I was close friends with the Chief of Police at the time, and he told me they suspected a double homicide and that Russell murdered Tubbs, of course, and went back to the carnival and searched the mermaid display inch by inch by inch.

"That, however, didn't befuddle them nearly as much as the indecent little mystery they never leaked to the public. I'm not sure I believe what the Chief told me many years after the fact, and have never repeated it to anyone until today."

"Is this something I should add to my paper?" asked Sangor.

With his head slightly lowered, Schlomo looked up under the fringe of his eyebrows and picked up his paper napkin from the side of his plate and began to wipe his mouth.

"They found his bloody razor, of course, fallen just below the rear-projection movie screen. But the rest falls into the category of what they didn't find, really, doctor. They didn't find a knife or anything that could have severed Russell's hands just below his horrible slashed wrists. They never really found a motive, either."

Schlomo laid the napkin on the table without raising his head.

"But the greatest enigma," Schlomo continued, "is what they didn't find behind the back-projection movie screen."

"What was that," asked Sangor.

"A projector."

The End

About Our Creators

Michael Vance was first published in The Professor's Story Hour chapbook at the age of eleven and became a professional freelance writer in 1977. He has been published in dozens of magazines and as a syndicated columnist and cartoonist in over 500 newspapers. His history book, *Forbidden Adventures: The History of the American Comics Group*, has been called a "benchmark in comics history".

His magazine work has been published in seven countries, and includes articles for *Starlog, Jack & Jill* and *Star Trek: The Next Generation*.

He briefly ghosted an internationally syndicated comic strip, and wrote his own strip for five years called *Holiday Out* that was reprinted as a comic book. Vance also wrote comic book titles including *Straw Men, Angel of Death, The Adventures of Captain Nemo, Holiday Out* and *Bloodtide*. His work has appeared in several comic book anthologies, and he is listed in the *Who's Who of American Comic Books* and *Comic Book Superstars*.

His stories about a fictional town called "Light's End" have been published in *Media Scene, Holiday Out Comics, Dreams and Visions, Maelstrom Speculative Fiction, Whispers From the Shattered Forum, On Spec, Whispers from the Shattered Forum, Lovecraft's Mystery Magazine* and many others. They have also been recorded by legendary actor William (*Murder She Wrote)* Windom. One of these stories was nominated for the international 2004 SLF Fountain Award for Best Short Story.

The book *Weird Horror Tales* from Cornerstone Publishers republishes thirteen of these short stories. The second volume, *Weird Horror Tales: The Feasting*, featured 15 tales. You hold the third and final volume of the Weird Horror Tales trilogy in your hands.

Reviewers write: "Vance has produced a terrific cycle of tales, inspired by but not slavishly imitative of Lovecraft's Cthulhu Mythos. [He] has assembled those traditions in a new and deliciously creepy way. Highly recommended." The first two braided novels have favorably been comparied to the work of H.P. Lovecraft and writer Ray Bradbury. As well, Vance has been called "the Christian H. P. Lovecraft".

With novelists Mel Odom and R.A. Jones, he co-wrote *Global Star*, a tabloid in a world where werewolves and babies born with bowling balls in their stomachs are reality, and the New York Times and Washington Post are "trash journalism."

Vance's weekly comics review column, *Suspended Animation*, was continuously published for more than twenty years reaching more than 4,000,000 readers in fanzines, newspapers, and on over eighty websites at its height.

In addition, he worked in newspapers for twenty-two years as an editor, writer and advertising manager, creating three successful newspaper magazines.

Vance also created the new *Oklahoma Cartoonists Collection* housed in the *Toy and Action Figure Museum* in Pauls Valley, Oklahoma, and was a keynote speaker at the "Uncanny Adventures of Okie Cartoonists" exhibit at the Oklahoma Historical Museum in Oklahoma City .

He is currently communications director of a nonprofit agency, the Tulsa Boys' Home, in Tulsa, Oklahoma. He is a Christian.

Eric York is an artist living high up in the mountains of northern Arizona. His work has appeared in books, zines, and comics including *The Fantastical Worlds of H.P. Lovecraft, The Shadow Over Santa Susana, Malafact, Besmirched, Terminal Brain Rot* and many others. He also puts out his own material under the Maggot Global Publishing imprint and has published *The Hungry Maggot, Vermis Rex, Tillinghasts' Moribund Fairy-Tales, Eldritch Pulp Adventure, The Erebus Tarot*, as well as the upcoming *Zygote's Fables* and his 100+ page graphic novel adaptation of H.P. Lovecraft's *Fungi From Yuggoth*. He has played in numerous bands with names like *The American Deathtrip, Scar Strangled Banger, Anyface, Shrunken Monkey Paw, Super Colossal Beast, The Baskervilles, Evilsaurus Rex*, and his current one, *King Omega*. He works as the night manager of an old haunted hotel and lives with his girlfriend, Sharlene. You can see 500+ examples of his artwork at tillinghast23.deviantart.com and can contact him at hungrymaggot@netscape.net.

K eith Birdsong is famous for his extremely realistic covers for *Star Trek* novels, featuring the actors from the movies and television series. He has also done work for *Star Wars*, the cyberpunk role-playing game *Shadowrun* and a children's book *The Halloween Hex*. In addition, Birdsong's work has been featured in films, on Hamilton Collection collectors' plates and on U.S. Postage stamps.

F or Dianne Savage's actual photographs of Light's End, and much more, go to *http://www.flickr.com/photos/27498787@N04/*

MORE PULP CREEPINESS
FROM THE PEN OF MICHAEL VANCE...

Somewhere on the rocky coast of Maine there exists the small, quiet town of *Light's End*. Built along a metaphysical fault line between the universal forces of good and evil, it has been the setting for countless episodes of mind-numbing horror and depravity.

Award winning writer, Michael Vance serves up horrific and deeply moving stories of people caught in unimaginable horror. Douse the lights, bolt the doors and get ready to be frightened by these two collection of the macabre by a true master. Illustrated throughout by fantasy illustrator, Earl Geier, *Weird Horror Tales* and *Weird Horror Two: The Feasting* are custom made for the jaded horror fan wanting something new. Here is pulp horror at its finest.

PULP FICTION FOR A NEW GENERATION

WWW.GOPULP.COM OR FOR YOUR E-READER, PDFS AT: WWW.AIRSHIP27HANGAR.COM

Situated in the rural back country of Edwardian England is an old, mysterious house whose unique owner earns his living as a Spirit-Breaker, a hunter of ghosts. A former military veteran, Sgt. Roman Janus has devoted his life to aid those haunted, both emotionally and physically by obsessive wraiths whose spirits are still anchored to our world.

Airship 27 Productions is thrilled to present *Sgt. Janus – Spirit Breaker* by Jim Beard. Part detective, part occultist, Janus is himself a man of mystery whose own past is shrouded and the motivations behind his calling kept hidden. Within this volume you will find eight tales as narrated by his clients, each with his or her own perspective on this uncanny hero and his amazing career. Filled with suspense, terror and agonizing pathos, each a solid mesmerizing journey into the unknown world beyond.